D. G. Compton was born in 1930 and lives in London. His many critically acclaimed novels include *The Steel Crocodile*, *Chronocules*, *The Continuous Katherine Mortenhoe*, *Ascendencies* and *Nomansland*.

JUSTICE CITY

D. G. Compton

Distributed by
Trafalgar Square
North Pomfret, Vermont 05053

GOLLANCZ CRIME

First published in Great Britain 1994
by Victor Gollancz

First VG Crime edition published 1995
by Victor Gollancz
An imprint of the Cassell Group
Wellington House, 125 Strand, London WC2R 0BB

ISBN 0 575 05840 4

Printed and bound in Great Britain
by Cox & Wyman Ltd, Reading

'We understand too much and punish too little.'

John Major, 10.8.1993

JUSTICE CITY

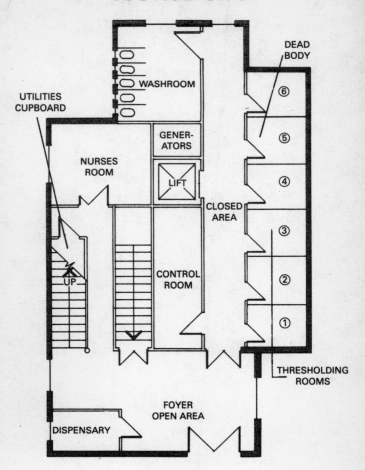

PUNISHMENTS BUILDING

tuesday

one

Look up there. Those burnished black ramparts hacked into the side of Skagg Tor – that's Justice City, firstborn and flagship of the nation's Punishment and Protection Centres. Two hundred thousand square metres of crag and bracken, levelled, terraced, built over, populated, five thousand inmates to three hundred prison staff (a uniquely cost-effective ratio), the entire P & P area enclosed in black steel walls ten metres high, windowless and intricately riveted, with a gaunt black road zigzagging down from them. At the bottom of the road lies the main Manchester–Huddersfield autoroute; at the top of the road, looming over a gravel turn-around laid out with armoured trucks in mind, stand the windowless black steel gates, in the windowless black steel walls, of Justice City.

The name, of course, is a political statement; so is the building material. Both were intended six years ago as vote-getters, did the job then, and still do now. Of the two, the steel is the more truthful. Justice City isn't a city, and the justice it delivers is maybe debatable, but its walls, although six years old now and rusting a bit round the door sills, are still basically as unassailable as their steelness and blackness and windowlessness was intended to suggest.

In many ways, especially when seen from down here on the main autoroute, Justice City does a fine job. Ordinary decent citizens passing in their cars can see that: they can see

11

how it subjugates the land. They can look up and see for themselves how big and black and unassailable it is, and people they believe have told them it's also cost-effective. It's right-thinking, too. The name says it all: Justice City. Wrong-doers are brought to it and, profoundly, they receive it. It's more than just a prison. Ordinary decent citizens, as they pass in their cars, understand its significance very well. They can see that it's more than just a prison. It reassures them and at the same time, secretly, it terrifies them. It's Justice City.

Seen from inside, too, the City is reassuring. There are gates and granite within its steel-walled two hundred thousand square metres. Grids of Long Term Incarceration (LTI) Blocks, a Hospital Wing, a Punishments Building, a Prison Procedures Research Unit, exercise yards and running track, chapel, library, ornamental gardens, vegetable gardens, motor transport pool, staff quarters, staff canteen, staff leisure centre, staff cinema, staff swimming facility ... And then there are the famous walls, battleship Victoriana eight metres high, their black steel plating ten millimetres thick and riveted at fifteen centimetre centres, the rivets marching three abreast in clanging ranks up and across and down ... It's impressive. Did anyone mention trees? There are many trees, fruit and ornamental, deciduous and evergreen, and in another season there'll be roses blooming.

So what's the snag?

Is there one?

As has already been mentioned, Justice City has five thousand inmates and three hundred resident staff. There is also the occasional short-term ministry-approved visitor. Four times a day, however, the permitted number of inmates is exceeded. At five a.m. and ten a.m. and one p.m. and three a group of no more than six new inductees is booked in from Manchester: one hour later, at six a.m. and eleven a.m. and two p.m. and four, a similar number of long term inmates (LTIs) is discharged. New inductees are scrupulously balanced by LTI discharges. The staff/inmate ratio is pared to the bone, the prison officers' union is watchful, and the governor, Mr Ransome, has made a commitment to his men never to exceed it for longer than one hour.

At this grey hour of a January morning few men are out of doors. The eight o'clock exercise detail (ten inmates) is exercising, the eight o'clock running detail (six inmates) is running, and twelve prison officers armed with shot-guns can be seen, supervising them. (No more than sixteen inmates are ever outside their cells at any one time: free association isn't allowed. This is what makes such cost-effective staffing levels possible. This and the politically unfortunate guns.) Inmates wear fluorescent orange City tracksuits as a further disincentive to escape, and officers wear regulation blue. This morning the flat waterproof tops of their caps are damp and shiny. One visitor is in sight, marching from Inductions to the Prison Procedures Research Unit: identifiable by his khaki greatcoat, and his march, he's a military policeman on secondment from the army jail in Oswestry. He's observing prison management methods here, and he doesn't belong. Neither do the inmates, but the staff treat them as if they did. Only the staff belong in the City.

It's coming up to eight thirty, time to go indoors. Through the first floor window, third from the left facing south, of the Punishments Building, the back of Margaret (Peggy) Landon's head is visible. The Punishments Building is the smallish granite-faced block with barred windows (not helpful: most of the buildings here are granite-faced, with barred windows) over there by the rose garden to the right of Inductions, which is just beyond Reception. Peggy Landon is going to be important to this story – she and Chief Inspector Alexander (Alec) Duncan, a CID man who's a hundred miles away at present, driving home from an overnight stake-out, along a Liverpool street.

On the other side of the window, with her back to it, in a crispish white coat, Peggy Landon is sitting at a cluttered government issue desk. The room she's in, neon-lit against the dreary morning, is bare but decent-sized. She seems only recently to have arrived. Judging from the way she sits at her desk, she's hating it. She sits at it but she isn't yet of it.

This is clear because, her back straight and her stomach pulled in, she's making a pointed distance between herself and the central drawer-front. Her legs in their brown paisley tights are curled back distastefully under her chair and she holds her arms out over the desk top, elbows fastidiously raised, fingers and thumbs together, as she scans its littered surface for some reasonable starting point to her day.

On the desk are papers and ballpoint pens and file cartons, junk-mail drug promotions, a smeary computer terminal, an out-tray (no in-tray in sight), dirty coffee mugs and tangled elastic bands, a scuffed leather photograph frame containing a sunny colour picture of a pipe-smoking middle-aged man, two telephones, a plastic swimming cap, newspapers, an ophthalmoscope missing the screw-end to keep in its battery, and a number of empty potato crisp packets.

Chief Inspector Duncan, Alec, will learn a lot, in his close-up way, from this desk. The chief inspector is good at seeing things close-up, and less good at the panoramic. On some cases this gives him an edge. On others it makes him a walking disaster area. The trick for his superiors is to tell in advance which sort of case it's going to be.

Alec will be good, for example, at the photograph in the leather frame: from the man's likeness to Peggy Landon he's a relative, and from the pipe and the scuffed frame it's an oldish picture, carried round a lot, and therefore loved. From his age, he's probably her father, and – in the absence of a more recent picture – he's probably several years dead. But there seems to be no mother's photograph, and no boy- or girlfriend's. Does Oedipus rule, then? Alec will cautiously think so.

The picture is indeed of her father. Peggy Landon is thirty-two years old, an only child born in west London, now a

14

trained psychiatric nurse who likes to call herself a psycho-therapist. She joined the prison service after six months at a private psychiatric institution, she's worked in Justice City since it opened, and now, with four nursing assistants in two shifts, she administers thresholding in the City's Punishments Building, generally known as the House.

Her father was certainly well-loved, and is now fifteen years dead. He was a delusional schizophrenic and he died in a car crash which involved nobody else and was probably intentional, while driving under heavy medication on a long straight country road at two in the morning. There'd been a bitter family quarrel earlier that night, and the episode left Peggy and her mother with so many guilts and mutual recriminations that they've never addressed each other reasonably since. She has no boy- or girlfriend in the roman-tic sense, but she and Dr Karl Stanna, senior neurologist in the Prison Procedures Research Unit, have laughs together, and often sex.

Peggy Landon is, finally, not likeable. But she's of her time and, given the pressures on her, it's hard to see how she could have turned out all that differently. She lives within the black steel walls of Justice City (all staff do), she enjoys taking part in amateur TV theatricals in the staff leisure centre, and she swims twice a week in a vain attempt to plump up her breasts and plump down her legs. She's short and dark, her face is prettier than her nature, and she wears short skirts and patterned tights that don't suit her. She—

Just now that's all the background information there's time for. Peggy's finished scanning her desk and she's found what she was looking for. It was under the newspapers, in her in-tray where it should have been: the file brought up to her office from Inductions that morning by a City messenger, detailing last night's four new inductees, ready now for thresholding.

She leafs through their papers, going first to the duty prison medical officer's report sheets. All the inductees are in good health. Sufficiently good, that is, for the City's purposes. Peggy looks next at their sentences. These are not her responsibility, they're emphatically non-medical, but naturally she liaises with Captain Wilson, the punishments officer downstairs. There are never enough punishment rooms, and never enough hours in the working day. Scheduling is tight, and if any of this intake have to be laid over he'll need to organize them into the Holding Block.

Reconciled to her desk now, she shunts clutter back out of the way, making room for the papers. One man's sentence catches her eye – it's unusually severe and she frowns and checks the crime. The inductee's crime is rape and murder. The crimes of the other three are minor: non-payment of child support, indecent exposure, computer fiddle. Sentences of an hour or two, for a week or two, no problem. Peggy goes back, curious, to the rape and murder.

She remembers radio reports of the case. The victim had been a young black prostitute, beaten up, then raped and cut about. Seriously disfigured, the radio said, with a razor. She hadn't died quickly or easily. The convicted man was known to have kept a string of prostitutes so she was presumably one of his and she'd stepped out of line. Peggy turns back to the inductee's medical report sheet: name, sex, age, race, religion, height, weight, build, colour of hair and eyes, condition of teeth, distinguishing marks or features, trade or profession, addresses of next of kin . . . then the examining doctor's comments, down finally to *any known allergies*. The inductee's name is Albert Beech. He's twenty-nine and Caucasian and big and muscular and blond, and healthy in every physical particular. As to his mental health, or lack of it, it doesn't rate a mention. It's none of the City's business. Albert Beech has no religion, no trade or profession, and his next of kin live in Clapham, a mother and a sister. The sole distinguishing mark listed is his beard.

Peggy looks at the Albert Beech polaroids taken down at Inductions, full face and profile, early this morning, fully conscious, before the barbiturates in his pre-thresholding hot beverage. The eyes are mean but the beard is golden and luxurious. It doesn't fit with a raped and murdered black girl and was probably grown at his counsel's suggestion while Albert Beech was on remand, awaiting trial. It didn't do him much good apparently: not with the jury and certainly not with the judge. The severity of Albert Beech's sentence will bring the punishments officer's room schedule to its knees.

Peggy stares at the polaroids – she's seen this man before. Without the beard? It's difficult to tell. She'll have seen pictures of Albert Beech after his trial, on TV or in the papers. Or is this an older memory? But in any case, Manchester should warn them before sending on inductees with sentences like this. Room availability doesn't grow on trees.

She bows her head, eyes closed, two fingers supporting the bridge of her nose, and shudders slightly. Judges don't see what these sentences *do*. Concern for the victim is a good idea, of course it is, but nothing's going to bring a young black woman back to life, or ease her pain. Some days she hates her job. Hates it.

She turns to the other three sets of papers, firmly displacing Albert Beech from her mind. It's eight forty now, nearly time she went downstairs.

The polaroids show three total strangers. They're all in good health, except that the indecent exposure claims he has a feather allergy. Peggy makes a note to tell Carole to find him a polyfibre pillow. Carole is kind-hearted. Jake, this morning's other nursing assistant, is less so. Mention an inmate's feather allergy to him and he'll scour the City for a moulting parrot.

The computer fiddle says he's a Christian Scientist. If that means he never accepts drugs, not even pain-killers, then the barbiturates in his breakfast hot beverage will have laid him out. Peggy makes a note that she may have to recalculate the thresholding dosage.

17

The non-payment looks as if he's the perfect patient. Nothing to be noted – even his *Comments* section is blank. But she recognizes the examining PMO's initials: Dr Peck is a sod and he•often can't be bothered. She taps the papers together, adds Albert Beech to them, and puts them back in the file.

It's an odd thing. She'd like to be able to jargonize Albert Beech like the others, think of him as a category, as the multiple rape and murder, but she can't. He isn't a category, he's flesh and blood. He's Albert Beech, flesh, blood, and she's seen him before . . . She sighs, pushes back her chair, gets up from her desk, goes to the window. She hopes to look out through the bars and over the City's walls, to see the moor beyond, but the morning's too dark and the window glass simply gives her back her reflection, and the precise bright office behind her. The electricity generating station is in the way, in any case, all four storeys of it, but that never stops her hoping . . . The mirror image of the clock on the wall above the copier catches her eye and she interprets it. Eight forty-five. It's time she went downstairs.

The Punishments Building has three floors. There's an unused top floor with a toilet, inventoried as *spare capacity*; a first floor for offices; and a ground floor with entrance foyer, a tiny dispensary, and a nurses' room: this is the ground floor Open Area. Then there's the ground floor Closed Area, thresholding rooms, a control room, and a machine room for the air-conditioning and the EAT (Extreme Audio-frequency Treatment) generating equipment. There's also a lift down to Punishments, the large basement floor that extends out under the gardens and accommodates the EAT rooms, monitored from a central observation station. If the capacity's available, inductees go straight down from thresholding to EAT; otherwise they're moved to the Holding Block, known among the staff as Limbo, which borders the west-facing rose garden. Punishments has secondary access, into the City's tunnel system which has exits in the LTI compounds as well as in Holding. No staff members like the Holding Block. They'd need to be sick to enjoy the fear that lives there.

From the ground floor entrance foyer of the House short covered walkways lead west to Inductions and Reception. It's a compact arrangement, convenient for the staff. But the walkways have open sides, and on this January morning wet freezing winds gust across them. Daylight will scarcely reach the sour sodden gardens on either side of them until eleven or so, and the cheery electric glare that spills out through the armoured glass doors to the House is smothered before it's gone two metres.

Like Peggy Landon, the old man now hurrying along the walkway from Inductions to the Punishments Building is important to this story. He's a sight to see. He wears his regulation blue cotton staff coat over flared American red plaid trousers, a greasy yellow tie shows in the vee of his coat against a pink shirt much too large for his stringy neck, and on his head a Balliol college straw boater sits above faded wind-blown hair at a jaunty Chevalier angle. His feet bulge out through holes in his trainers and his large hands flap anxiously, scarcely connected to his arms, which are scarcely connected to his shoulders. Most people tighten up as they grow older. This man has loosened. He hasn't shaved today, his false teeth whistle, and the badge pinned on his breast pocket, behind a row of different-coloured ballpoint pens, identifies him as GRANNY and his prison rank as PORTER.

None of this means that he's a figure of fun to the City's inmates. Granny Porter's to be seen all over the place, cleaning brasswork, replacing light-bulbs, and newcomers may laugh at him, but there's always a wiser man around to set them straight. Granny Porter is a City institution. He's the oldest lag in Justice City. His presence there helps Governor Ransome, on his bad days, to live with himself, for it was the Governor, a couple of years ago, who finally took pity on him. He's got form as long as both your arms, and one of your legs as well. He once drove cars for Albert Beech, and he was arrested by Chief Inspector Duncan (but never charged) back when Duncan was a detective sergeant. He dresses the way he does for very good reasons: he buys his clothes in Manchester's charity shops, he likes bright colours, and he stopped looking at himself years ago.

This morning, as always, Granny Porter's in a hurry. Maybe he hunches his shoulders and clutches at his boater because of the wind across the walkway, but he hurries because that's what he does. He always hurries. He thinks it shows willing and he thinks that to show willing is the best way of making his luck last.

Before the governor gave him this portering job instead of flinging him out at the end of his sentence, he'd known this and other, lesser prisons on and off for fifty of his seventy-odd years, from the other side of the bars. He'd got his name *Granny* for tidy housekeeping on cell blocks the length and breadth of the land. Giving him this job was the best thing Mr Ransome ever did. Since he was hired Granny Porter hasn't nicked so much as a mop-head. He's no need to. He's where he wants to be. He'd kill anyone who tried to shift him.

He's on his way back to the House now after returning the last empty stretcher trolley to Inductions. Some men are still able to walk after their hot beverage, but mostly they need the trolley. Escorting inductee trolleys is one of Granny's better duties. He can lean on the trolley handles without people noticing.

As he bangs in through the foyer doors Missy Landon's coming downstairs from her office, the red inductees folder on its clipboard in one hand. She's a friendly soul but he touches his boater and slopes on by, making for his buckets and brooms. He's showing willing.

Peggy looks up from the folder. She notices the musak that will play all day in the foyer. Granny Porter turns it on first thing, when he gets in at six, and she wishes he wouldn't but she's never asked him not to. This morning his coat is spotted with rain and he brings with him the smell of wind off the moors, and she forgives him his musak. She calls after him, 'Morning, Granny Porter.'

'Morning, Missy Landon.'

It sounds, with the whistle, more like *Mishy*.

'And how are you today?'

'Fine, ta, Missy.' Disappearing through the door to thresholding and the washroom. 'Lovely BM this morning, Missy. Lovely BM.'

'Good, Granny. Very good.'

Very good . . . She grimaces. Christ, the social round. But she checks herself – no, that's just the dark day getting at her. These things matter to Granny Porter; his bowel movements make the difference between happiness and misery. She's bloody sure she'll never linger on so long, but that's another question.

Tapping the inductees folder, she descends the last few steps and looks in at the dispensary. It has a half-door, the bottom half incorporating a small counter-top, and it opens directly out of the foyer, to the right of the main entrance. In a few hours the vantage point it offers is going to be significant.

Jake is in the dispensary, sniggering at Granny Porter's BM. That's Jake de Carteret, lovey – it's a Channel Islands name. Peggy doesn't usually like Jake's sort of gay but she's used to him now and he keeps it away from the bedside. He's a good nurse. She's lucky to have him and Carole – both members of the afternoon shift are Hospital Wing rejects.

Jake catches her eye, stifles the snigger. He's preparing the treatments wagon. He doesn't usually like Peggy's sort of straight but he's used to her now and she doesn't push it. They've worked together for a couple of years, she knows her job, and she's never sloppy. It gets up his nose the way most people piss around.

21

Like Peggy and Granny Porter, Jake is important in this story. He's twenty-seven, pony-tailed, quick, small, sharp-featured, and he arrived at the House via a young designer friend who died of AIDS. That got him out of the design scene and, wanting to help, into hospital nursing. Four years of not being able to, of deaths and more deaths, got him out of hospital nursing and into the prison service. He couldn't bear to see another Kaposi sarcoma, and someone had told him that prison inmates were shipped out before they reached that stage. And once he was in the prison service – because he's smart and bright – it was only a short step to Justice City, and once he was in Justice City – because he's happy with the work the House does – it was only a short step here.

There are two ways of getting on to the staff of the House. Either you're drafted here because the Hospital Wing wants to get shot of you, or you apply because you're happy with the House's work. Jake applied. He's done his punishments stint downstairs and now he's thresholding. He's happy with the House's work; he sees its point. He doesn't enjoy the reality of it, to be blunt, the pain, but he sees its point. This might be thought a narrow distinction, but both for him and for the House's director (who screens out the enjoyers) it's sufficient. The way the system works there's precious little sadists could go for, but no one wants to take the risk.

As far as Jake is concerned it had been a brilliant idea, officially separating off two of the traditional prison functions, retribution and incarceration (the two Ps, Punishment and Protection), from the rest. The other four functions, denunciation, deterrence, reparation and rehabilitation – especially rehabilitation, which had long been discredited – simply confused the issue. It was obvious, really. People wanted to be protected, and they wanted villains to be punished – the rest was élitist egg-head shit. Even so, it had needed the government to be in serious trouble, its electorate genuinely pissed off at the apparent avalanche of crime engulfing them, much of it drug-related and seemingly unstoppable, before ministers realized that maybe a concentration on the two Ps was the answer.

If justice was to be seen to be done (vital in any democracy), and at reasonable cost (equally vital), then quite short periods of Punishment (provided it was sharp enough) would do the trick, as long as they were balanced by quite long periods of Protection (provided it was cheap enough). That way both the public and the Treasury would be satisfied. The liberal lobby, it was thought, could bleat to its heart's content: bleat, and be out-voted.

Cheapness was the crux of the matter (sharpness was simply a question of finding something the bleeding heart couldn't get too exercised about), and cheapness most of all meant low staffing levels. Conventional prisons are ruinously labour-intensive. Hence the government-sponsored psycho-sociological research team that came up with LTI (Long Term Incarceration) as secure but lightly staffed protection, and the government-sponsored neurological research team that came up with EAT (Extreme Audio-frequency Treatment) as sharpish but reasonably bleeding-hearts-proof punishment. And hence, finally, the government-sponsored P & P programme that builds centres like Justice City, where Punishment really does punish and where Protection really does protect – life imprisonment means what is says here, and shorter sentences average out at around twenty-seven years. No riots, either – lack of free association takes care of that, plus individual self-contained cell suites for every inmate.

Jake approves. He didn't enjoy his time downstairs in Punishments, and he's glad to be working up here now, and LTI gives him the creeps, but he sees the point of both.

Peggy Landon opens her folder and checks the two brief notes she made upstairs. She asks Jake, 'How's Marsden three-two-seven?' (That's the Christian Scientist.) 'Looking good?'

23

'Looking very good.' Jake tosses his pony-tail. 'He's a dish.'

'He's married, Jake. I gather, happily.' These saucy rituals bore her. She's not getting old — they always did. 'I was referring to his signs.'

'Some of my best friends are married, lovey. I gather, happily. His signs are fine.'

She watches Jake break open a glass ampoule and hold it up to the overhead light as he fills a disposable syringe from it. He has slender, feminine hands that a few years ago, on a man, would have been called artistic. He puts the prepared syringe on the stainless steel rack with the others.

'He isn't used to barbiturates, Jake. Perhaps I should take a look. If he's gone too deep I shall have to recalculate.'

'He has and I already have.' Jake indicates a tagged syringe among the others on the rack, and hands her the chart. 'I'd hate him to miss out on anything.'

'So would I.' Thresholding requires exact levels of drug-induced amnesia, paralysis and narcosis. Jake's chart will be faultless. Marsden will be borderline conscious for his thresh-olding, yet paralysed and totally amnesiac. She passes the chart back across the counter, unread. 'Just so long as he's firing on all six.' She looks over Jake's shoulder, into the dispensary. He's irritated her, she's not sure why, and she tells him waspishly, 'Those shelves are a mess.'

His hands are still for a moment. He knows, as she does, that the state of the shelves is neither his fault nor, solely, his responsibility. But he also knows that a guy like him, especially this early on a grey morning, can be too perfect.

'It's time I checked the stock,' he says. 'Two birds with one stone, lovey. I'll see to it later. I promise.'

Granny Porter hurries by, his knees hurting him, carrying a broom and a long-handled dustpan and a bucket full of dusters from the cupboard under the stairs. He's making for the corridor to the thresholding rooms. Carole's coming the other way, retying her nurse's apron round her large waist.

They meet in the entrance to the corridor and pass economically.

Carole Serote – that's Carole pronounced as in *parole* – is very black, Nigerian black, and in Granny Porter's eyes she's a fierce wild woman. In Carole Serote's eyes Granny Porter is a man in need of a good hot bath that she isn't allowed to give him.

They pass. Carole sees Peggy Landon outside the dispensary. 'Morning, Dr Landon,' she sings out. 'How are we this blessed morning?'

Don't worry – Carole Serote isn't the cliché Bible-bashing black: she's no more godly than anyone else in Justice City. The *blesseds* are left over from her parents in evangelical Hackney. But she does bring genuine enthusiasm to her mornings. She's broad and she's brave. She laughs at simple things and she takes lip from no man. She survived Hackney housing and Hackney schools, and she's seen from inside the anger and despair of the unconstrained human condition. Growing up among men with neither discipline nor hope, she quickly figured out how the lack of the first caused the lack of the second. And now, in the nursing service, and the prison service, she can try to give men both. It doesn't always work out that way, in fact it hardly ever does, but she believes she's in the right place. If she offers joyful phrases it's because she's joyful.

She takes in Peggy Landon's white, wary face: white in the sense that it isn't black; wary in the sense that, like most white faces meeting hers, it's wary.

It suggests that she should tone down her greeting. 'I'd say you're doing all right, Dr Landon.'

Peggy is mollified. 'Running to catch up, Carole. It's going to be a long winter.'

She knows she ought to correct Carole when she calls her *Doctor*, and she occasionally does, but Carole takes no notice. To Carole flattery is clearly common courtesy; also, *Doctor* raises the tone of the establishment. Peggy's boss doesn't like it, and complains, but the Herr Direktor spends most of his time at meetings, and government hearings, and overseas seminars, and she seldom sees him.

The Herr Direktor (Jake's name for him) has a genuine, if lowly, medical degree. But Dr Mellish's ambitions, which are enormous, lie in the field of hospital management. He's in Chicago at the moment, at a hospital management seminar, which he'll soon discover is a good place for him to be on this particular Tuesday.

Peggy tells Carole about the indecent exposure's allergy, and sends her to the store upstairs for a polyfibre pillow. Granny Porter comes back with his dustpan and broom and bucket of dusters and disappears through the door to the thresholding rooms. The musak plays. She asks Jake, 'Do you know anything about a man called Albert Beech?'

'*Albert* Beech? That's who this morning's Beech is? Of course I do.' Jake fills the last of the syringes and puts it on the rack. That's four syringes for the inductees and a couple more for back-up. 'Too quick with his prick and his razor, our Bert was. A real sod. When he wasn't running half London's crime. DNA matching got him. Tried to get it thrown out on appeal – dodgy procedures, all that shit – but he didn't stand a chance. The appeal court verdict came through a couple of days ago. I saw it on the tube. They were dancing in the streets. I mean that. Really dancing in the streets.'

Peggy frowns. 'I missed it. Yes, that's our Beech. Didn't you recognize him?'

'Do me a favour. All the tube ever gives you is a blanket leaving the courtroom, and a solicitor rabbiting on about his client's innocence.'

'The papers?'

'*Your* papers, lovey. Me, I stick with the qualities. Recipes I can't afford and London restaurants I'll never eat at. Never pictures of mad rapists.'

Peggy shrugs. She seldom reads the tabloids. She seldom

looks at a paper at all. There's never time ... She flicks through the folder on her clipboard to Albert Beech's sentence and holds it out to Jake. 'He's going to be sorry,' she says.

Jake doesn't look. He's checking the contents of the wagon: surgical spirit, swabs, cotton wool, adhesive tape, mouthguards, electrode contact jelly, blood pressure cuff, stethoscope, thermometer, all the pre-thresholding paraphernalia. There are inmates Jake would have a shorter, sharper way with. And he'd pull the switch himself.

He unlatches the half-door and pushes it open. As he gloves up Peggy steps back to let him pass with the wagon. She asks, 'Who's in number six?'

'Petersen, six-six-three.'

She goes through the swing door out of the foyer and down the passage to the washroom where she scrubs her hands. Then she joins Jake and his wagon outside the end thresholding room, number six, just across the passage. These spatial relationships are going to be important. The folder Jake hands her confirms Petersen six-six-three as the unpaid child support and, according to the examining doctor, the perfect patient. Maybe she should check. Rain lashes briefly against the window beside her. She sighs. Who does she think she is, on a foul morning like this, to question the wisdom of the examining doctor?

Jake bangs his wagon through into the thresholding room. The man on the bed is prepped and Jake's noisy arrival doesn't shift him. The door flaps shut behind them and they leave the musak behind. Peggy formally checks the plastic ID bracelet on his right wrist: Petersen, six-six-three. She also checks his appearance against his description on the medical report sheet. They tally. Unconscious on a waterproof plastic sheet, Petersen six-six-three is stripped to the waist and contact electrodes have been taped to his chest and his jaw and his temples. Fine wires lead away from the electrodes to monitors above the bed, and on to the screens and recording

27

equipment in the work station across the corridor, outside the soundproofed room. Petersen's wrists and ankles are strapped to padded supports around the bedframe and Petersen's head, on its pillow, is distanced from any hard surface. Peggy's pleased to know that in all her time at the House these regulation precautions, and the mouthguard she will now insert, have never been needed. They're specified in order to protect inductees from convulsions due to sloppy thresholding.

She puts her clipboard down on the bed by Petersen's legs, snaps on a pair of plastic gloves from the wagon, and inserts the mouthguard. Jake gives her the stethoscope and she listens to Petersen's breathing, checks his vital signs, and compares her findings with the on-going read-out above his bed.

The room, although windowless, appears friendly. Like the musak-filled foyer, it has a friendly air to it. Very occasionally an inductee arrives *compos mentis* from Inductions, having dodged his hot beverage or whatever, and nobody wants to risk a rough-house, so the approaches to thresholding look friendly: the colours of the rooms are oysterish and rosy, the soundproofing is invisible, the EAT diffusers resemble heating vents, and the bed is superficially of standard hospital design, with a rosy candlewick spread covering the plastic sheet. TV surveillance is through a small one-way mirror, nicely framed, above a wooden console table, the monitors above the bed are concealed until needed behind tactful cupboard doors, and there's a vase of very presentable plastic flowers on the table under the mirror. The vase completes the domestic picture, and the National Health Service anti-smoking posters on the walls keep things plausible. Friendly, but not effusive.

Carole comes in from a room up the corridor, where she's been changing the indecent exposure's pillow. She's late, but it's Dr Landon's fault for not waiting. Two nurses are supposed to be with the doctor at all times when she's in a room with an inductee.

Carole stands at the foot of the bed, arms folded, watching as Dr Landon rotates Petersen's left arm, exposing the smooth skin inside his elbow. She taps it, looking for a vein, then cleans it with surgical spirit and inserts the needle of the disposable hypodermic syringe Jake has handed her from his rack. She depresses the plunger slowly, then removes the needle. A tiny spark of blood shows. She keeps an eye on it, meanwhile dropping the used syringe into the waste sack slung at the end of Jake's wagon. The spark stays tiny, and dulls. Jake's drug cocktail takes effect very quickly: Petersen's breathing slows and, although there's no other obvious change in his condition, Carole gets a sense of him settling, of him giving up as he will one day in death. Carole is sorry for him, as she always is for inductees no matter what they've done, genuinely sorry. She asks him in her head, as she always asks inductees, genuinely asks him to forgive her. She knows that what happens next, and next and next, although not nice, will be for his own good, but in her head she doesn't tell him that. It wouldn't be helpful.

Peggy assures herself that Petersen is responding correctly. The electronics will be confirming each specific effect, but she likes to believe that clinical experience can contribute. She checks reflexes, skin temperature, colour, flaccidity, that sort of thing. Jake clicks his tongue and points, drawing her attention to Petersen's right hand, which has relaxed and opened: there's something in it. An acorn, stuck to the sweat. Peggy reaches across his rib-cage, takes the acorn and examines it. That's all it is, an acorn. She's moved – it's a curious treasure to have brought so far. As she leaves the room she puts it on the table under the see-through mirror, by the vase of plastic flowers, ready for Petersen when he wakes.

Carole and Jake, with his wagon, join her outside. In the room across the corridor at the foyer end is the work station where the EAT programmes for all six thresholding rooms are monitored. This morning only the four end rooms are in use, numbers three to six. Jake leads the way to number five, thumps its door open with the wagon, crashing into Granny Porter who's standing just inside and hasn't heard them coming on account of the soundproofing.

'Fuckin' arseholes. Don't you never look where you're goin', prick?'

It's a fair, if needlessly anatomical question. There's a glass port hole in the door for Jake to see through, and Granny was dusting off the flowers, and now they're all across the floor and the trolley's run over them. It's only luck he hasn't dropped the vase and broken it.

Jake doesn't answer. He offers 'Sod off' and pushes past. The racket with Granny and the door, or something, has roused the man on the bed. He's Beech nine-seven-seven, and he's bigger than Petersen, and maybe Inductions didn't get his dosage numbers right. He's awake enough to twist his head on the pillow and his bare feet spread their toes.

Jake reaches the bedside, Peggy close behind him. He already has a swab and a syringe ready. Beech's hand, below the padded strap, is clenching and unclenching. There's no danger of his getting loose, the bed and the straps are stronger than he, but injecting an unwilling patient can be messy.

Carole is at the other side of the bed now, her hands on Beech's shoulders, leaning. Granny Porter has gathered up the flowers – the trolley squashed one and it's shed all its petals – and now he gapes at Beech, and sidles closer. Beech lifts his head, his chest heaves, and his eyes above his beard open very wide. His chest is so hairy that areas have had to be shaved for the contacts.

As Jake steadies his arm and Peggy inserts the needle and depresses the plunger, Beech smiles in astonishment and says, quite clearly, 'Wishbone?'

30

And again, trailing off, '*Wishbone* . . .?'
After which he's safely unconscious.
Two words. No, the same word twice.
His last.

two

Forty minutes earlier, when this story began, Chief Inspector Alec Duncan was driving out from the centre of Liverpool, south along Strand Street past the law courts, making for Toxteth and the Aigburth Road. He'd come from Birkenhead, through the Queensway tunnel under the river, and his eyes were still smarting from the fumes. Running the car fan didn't help much: the morning rush hour was building up, the sodden clouds lay on the roof-tops down there in the city, and what the fan sucked in was as poisonous as the air already in the car.

Alec Duncan had spent the night backing up the Terrorist Squad on a stake-out in Bidston, outside an IRA bomb factory in one of a crumbling row of terraced houses more or less under the M53. They knew about the factory; they wanted the men. But tip-offs worked both ways, and Alec's team had passed a fruitless night. He'd sent them home at eight, after the grudging January dawn had revealed their operation for the farce it was. Grown men playing cops and robbers in draughty inadequate doorways while matey stayed snug at home, pissing himself laughing.

Alec, come to that, was close to pissing himself now, with the coffee he'd drunk. Frank Grove's good lady was generous, provisioning both her Frank and her Frank's gaffer, and she did a good pair of thermoses, freshly ground, none of your instant. Her sandwiches were less chic, though, very

Chapel, reflecting her Betws-y-coed childhood, and the supermarket bread lay heavy now, adding to his problems.

He glanced at his watch. He ought to be reporting back to the station. That could wait. He'd phone in when he got to May's. Cluttering the radio wasn't welcome and his carphone was in one of its moods. The station sparks had been promising to look at it for weeks.

He turned his Rover into the Aigburth Road. Some hot-shot hurtled past him, horn blasting, doing maybe seventy. Alec closed his eyes. If he saw the hot-shot's number plate he'd have to do something.

He put a hand inside his jacket and massaged his belly. At least Sergeant Grove still had a good lady, which — what with the hours and the company they kept — was more than could be said for most coppers. As for him and his May, they came and went: in emotional terms he wasn't much more than her lodger, and in practical terms he was even less. Certainly not regular hot meals, a coffee thermos, sandwiches. She had a full-time job of her own in town. He'd been married once, properly, in a registry office, but years ago and not for long. May suited him, they suited each other, and there was always his sister Morag's place for when things got hairy. The station canteen served muck and he ate out a lot, at decent restaurants. A couple of pubs in town would feed him any night in exchange for a set at the piano — imitation Nat King Cole, with Art Tatum decorations — but he went to them less and less. He enjoyed the jazz he played but he enjoyed expensive food more these days, and he'd not got much else to spend his chief inspector's salary on.

He was young for the rank, only forty-one, and the wrong colour too, black. He'd been the youngest sergeant on the Merseyside force, black or white, and the youngest inspector, and now he was the youngest chief inspector. Positive discrimination? Not his problem. If anybody's, then it was other people's. He'd done the job, got some breaks, and seen a whole echelon above him go on corruption charges. When they'd promoted him he'd asked for Frank Grove as his sergeant. Frank was Liverpool born. Alec was only fifteen years down from Edinburgh, and he knew he needed a Scouse if he was to get in with the locals.

Left off the Aigburth Road it was a short jog to Lark Lane, then the beginnings of snobby Sefton Park. Alec stopped for his paper at the Love Lane newsagent. While he was waiting to be served, other front pages on the rack caught his attention. MUGGER'S DELIGHT ... GRANNIE GET YOUR GUN ... RAPIST'S CHARTER ... A legal commission of inquiry was recommending slight liberalizations to recent changes in court procedures. Alec hadn't bothered with the details – the tabloids had taken off against them so there wasn't a chance of their going through. His own paper, his and May's, was headlining the effect a big arms sale to Egypt had had on unemployment figures.

Alexander Duncan from Edinburgh ... black skinned and a Duncan, and not just from Edinburgh but actually from one of the nice squares up by the University. Nice people lived up there, raising nice daughters with names like Jean. It was all the Festival's fault – the Festival and John Knox's loss of clout in the middle 1950s. Plus a daring nineteen-year-old girl's passion for jazz, a poorly attended Fringe event from Philadelphia, a bass player who was smooth and beautiful, and a rare spell of fine weather. Jean never regretted her bass player. In West Princes Street Gardens he shared with her the two most sinful and resplendent early mornings of her life. The blackness of her son, if she wasn't expecting it, often shocked her, but never the blackness of his father. His name had faded in her memory, but never his voice or the beery smell of his breath, or his body.

Jean's husband John, a liberal-minded local journalist acquired when Alexander was four, was understanding. More than that. Romantic, and a versatile sexual fantasist, he was secretly in love, and making love, through her, with the bass player. He took off, after a couple of years or so, to live with a bass player (or at any rate a man) of his own. Jean was distressed, but grateful for the daughter he laid on her before he left. She never told her parents, respectable Edinburgh people, the details of the separation, and they went to their graves congratulating themselves on having found him for her – before John they'd been more or less reconciled to a shamed daughter and an illegitimate grandson who they were additionally obliged to admit, when pressed, was 'dusky'. They lived, as has already been said, in one of the nice squares up by the University. Jean acquired 'good lady' from them, and more of the sort, and passed them on to Alexander. The West Princes Street Gardens apart, she was a respectable Edinburgh person herself.

Alexander's half sister Morag, born when he was five, grew up believing herself the only girl in the world with a nig-nog older brother ('dusky' had been laughed to bits on her first day in the big girls' playground). She was passionately racist. She hated whites and never thought she'd marry one, but these things happened. She had a white husband now, a socialist science teacher, Iain Hardy, and two white children. It was Iain's job in Liverpool, in the big central Comprehensive, that had made Alec apply for a transfer south. He and Morag were very close.

Such transfers were seldom authorized but he was pushing for promotion even then and the Edinburgh force had run out of excuses. They wanted his sort, but not above the rank of sergeant.

He wondered sometimes why he'd gone into the police. His grandparents had hoped for a nice university degree, and then accountancy. Perhaps that was why. His mother, for once, had supported his decision. So, of course, had his twelve-year-old sister. He was going to set the world to rights for her.

Now, nearly twenty-five years later, there was always a bed for him in Morag's house. For the moment, though, he was with May in Sefton Park. His lodger status wasn't much, but it might improve if he worked at it. He saw the clock above the newsagent's counter and left in a hurry, one heel skidding on 'the greasy black pavement. May would be leaving for work soon and he didn't want to miss her. He drove on up Lark Lane.

The name was long past raising a laugh: boarded-up shops, a few sooty trees, a sour residue of dead leaves in its unswept gutters. Even the kebab take-away had failed. Alec drove slowly, steering with his knees as he looked at the crossword on the back page for a couple of words he and Frank hadn't got. At the end of Lark Lane, before Sefton Park proper, there were three ambulances and a police road block.

Alec drew in to the kerb and wound down the Rover's window. By the time the constable in his green fluorescent waistcoat reached him he had his wallet out and was showing his warrant card. The routine he got, when in plain clothes like today, as just another coon, nigger, groid, black bastard, no longer amused him. The other officers' faces, when he finally got round to identifying himself, no longer amused him. Caught out, not shamed, just caught out, they'd never amused him.

'What's going on, Constable?'

'A purge on Needle Heaven, sir. The local Residents' Association has been camping on the super's doorstep.'

Alec didn't altogether blame them. If you had a park you'd like to be able to sit in it without gangs of addicts bollock-naked, spoiling the view – the men shot up in their penises these days, when the veins in their arms had died. There was a fine Victorian glasshouse in the middle of the park, near the lake, a wintergarden with a pretty wrought-iron staircase and a gallery up among the palm fronds: these days you couldn't breathe in it for the piss and the vomit, you couldn't walk in it for the condoms and the syringes, and the staircase had been closed since some girl threw herself off the gallery.

The ferms underneath had been damaged more than she, but you couldn't count on it.

'It's a seasonal event, Constable. Like the Teddy Bears' Picnic. I wish you well of it.'

'Thank you, sir. Fact is, sir, I'm glad I'm on traffic. What's going on in there is no picnic.'

'Very true, Constable.' Sanctimonious bastard. 'You've been here before.'

'Last year, sir. Didn't sleep proper for nights.'

Alec nodded. The constable was very young. From behind him came distant sounds of shouting, screams, breaking glass, dogs barking. Alec wound up the car window and drove on slowly. He could think of better uses for the police. People who had reached Needle Heaven had nowhere else to go. A day or two down by the ferry terminal, maybe, then they'd be back. For those sent on detox, a week away, even a month, then they'd be back too. Cosmetic policing. He did too much of it. Showing the Blue.

He turned into the road that circled the park. On the right, big Victorian houses behind dark laurels, made into flats, one of them May's, and on the left low spiked park railings and more laurels. The laurels might have been something else, but to Alec anything shrubby and evergreen and depressing was laurel. The time was eight fifty, just about when Peggy Landon, in Justice City, was dosing Petersen six-six-three, the unpaid child support.

Alec squinted through the windscreen. His sleepless night had caught up with him. His eyes hurt, his stomach was full of cold ball-bearings, and his urethra had gone into spasm. A hundred yards ahead of him, on the right, the laurels in the park were agitated. They parted and a young man, stubbly-haired with wisps of ginger beard, backed out through them. From his clothes and his filth and his emaciation, an addict. He turned, lurching, and found himself up against the waist-high railings. He tried climbing over them,

37

hopped and strained, and dropped back on to the wet mossy earth. Alec stopped the Rover a few yards short of him.

The addict looked back over his shoulder, probably hearing voices on the other side of the bushes. His head movement was a spasm, a jerky scooping motion with his jawbone. All his movements were spasms. He flung himself at the fence again and scrabbled to get over, hooking one foot up between two spikes. He hoisted his body, shuffled the other foot up, both out on the same side, and teetered. A shoe stuck between the spikes and he eased it, swaying. Then he braced himself and lunged forward, one arm collapsing as the other flailed for balance above his head. His painted felt waistcoat caught on a spike and tore. One foot pushed out successfully from the railing but the other lost purchase and flew away behind him. He fell heavily, gouging his shin, and lay sprawled on the pavement, suddenly still. Alec put his paper away and got out of the car. His bladder had waited so long it could wait a bit longer. It was a draughty, grey, miserable rotten day to lie bleeding in the street.

The addict was grunting. Behind him, in the bushes on the other side of the railings, men crashed about and called softly to each other. Alec ran to the man on the pavement, crouched down beside him. His eyes, startlingly blue, were wide open, and wild.

'Fuck off, man. I mean, fuck the hell off.'

Alec experimentally straightened the young man's legs. Nothing seemed to be broken. His bowels had leaked, perhaps as a result of the fall.

'I said, fuck the hell off. I don't need this.'

His voice was gone, his whisper a blast of sour heroin in Alec's face. Speaking had revealed a broken front tooth, the others slack and yellow. Alec eased an arm under him and sat him up. One jean leg was ripped almost to the crotch and blood flowed sluggishly from the gash made by the spike of the railing.

'That's going to need attention,' Alec told him. 'I've got a car.'

The addict hit at him feebly, and fell sideways. 'What the fuck d'you think you're doing? Who the fuck d'you think you are?'

The hate was general. Racism was one thing being an addict beat out of you. There was no black or white, OD-ing on some piss-soaked mattress.

Alec heaved him to his feet. 'My name's Alec. I'm taking you to get that leg seen to.'

'Fucking railings. I was the school's champion fucking high jump. D'you know that?' He tried to stand on his own and failed. 'That's Toxteth fucking Grammar — we aren't all idiots, you know. I was Toxteth Grammar's champion fucking high jump.'

Alec was leading, half-carrying him away. As they reached the Rover the men's voices behind them grew louder. Alec unlocked the car door, tipped his burden in, slammed it shut.

'Sir? Excuse me . . . Sir? Sir . . .?'

One of the men behind him, one of the policemen, was calling. Like the addict, Alec didn't need it. Head down, he went slowly, purposefully round the car and sat in the driver's seat. He could see the two policemen now, standing behind the railings. One of them was restraining an Alsatian; the other vaulted over the railings. Alec started his engine and flicked the right indicator. The addict was swearing hoarsely, crumpled sideways, his knees above the dashboard. Alec leaned sideways, pounded them down, and heaved the seatbelt across him. The two policemen were watching, uncertain, one on each side of the railings. Alec fitted his own belt, looked carefully in the mirror at the deserted road, and drove off, decent and slow. When the two policemen came into view in the mirror they were still watching the dirty blue Rover but neither of them seemed to be making a note of its number. They had enough in the bag — they didn't need his friend here. Personal arrests made paperwork. And anyway, what would they arrest him for?

Alec glanced sideways at his passenger. A dealer? Too poor and too destroyed. A user. Charge him for possession – half a gram stuffed in his Y-fronts? Run that past the sergeant and see what it did for him . . .

Looking at the addict, at his unshaven skeletal face, his filthy black felt jacket hand-painted with silver pentangles, his layers of greasy shirts, Alec wondered why the hell he was bothering. There'd been a risk, ignoring the Drug Squad officers – he could have said he hadn't heard them, and was taking the addict into custody, but why had he bothered? The addict's total wretchedness? Past hope, past help, shitting himself on the pavement? Why not be the copper with the heart of gold for once? Alec wondered if he'd have done the same if the young man had been black.

No. He didn't wonder because he knew. If the addict had been black he'd have driven straight by.

'Nice wheels you've got, man.' The addict had been in shock. Now he was coming out. 'That was great, y'know. What you did there – that was great. You saved my fucking life.'

Alec grunted. 'Nothing so fancy.'

The breathy croak continued. 'In China, if you saved someone's life it used to make you fucking responsible for him for ever.'

'This isn't China. I'll see your leg gets fixed. That's my limit.'

'No offence meant . . . I tell you, man, the last fucking time the Blue lifted me I ended up less a couple of fucking gnashers.' He pulled up his lip with grimy fingers to show the gap. 'See that? Blood all over the fucking place. And they made me scrub out the fucking cell.'

Alec had heard it all before. 'Did you enter a complaint?'

'You must be joking, man. I wanted to get out of that fucking place alive, didn't I?'

Alec let it go. He didn't want to sound like a copper. He didn't know why he was doing this, but now that he was he'd rather keep things simple. Matey here would need to be sharp before he spotted the gun under his left arm. Alec hated the bloody thing but villains had a lot at stake these days – and at least the new government issue holsters fitted properly. You didn't walk around announcing your profession.

The addict was looking round, fingering the Rover's walnut trim. He got to the centre console, the telephone between the front seats. 'So what's the mike and stuff? You with Merseyside fucking radio, or what?'

Alec was guarded. 'Do you listen?'

'I could tell you a thing or two about Sefton Park, man. Shock horror. Sex games in net curtain land. Make a good piece. TV would be better . . .'

May's flat was just up ahead. Alec indicated early and pulled out to the right, glad of the distraction. 'I've a friend here,' he said. 'How's the leg?'

'Fucking terrible.'

Alec drove in between stone gate pillars and parked at the side of the house, on mossy green gravel. 'We're going in here for a wee while and we'll clean up your leg and bandage it. And listen – I want you to spare my friend the *fuckings*. I cannot believe your vocabulary is that impoverished. Right?'

'Moving in high society, are we? Pardon me for fucking breathing.'

'Listen to me. Her name's Calcott. And she won't be shocked, only bored, and we need her help. So shut your mouth.' Alec opened the car door, looked back over his shoulder. 'What shall I call you?'

'Humphrey. Why not call me Humphrey? It sounds like a name with connections.'

Alec got out of the car. Humphrey, which wasn't his name, showed no sign of moving. Alec went round to him, opened the door, released his seat belt, hauled him out. The sparky talk had been all sparky talk – Humphrey could scarcely stand. He leaned on the roof of the Rover and shuddered.

'You're a mess,' Alec told him. 'Let's be glad your mother can't see you.'

He supported Humphrey to the side door of the house, May's entrance. Branches dripped on them. May's little Ford was still parked in the drive out front, so she hadn't yet left for the office.

Humphrey propped himself against the wall by the door, gasping. 'A man like you, y'know, black, y'know, why the fuck are you doing this?'

Alec hoisted him up the wall by a fistful of shirt. 'One more *fuck* out of you, matey, and I'm not.'

There had to be, somewhere, a limit.

May opened the door. Alec hadn't rung the bell – she'd heard the commotion. 'I'm just on my way out,' she said.

'Humphrey here's hurt his leg. I said we'd bind it for him.'

May, in her neat solicitor's outfit, considered the two of them. She allowed only just so many irregularities in her life, and Alec knew that on his own he was already stretching things. Especially in a suit he'd slept in. She glanced at her watch. So did he. The time was nine o'clock.

'You'll have to help yourself, Alec. I hope you know what you're doing.'

'No big deal, May. Ah . . . May Calcott, this is Humphrey. Humphrey, this is May Calcott.'

From behind them, even at this distance, there were faint sounds of the police operation over on the other side of the park. May looked past them, then asked Alec, 'Is that anything to do with you?'

Her choice of words, mercifully, omitted his profession. 'Me personally, no.' He edged forward. Humphrey wasn't contributing. 'May we come in?'

She stepped back. 'I was just on my way out.'

But she let them in. Alec tooked Humphrey into the kitchen, sat him down by the table, and crouched to look at

42

his leg. May stayed out in the hallway, watching. As if he sensed her hostility, Humphrey stirred himself.

'You've got a nice fu – you've got a nice place here, Mrs Calcutt.' His speech rhythms were shot without the decorations.

May didn't answer. 'If they're bad enough,' she said to Alec, 'it lets you love them.'

He frowned. He was rolling up the ripped trouser leg, out of the way. His hands jerked, then stilled. Why was she so hard on him? 'Stay here,' he said to Humphrey. 'I'll get hot water.'

May joined him at the sink while he was running the water and filling a plastic bowl. She put a hand on the back of his neck and gently kneaded the muscles. 'I'll call you when I reach the office.'

'Don't leave it too long. When I'm done with this wee bastard I'm for my bed.'

She kissed the back of his head, went out past Humphrey without a word, and left the house. She knew an addict when she saw one. She made no secret of where she stood – she had nothing to say to addicts. If they wanted to kill themselves there were tidier ways. He heard her rev angrily as she drove away.

He fetched disinfectant, gauze and a bandage from the bathroom, had a long overdue piss while he was there, cleaned out the wound as thoroughly as Humphrey would let him, which wasn't much, and bound it up. The flesh was bloodless and flaccid and probably wouldn't heal. If it went rotten enough, in a week or two it would land Humphrey in hospital. Addicts let things go. It could lose him half his leg if it went rotten enough.

He made Humphrey a mug of sweet instant coffee and tipped shortbread biscuits on to the table beside it. May's words rankled and the joy was gone from the morning. He wasn't the addict – why take it out on him?

'You could be done for indecent exposure,' he said, 'wearing those jeans.'

He went into May's bedroom, their bedroom, where he had wardrobe space, and hauled out a beat-up pair he used for gardening. But when he held them up he saw that Humphrey was far more May's size than his, so he found a pair of hers. While he was there he remembered the station and rang through on the phone by the bed. He'd be in around four, he said, when he'd had some sleep. He spoke softly, in case Humphrey should hear him, but he needn't have bothered. Humphrey was a mess. His hands were shaking and he'd spilled the coffee. Alec flung him the jeans. May wasn't fat, nudging a hundred and ten pounds, but they had to be furled in round Humphrey's waist like a sail.

Alec checked in his wallet, took out three of the four tenners and stuffed them into Humphrey's waistcoat pocket, on top of the tin box he'd already felt there, containing Humphrey's gear. Not a hand-out – basic crime prevention. One fewer little old ladies mugged in Aigburth that Tuesday for the price of a fix.

He took Humphrey, limping, to the door. Humphrey asked for the toilet first. He came out feeling better. Alec took him to the door again and he stood jauntily in the open doorway, looking round.

'That's it, then? No fucking lecture?'

'No fucking lecture.'

Humphrey turned and backed away, little steps on his toes across the gravel, looking up at the house. He'd shot up in the toilet, as Alec had known he would, and he was flying. Even his voice was better.

His bright blue eyes took in the downstairs windows, the many drainpipes, the red alarm box. 'That's nice . . . Work nights, do you?'

'Not if I can help it.' Humphrey might be mocking him but his drift was clear. A woman on her own at nights, no bars on the windows, a medieval alarm system . . . This

44

whole Samaritan thing was a mistake. The man who fell among thieves had been a law-abiding citizen. 'Miss Calcott is wired direct to the station,' Alec said, lying. 'All the flats along here are. I'd have expected you to know that.'

Humphrey made fluid calming gestures. He might have been a dancer. 'Only kidding, man. Only kidding . . .'

'Of course you were. And Humphrey . . .' He tried, one last time, to reach him. 'Do me a favour, will you? Keep out of trouble. OK? If you meet a copper, walk straight? OK?'

'What for, man? The Blue can't touch me.' He twirled round and round, scattering mossy gravel. 'You don't think I'm still in possession?'

Alec sighed. 'I suppose not.'

'Right on, man. Right fucking on. The Blue can't touch me.' He sauntered away down the drive, pausing at the end to hitch up his trousers, May's trousers, and wave. Four hours, six maybe, then his veins would be hungry again.

Alec watched till he was out of sight, then closed the door and leaned against it, bone weary. The telephone rang, startling him. He nearly didn't answer it.

'Chief Inspector Duncan . . .'

'Alec. I said I'd call. Are you all right?'

'I'm fine, May. Fine . . . And May, I'm sorry I stuck you with matey.'

'And I'm sorry I said what I did. It wasn't true.'

Silence. They'd spoken too quickly for it to signify. Too easily. And besides, it probably *was* true. Alec cleared his throat.

'I'm for my bed, then.'

'Have you eaten? You should have eaten.'

'I'll eat this afternoon. What does your day look like?'

'Magistrates' Court. Traffic offences, shop-lifting, a GBH . . . Oh, and a Commercial Premises Health Act prosecution that might be interesting.'

He didn't want to know. 'We'll eat out, May. Try to get home early.'

'Not a hope. Hold things with some soup. There's a carton of that lentil stuff in the fridge.'

'Sounds fine. Fine. Well then . . . See you.'

'See you.'

He half lowered the receiver, then raised it again. 'Thanks for calling, May.'

The line buzzed at him. She'd already rung off. He went through to the bedroom, removed his jacket and his gun, flung himself on the bed, on top of the duvet, still wearing his shoes, and instantly fell asleep. The time was half past nine.

At half past ten, over in Justice City, Albert Beech's death would be discovered.

three

Jake de Carteret dandles his herbal teabag on the end of its piece of string. He counts the dandles: too few and it's nun's piss, too many and it's paint remover. Twelve is the ideal number, if the water's hot enough — which it bloody well ought to be, coming from the sterilizer. The sterilizer's used for little else these days, since the arrival of disposable syringes, disposable forceps, disposable scalpels, disposable everything. Disposable nurses, he thinks some days, when he's feeling particularly unnecessary. Is that what he did his training for? They'd computerize him easy as kiss your arse, if the union'd let them.

It's coming up to ten fifteen and Jake's in the dispensary. Since he left Peggy Landon in the control room at the start of the thresholding cycle he's been over here stock-taking. He keeps his promises. The shelves are neater now than they've been in months and he's filled up half an indent form with orders for Herself to initial. He's been on duty in the House since six and now he's having his break. There's a book on the counter by his tea mug, a paperback classic, E. M. Forster, but he isn't reading it. He's planning a dinner menu on the back of the indent form pad. The coming Friday will be Davey's birthday.

At senior administration levels in the prison service homophobia is acute. Maybe it's to be expected that gay lovers won't get married quarters, but discrimination extends from denying shared leave arrangements right down to questions of clothes and appearance. Jake's pony-tail gets by, just (on a nurse, not a warder), but to senior administrators an earring would be a disciplinary matter. Displays of affection between gays they consider very serious offences.

On the ground, though, life is more relaxed – and particularly here in the service's flagship, Justice City. The City leads not only in its treatment of prisoners but also in its personnel relations. A discreet word to the accommodations clerk got Jake and Davey adjoining rooms in male staff quarters, a blind eye was turned to the arrival from a Manchester furniture store of a double bed, and by common consent the other men leave the two of them most of the storage space in the wing's self-service kitchen. This is no big deal for the other officers – most of them prefer to shovel down canteen food and wouldn't be caught dead whipping up an *omelette aux fines herbes* – but it's transformed Jake and Davey's attempts at home-building.

His menu fixed, Jake starts a shopping list. He'll phone it through tomorrow, for delivery on Thursday. There's a prison bus that would take him in to Tesco any day after work, but City people tend to stay put. They keep themselves to themselves. If they go out in uniform they get sidelong looks in the street, children called away back to their mothers, and if they're in civvies there's always the fear of being found out. Telling what you do is a sure-fire conversation stopper.

Jake writes down *aubergines, cheddar cheese, soya protein* ... He and Davey are vegetarians and he's planning a moussaka. Eggs baked in ramekins first, over hazelnut purée. Fruit salad for dessert. Davey has to watch his weight. Even so, a good Australian Chardonnay, just one bottle. . .

Jake pauses, drinks his tea. The dispensary is tiny, not much larger than a walk-in larder, and windowless, so he leaves the top half of the door open, hooked back against the wall. He looks out into the deserted foyer. It's been a quiet morning. With the Herr Direktor away in Chicago they've been left in peace to get on with the job. No visitors. No MPs, no Howard Leaguers on the prowl, no military policemen picking up a tip or two. Jake was over in the control room when Inductions called Herself at around nine forty-five, wanting a progress report on the morning's first batch of inductees. No snags, she told the receiving officer. They'd be ready for their second batch on schedule, sharp at eleven. The control room was peaceful. Their thresholding nearly over, the four in the first batch had less than an hour to go before they were surfaced.

Nurse Serote is servicing them now as they come round, removing electrodes and mouthguards, and Granny Porter is sweeping up. The warders will be up in the lift from Punishments at ten thirty to collect the first.

Herself — Peggy Landon — has gone off for her morning confab downstairs with the punishments officer. She likes to deliver treatment profiles in person, and discuss them. She takes her work seriously and Jake approves. Treatments tread a razor edge of the permissible — he's worked down there and he knows. He thinks of blond bombshell Beech: maybe for him there isn't an impermissible, but do judges have any idea how much that many days of EAT *cost*? In terms of money, never mind the stressed-out warders . . .

Outside in the deserted foyer the musak plays. Jake finishes his tea and listens to it, and loves it. He loves it because it's a secret insult. An insult because it speaks sweetly to men brought here to suffer, and secret because they're not supposed to notice it. Jake grins at the thought.

He knows he's malicious. He genuinely wishes he wasn't, and often — especially with Davey — he isn't, but it's a malicious old world.

He puts down his mug and returns to his shopping list. *Tomatoes, mushrooms, garlic* . . . Nurse Serote comes in from the Closed Area. She leans on the top of the half-door.

'We've got trouble,' she says. She hasn't hurried, and her

voice is as round and musical as always. 'We've got big trouble.'

Jake looks up from his list. 'Where do tomatoes come from at this time of year? Mexico? Maybe I should buy tinned . . .'

She reaches across the counter and turns his list so that she can read it. She's wearing plastic gloves. 'Beech nine-seven-seven,' she says. 'The man's died on us.'

Trouble indeed. Jake gets down off his stool. He believes her immediately but he has an understandable wish to see for himself. He pushes his stool back, opens the door, goes out into the foyer. He asks her, 'Still wired up?' over his shoulder as he goes and she answers, 'Hasn't moved an inch.'

Jake is putting the top on his ballpoint pen and clipping it into the breast pocket of his coat. He leaves the foyer and goes through into the monitoring room. Chief Inspector Duncan will find it interesting that he comes in here rather than going to see the man himself. He turns on the screens – Beech nine-seven-seven's vital signs are all silent flat green lines. Jake slides levers, increasing amplification. Beech nine-seven-seven's lines stay flat and silent. Beside them the other three subjects' lines dance up and down, and beep. It looks as if Beech nine-seven-seven has been disconnected, but Nurse Serote says he hasn't.

He has been, of course. Permanently.

'How long has he been like that?'

She shrugs. 'He was warm when I found him, but he didn't respond. I beat the hell out of him but he wasn't about to come back.'

There's no resuscitation unit kept in the House. They're expensive and nobody's ever seen the need. New arrivals are vetted by the PMO before they get here. EAT isn't fun, but it's more or less guaranteed not to bring on cardiac arrest.

'Have you called our Peggy?'

'Dr Landon isn't in her office. I came straight out to you.'

50

'Of course she's not in her office, lovey. She's downstairs with the profiles.'

She goes down with the profiles every day. Nurse Serote knows that perfectly well. It's the first sign that she's not as much on the ball as she seems to be. Jake pushes past her, crosses the corridor, and goes into Beech nine-seven-seven's thresholding room. She follows him in and they stand on either side of the bed. To an outsider's eye there's desperation in the big, blond-bearded man lying between the two nurses in their hospital uniforms, quite still and quite silent, his bare chest a network of coloured wires and terminals, his blue eyes staring. He's trapped there. The hotel-style room only adds to his despair, and the nurses move closer to him helplessly, and away again.

Jake unstraps a wrist, tests the joint for flexion. He ought to have gloved up but on a dead man he doesn't bother. His eye travels on up the bare arm and he stoops, peering. Then he straightens and gestures for Nurse Serote to come round to his side of the bed and see for herself. This is Beech's left arm, where Peggy Landon gave him his injection, and beside her neat puncture mark there's another, far less neat, and signs of bruising.

Nurse Serote touches the marks as if she can't believe them. As if to brush them away. They won't be brushed.

There are no signs of rigors or discharges. Beech nine-seven-seven seems to have died quite peacefully.

Jake says, 'You stay here and keep any eye out. I'll call downstairs – our Peggy's going to have to tell someone.'

He hurries away. Nurse Serote stops him by the door. 'Get the duty PMO, Jake. There'll be hell if you don't.'

Jake flounces. 'There'll be hell if I do, lovey.'

He continues on through the door, across the passage to the telephone in the control room. He rings the punishments officer, twitching as no one answers. He knows, as does Nurse Serote, that the clumsy second injection mark will take some explaining. That's why he's left her with the body. He can think of no reason for it. No medical reason. No legal reason.

'Punishments officer.'

'Jake de Carteret here. Can I talk to the boss?'

'She's gone. Fifteen minutes – maybe twenty.'

'Did she say where?'

'I didn't ask. I'm trying to sort out that fucking Beech's schedule. Is it important?'

Jake is tempted to give him the good news. To spread himself. He resists. 'Nothing that can't wait. Maybe I'll page her.'

'Do that thing.'

' 'Bye now.'

Jake rings off but the line's already dead. He and that particular punishments officer are old enemies. When he did his stint downstairs as duty nurse he and that particular punishments officer didn't always see eye to eye. Punishments officers as a breed, although necessary, aren't his sort of people.

He hoists one bum cheek up on to the stool and stares at the telephone buttons, his finger poised. Keeping Beech's sad fate within the department is all very well, and Herself really ought to know about it first. But the duty prison medical officer has his rights too, and if Herself chooses to go walkabout, that's her problem. He rings the PMO's people first, knowing that his call will be logged to the nano-second, and only then puts out a bleep for Charge Nurse Landon via the central exchange. The time is ten twenty-two.

Jake goes out to the dispensary. He washes out his mug, drops the dead teabag in the bin, and puts the mug and the Celestial Infusions box back on the shelf. Today's duty PMO is Dr Peck, and he's a stickler. Also, Jake is in no hurry to get back to Nurse Serote and the dead man. There'll be conversation to make and he'd rather get his thoughts in order. He's realized that he ought to be worried about the medical wagon, which is his responsibility. No firm procedure is laid down, but he's left it in one of the thresholding rooms, he can't remember which, and Dr Peck may well argue that any source of potentially dangerous drugs should be looked after more carefully.

Jake always leaves the wagon outside one or other of the thresholding rooms – it carries towels and swabs and drinking water and mouthwash and other such things that may be useful when a subject is surfacing. But it also carries the two spare disposable hypodermic syringes pre-filled with the thresholding cocktail that he prepares as back-ups, in case of accident, and Dr Peck may well argue that these should be returned to the dispensary. There's no evidence yet that one of these syringes has been used to cause Beech's death, but that's obviously what's happened, and Jake can see a charge of negligence coming up that will do his record no good.

The greater charge, of murder, which he's been thinking about too (that second injection could never have happened by accident), he's sure he can weather. Admittedly there's no proof that after leaving the control room he was here in the dispensary until Nurse Serote came to fetch him, but he'll say he was and there's no proof that he wasn't.

It's too late now, of course, for him to retrieve the wagon. But in any case – and the realization strikes him like a golden sunbeam, so that he smiles – in any case, he needs the wagon out there somewhere. Out there somewhere, anyone could have got to it and snaffled a spare syringe. In here, only he could have.

Dr Peck strides in, bag in hand. It's less than two minutes since Jake called his people. He must have been just down the walkway, in Inductions, and of course that's where he would have been – ten o'clock is when the morning's second batch of inductees start checking in from Manchester. Like Nurse Serote, Jake isn't fully on the ball. Murder does that to a person. If he'd been fully on the ball he'd have called Inductions direct.

Dr Peck steams past, stops, back-tracks. He's small and

skinny, with shabby hair and an extraordinarily benevolent smile – mouth, eyes, cheeks, his whole face, even his ears – that he was probably born with and means nothing. He smiles just as prettily when he kicks a man in the crotch as when he gives him lollipops. Or he would if he ever gave anyone anything, which he doesn't. The word is that in the past he's suffered from serious ill-health (unspecified), which obliged him to give up a rewarding career in general practice for the regular hours and lighter workload (and smaller pay-checks) of the prison service. He has found that a permanently grudging approach can reduce the workload still further, till it almost matches the pay-checks.

He leans in the doorway to Jake's dispensary, his bag held against his chest, smiling.

'My secretary tells me you have an emergency, Nurse de Carteret. I have to say it doesn't look like it.'

Jake stands up straight. 'A inductee has died, Doctor. In number five thresholding room, sir.'

'Died?'

'Nurse Serote found him. She's with him now.'

'You've seen him yourself, this dead inductee?'

'Yes, Doctor. In number five thresholding room.' Jake starts forward. 'I'll show you the way.'

'Thank you, Nurse. I *have* been here before.' He lingers – a corpse can wait – his smile broadening as he looks round inside the dispensary, hoping for fluff, dirty bottle labels, failure. 'And where is Charge Nurse Landon?'

'She's been called away. The exchange is paging her.'

'And you've informed the governor?'

This is a trap. 'Not without your authority, sir.'

'In case the corpse takes up its bed and walks, you mean?' Briefly words and smile match. Then: 'I hope for your sake that it does, Nurse de Carteret. I very much hope it does . . . Room five, you said?'

He hurries away and Jake hurries after him.

Nurse Serote is standing by the bed exactly where he left

her. She seems not to have moved, but he's been gone four or five minutes, and that's a long time to be still. She's a still sort of person, though, so maybe she can be believed.

What else might she have done in the interval? Clearly there's been a crime — a chief inspector's promised — but its details aren't yet known so it's hard to imagine. A photographic record then, over Jake's shoulder, just in case: broad black Nurse Serote, bursting, here and there, from her immaculate white nurse's uniform, her immaculate white nurse's hat looking like a paper chop frill in her huge frizzy hair, her hands in disposable plastic gloves clasped modestly at her waist. She stands to the right of the stripped-for-thresholding bed, at its head, facing the door, her expression oddly sidelong and wary, her right hip some eighteen inches from the motionless left arm of Albert Beech's motionless body, which is shirtless, in prison issue trousers and socks (no shoes). Beech's shirt hangs on a hook on the wall by the head of the bed, Beech's shoes are on the floor under the bed's foot. Beech's eyes are still open, and fixed, and it's extremely unlikely that he's moved of his own volition since Jake left him. The floor of the room, like Nurse Serote, is immaculate — a significant fact — and on the wall above the bed the cupboard doors to the in-room monitoring screens and dials are open — an insignificant fact: they've been open since Beech got here.

Dr Peck, like Jake, has paused in the doorway. He observes Nurse Serote, Beech, the room.

'I remember examining that man,' he says. 'Unusually vigorous, I thought.'

'He ain't vigorous no more, Dr Peck,' says Carole Serote, niggering it up. She dislikes Dr Peck mainly for his lack of humour.

'I can see that, thank you, Nurse,' he actually tells her, bustling forward so that she has to melt out of his way quite sharply. He opens his bag just wide enough to draw out a pair of plastic gloves from the box inside. 'You suspect foul play, I presume?'

'You mean, why have I left him like this, Doctor, all cold and bare?' She's getting into her stride. 'I suspect foul play, Doctor. All I did was shift some electrodes, trying to start his heart.'

'Ah.' Dr Peck, gloved up, looks at the corpse, uncertain what to do next. No great medical skills seem to be needed on a patient so clearly dead. Besides, in the event of foul play, disturbing the corpse may get him into trouble with the police.

Nurse Serote leans round him and points unkindly at the marks on Beech's arm. Dr Peck fingers the bruise, stretching the skin indignantly. 'I hope no member of my staff is responsible for that,' he says through his smile.

Neither nurse answers him. They can't believe he said that. They wait while he fails to understand the reason for their silence.

There's a commotion out in the passage, the lift doors opening with their loud familiar *ping*, then voices and footsteps. Dr Peck looks up. He's suddenly decisive. 'Don't let anybody in. Don't you dare let anybody in.'

Jake tells him, 'It's the warders up from downstairs, Doctor. We have three other inductees in the thresholding rooms and they'll be surfacing.'

'Don't let anybody in.' He points dramatically. 'Go and head them off, Nurse de Carteret.' Then, as Jake is leaving, 'Come back. Tell me, Nurse, who knows of this . . . this . . . this. . .'

'Just us three, Doctor.' Jake saves him the need for definition. 'I've asked for Charge Nurse Landon to be bleeped but she hasn't called in yet.'

'Good. Good . . .' He snaps off his gloves and looks round for somewhere to put them. 'She'll have to be told, of course. And the director . . .'

'Dr Mellish is visiting the United States, Doctor.'

'Precisely.' He stuffs the gloves back in his bag. 'But no one else. You understand me? This could be very damaging. No one else. I must speak to the governor . . . The police will have to be informed, of course. But not until I've spoken to the governor. You understand me? This could be very damaging. You do understand me?'

Jake understands him. He goes out to head off the warders, two burly men in their shirtsleeves, acquaintances of his, who are at this moment coming out of the next door thresholding room. They're looking for someone authorized to hand over an inductee. As Jake walks towards them he hears the telephone begin to ring in the control room. It'll be Herself, he thinks, responding to her bleep. Poor lovey, he thinks, she's in for a nasty shock, and he goes on down the corridor to meet the warders.

four

At noon that Tuesday Chief Inspector Duncan was back in his Rover. He'd rung Sergeant Grove and spoken to Frank's good lady, and now he was parked outside the Groves' terraced house in Anfield, drumming his fingers. Frank knew he was there – he'd waved from the front window.

Alec blasted his horn. Two hours' sleep he'd had, not a minute more. Night duty in Birkenhead, two hours' sleep, and now a murder inquiry that by rights was Manchester's. 'Why me?' he'd asked the Super. 'It isn't even our bloody patch.'

'Why us?' Frank opened the nearside door and leant in. 'It isn't even our bloody patch.'

'Get in, man. What the hell've you been doing? Finishing the new sodding crossword?'

'That and the bridge page. I like a nice problem.' Frank lowered himself into the car, closed the door, unhurriedly fastened his seatbelt. 'So why are we off out to the City?'

Alec drove off noisily, looking all ways at once and clashing the gears. He beat the synchromesh and missed the next change altogether.

Frank heavily made no comment. 'Reckon they're wanting outsider talent,' he said. 'That's what I reckon.'

Alec breathed deeply, trying to relax, his sore eyes on the road ahead, his knuckles white on the wheel. He'd feel better in a minute. What he needed was some breakfast. He drove

58

in silence out through West Derby, making for the first service stop on the M62. Frank let him.

The partnership with Sergeant Grove was the first in Alec's police life that had stuck. A lot of people went through their whole Crime Squads with the same man, but not if they were black. Nobody wanted to be put with him, and nobody stuck. The same thing happened when he made inspector. You could argue that working with different men kept both of you sharp, that buddies got too comfortable. Certainly it hadn't kept Alec back. But when Sergeant Grove, who was able if a little stout, and no spring chicken, had stuck, it changed Alec's life. There was one rough corner the fewer, and it made a lot of difference.

With most of a plateful of baked beans and egg and bacon and fried slice inside him, and a cup of not bad tea, Alec felt human again. Motorway cafés weren't good for much, but they served a killer of a fry-up. Sergeant Grove sat across the table, picking at a warm-looking salad.

'This murder's a bastard,' Alec told him. 'A real career breaker.'

'Why us?' This time Frank didn't expect an answer. If the job was a bastard, sod's law said it would come his way. Even so, scabs were for picking at: 'The City's Greater Manchester's, isn't it? Hasn't the Super there got anyone he'd like to push off the end of the plank?'

'This comes from higher up, Frank. Manchester and the City's governor might be said to be too close . . . It's like you said, Frank – the Home Office wants an outsider.'

'The Home Office . . .' Sergeant Grove widened his eyes and puffed out his cheeks.

'More than that, Frank. An outsider's outsider . . . which is why Merseyside thought of me. This isn't just another jail killing. It's in the City, which is bad, and it happened under treatment, which ought to be fucking impossible. Governments could fall, Frank.'

'They want it natural causes.'

59

Alec shook his head. 'Governments could fall, I said. Apparently there's no way it's natural causes. They've hung up the prison medical officer by his toenails, but he won't help them. There's no way it's natural causes.' He forked fry-up into his mouth, spoke indistinctly. 'The victim died under thresholding.'

Grove nodded intelligently.

'You didn't hear me, Frank.'

Sergeant Grove conceded that the final word had been, well, mushy.

Alec swallowed. 'Thresholding. The victim died under thresholding.'

'That's terrible, Chief. Terrible.'

'You don't know what thresholding is.'

'We all went on that course, Chief.' Grove struggled. '. . . Thresholding's the first bit. Sort of the introduction.'

'You're right, Frank. It's the first bit. Supposed to be a safety measure. God knows how matey came to check out under it, but the Bleeding Hearts will have a field day.'

'Governments could fall, Chief.'

Alec reached across and patted his hand. 'Eat up your rabbit food. It's time we got on our way.'

The two men concentrated on their plates. In common with most policemen, they liked what the new programme did – kept villains off the streets – but didn't always like the way it did it. The government had caught them unprepared. A White Paper, a Bill, ten minutes in committee stage, two readings, a docile Upper House, and contractors were cutting the first turfs. To liberal outrage and general rejoicing. The last six years had given men like Alec and Frank chances to look into things, which they hadn't taken – there wasn't that much point. The reasoning went like this: a policeman was a public servant. If the public was in favour of the new P & P Centres, and it was, both of what they did and how they did it (even if in a sanitized version), then a policeman's likes and dislikes were neither here nor there.

Most people, afraid to go out at night, afraid to go out at all, had been sick of convict feather-bedding and the prison-as-holiday-camp syndrome. They'd pushed for hanging, a real deterrent, but ministers were uneasy. The European Human Rights Commission apart, there'd been too many unsound convictions discovered recently: men unsoundly hanged left wives unsoundly widowed, and compensation cost millions. The government settled for P & P and Justice City.

It still upset the Europeans, but for many citizens that was a point in its favour. Europe might outlaw the British sausage but it couldn't tell Britain how to run its prisons. Too much psychiatric clap-trap got talked. People had to be made accountable, responsible for their own actions. As a man sows, so shall he reap. Wrong-doers deserved to be punished. They were better for it. Ask any parent. And after they'd been punished they had to be put away. In decent conditions, if it wasn't too expensive, no point in being vindictive, but for a long, long time. Society needed protecting.

If Alec had his doubts, most people didn't, so he kept them to himself. There were protests – there were always protests – but decent ordinary citizens weren't hazed. They knew justice was being done and they slept easy in their beds.

Junior P & P Centres were under construction, two in the Scottish Highlands.

Frank Grove finished his salad. The salad, on account of his stoutness, was Mrs Grove's idea. She didn't know what she was going to do with him after his retirement but she wanted the chance to find out.

He yawned and stretched his arms. 'Did they name the matey? Anyone we know?'

'Not personally. By repute, however. A nice wee London matey, name of Beech. Albert.'

'Sod me.'

'Sod you indeed, Frank.'

'Wasn't he a local? Didn't his name come up a time or two when I was on the Manchester force?'

'Could well be. Beech, Albert, got about. Thievery, drugs, GBH, pimping . . . you could say his killer did the rest of us a favour.'

'Given the court's sentence, Chief, maybe the killer did Beech a favour.'

'The official view in a nutshell, Frank. But the public will want an arrest. It's not just Justice City's reputation – it's the whole system.'

Alec blotted up the last of the tomato sauce with bread, and ate it. His sergeant looked away, pained, and straightened his knife and fork on his wet empty plate. Alec pushed his chair back. 'Are you done then, Sergeant?'

He was about to get up when he became aware of a man and a woman, an elderly couple, threadbare, standing by the table. They were screwing themselves up to say something. He wondered what they'd come to complain about. His table manners weren't bad; not for a blackie. Then he saw that they were shy, wanting to be friendly, the old woman fussing with the clasp of her handbag and the old man smiling nervously. He must watch himself, he thought. His complexes were showing.

'Excuse me . . .' The old man reined in his smile. Someone had told him it showed too much false tooth. 'Excuse me . . . isn't it Inspector Duncan? Doreen said it was you. We were sitting over there. I wasn't sure. Doreen was, though.'

Alec stood up. He sympathized. All black guys looked the same. He stifled the thought. 'Your wife was quite right, sir. I'm Inspector Duncan. Can I help you?'

'Not at all. That's the whole point – you already have. You won't remember us, Inspector, but – '

'But indeed I do.' And suddenly he did. The public gallery, week after week, two years back. They'd never missed a day. 'You're Mr and Mrs Lawford.' He shook their hands. 'It's good to see you. Sit down, won't you? We've finished eating.

This is my sergeant. Sergeant Grove, this is Mr and Mrs Lawford. They – '

'No. No, really – we won't bother you. We can't stay. We're on our way to Huddersfield. Our daughter lives in Huddersfield . . .'

He ran out of steam. Alec waited, then turned again to Frank. 'Mr and Mrs Lawford lost their son a couple of years ago, Sergeant. In very tragic circumstances. He was – '

'We just wanted to thank you, Inspector.' Mrs Lawford had taken over. 'We never did, after the case. After the case it was suddenly all over and you'd gone. But . . . well, without all your good work, and the things you said in court . . . well, that wicked devil might of got away with it . . . If it hadn't been for you that wicked devil might of got away with it.'

'No prosecution's up to just one man, Mrs Lawford.' He was touched more than embarrassed. This had never happened to him before. 'The law got something right that day. That's all. I'm glad.'

'It didn't bring our Malcolm back to us. But – ' There were tears in the old man's eyes as he struggled to speak. 'But you saw that justice was done, Inspector. You hear such things about policemen – I always tell them, see how they went after that man who killed our son. He was a black man too.'

Alec smiled. At least he wasn't the only one with complexes. 'I can see you're both keeping well, Mr Lawford. That's good. And your daughter – are you going for a visit or just for the day?'

'For the afternoon, Inspector. There's a new grandchild and she's very busy. As you can imagine. That's three, now – the girls are seven and four, and now – '

'The inspector's a busy man, Harry. . . . We just wanted to thank you proper, Inspector Duncan. It don't bring Malcolm back, of course, but at least that creature's been put away. It restores your faith, Inspector.' She touched his arm. 'We just wanted you to know that. I sleep happy in my bed now, knowing he hasn't got away with it ... Well, we mustn't keep you. Goodbye ... Goodbye, Sergeant Grieves. I don't think people say *thank you* enough these days, do you? Perhaps they never did.' It was an apology for embarrassing them. She turned away quickly and Mr Lawford went with her.

Alec watched them shuffle away between the crowded tables. The Lawford murder had been his last case before he was made chief inspector. He'd appeared in court because his boss was off with kidney stones. Defence counsel had been aggressive, and good, but she couldn't make bricks without straw. Also, her client had been guilty.

'Sorry about that, Frank.'

'Why sorry? Me, I'd have asked for it framed, in writing. I've got just the place for it, on the wall above the sofa.'

'It's time we were on our way, Frank.'

'It's time we were on our way, Chief.'

As they were crossing the car park the Lawfords drove by, jerkily, concentrating on where they were going, in their ancient Austin Montego. Its tax disc was out of date. Alec hesitated. You're damned if you do, he thought, and you're damned if you don't, so he didn't.

In his car, out on the motorway: 'If I'm not chatty, Frank, it's because I'm knackered. If you cared for a kip then maybe one of us would know what he was doing when we got there.'

Frank grunted. He'd given up offering to drive. Alec had let him once and had sat in the passenger's seat for the rest of the journey, his right knee quivering as his brake pedal foot punished the carpet. Frank reclined his seat now and slept.

Alec drove soberly, no siren, no lights, seventy-three when the traffic and the thrown-up spray allowed it, in no serious hurry to get to Justice City. He was establishing his pace so that it would be firmly in his head by the time he reached his destination. In Justice City everyone would be screaming at him to find the killer, and he would need his own pace to keep to. Having a killer at large in Justice City was a national catastrophe.

He frowned at the broken white line flicking by. He was tired and he'd got his thinking wrong. Natural causes just weren't on. Nobody'd believe in them. The real national catastrophe would be to have an accidental death in Justice City. It couldn't happen. The government's entire P & P Programme, its New Approach to Crime, depended on Justice City. There wasn't much that was certain in life, but if the workings of Justice City weren't certain then maybe taxes and death would go next. No, any pressure on the prison medical officer would have been to declare an unexplained death. A killing. Foul play. Murder. Murder was fine. Murder took no account of excellent scientific test programmes, of rigorous safety margins, of well-trained staff, of good administration. They could all be beyond reproach. Murder didn't just *happen*, it was committed. Murder undermined nobody's confidence in the penal system. He'd got his thinking wrong. The prison MO had declared an unexplained death and he'd be required to agree.

Realizing that made a good starting point. Frank and he were entering a closed world, run by experienced professionals, from the governor on down, no fools, who needed an unlawful killing. He hoped that Frank and he would be able to oblige, but he was making no promises.

five

Carole Serote has her feet up. The time is two fifteen and she has the nurses' room to herself. She's been to the canteen for lunch and it's Jake's turn now. Carole doesn't keep many secrets from the world, but her varicose veins are a secret even from her doctor. They aren't serious yet, she's keeping an eye on them and she wears discreet special stockings, but after a long morning on her feet they hurt. Being overweight doesn't help, of course. They hurt a lot.

She knows what the doctor will tell her. Diet. A different job. Perhaps even surgery. But mostly diet. And honest to God, she doesn't eat enough to keep a flea alive.

Her feet are up and her eyes are closed. She's had lunch too. Bliss. It's been a terrible morning. She began it with such hate in her heart. Such hate, Granny Porter wheeling in that terrible man Beech almost before she'd got her eyes open. She's a slow starter, Lord knows, but she didn't need that to swing her motor. First the walk in the rain from staff quarters to the House, then Beech lying there on the trolley, waiting for her, pretty as a picture, ugly as sin. She knew that face straight off. Front page news, before the beard and after, she knew that face.

The girl's face too, the girl he done for ... What could you say? Honest to God, what could you say?

She didn't need to be told what her Pa said. It wasn't easy for him either, but he said it. Her Pa was some kind of saint.

There were plenty of sinners she could love, but not this one on the trolley. And she didn't reckon his time downstairs would do much for him. Nor for her. If he screamed, she wouldn't hear it.

Such hate she'd felt. Such a terrible morning.

Things were better by the time Dr Landon got in. Other inductees, other jobs. Work to do. She dealt with the hate — life was too short. Jake hadn't recognized Beech and she didn't tell him. She can never be sure how he'll react. He's a big heart but it scares him: bitching is safer. That's what the real gay disease is, if you'd like to know. Being scared into bitching. In any case, his not recognizing Beech made prepping him easier. It made the man just another inductee.

It didn't; he was Albert Beech and she wished him dead.

Three times dead for the girl, such a pretty girl, ten times dead for his other crimes, such ugly crimes, the robberies, the pimping, the drugs. But there was no dead times table. Dead was dead. So maybe downstairs was better.

It wasn't.

And then suddenly Beech wasn't going downstairs after all, and most of what she felt was this incredible relief. He was dead meat. Rotting. Meat did, it started instantly. It started rotting, and rotting was the worst thing she could imagine, and her hate was over. Poor Beech. Poor Albert. What a bloody awful life.

It was the Manchester police inspector who worked out the way Beech died. A nice young man, shiny shoes, well-chosen shirt and tie, classy suit. Carole notices these things. She likes a snappy dresser. The Manchester inspector talked to her and Jake in one of the spare thresholding rooms, while his experts were busy with the meat. He asked her about the disposable syringes, what happened to them. She passed him on to Jake who runs the wagon and its plastic waste sack. It hasn't been emptied and, sure enough, as well as the four syringes legitimately used on the morning's four inductees, there is a fifth in the sack. There is also one more pair of disposable plastic gloves than anyone can remember using. So it's clear enough – subject inevitably to the full post-mortem report, there seems little doubt concerning either the fact of the murder or the method. A fatal second dose of the thresholding cocktail was administered by person or persons unknown at some time between the end of the active thresholding, at nine thirty, and the discovery of the body, her discovery of the body, at ten ten.

The Manchester inspector was pleased with himself. Not an hour into the case and already he was well on the way to solving it. With method and time established, all he needed was motive and opportunity . . . He was called away to the phone. He took the call in the control room and he never came back. After a while a young bobby came to tell them they could go, but not to leave the House until some other big shot policeman had talked to them. Some Chief Inspector Duncan.

As Carole and Jake left the thresholding room she heard the Manchester inspector out in the foyer. Half the City heard him. He was very angry. By the time she and Jake reached the foyer he'd gone. Coppers stood around awkwardly and the double doors were still flapping.

She smiles at the memory. Her legs aren't hurting now. One of the coppers who were left had sealed off the thresholding rooms with tape, and then they went away too. The meat had already gone. The body. Beech.

Dr Landon's upstairs, talking on the phone to Inductions. They've had the morning's second batch of inductees on their hands for hours, and she can't take them in, and now she has this story she and the governor've cooked up between them. Seems an inductee's fallen and hurt hisself and now he wants to sue the City and they're trying to get him to change his mind. It explains the hold-up, and the police, and why they aren't even releasing his name.

They're trying to get him to change his mind . . . It's a

good line. It leaves enough unsaid to tell City staff everything they think they need to know.

Meanwhile, the afternoon's first batch will be arriving from Manchester at any minute, and the inductions officer hasn't the accommodation, and she can't take them either, and he's having a cadenza. Or he was when Carole left Dr Landon's office and came down here.

Dr Landon had given her one of her looks. '. . . Your best bet, Douglas . . . I said your best bet is to take it up with the governor, Douglas. He can talk to Manchester. The delivery officers have radios, don't they? Maybe he can turn them back . . .' She'd held the receiver away from her ear, letting it buzz as she shooed Carole out of her office.

That's Dr Landon all over. She keeps her sense of humour. She has a murder in the House, and Dr Mellish away in Chicago, and she keeps her sense of humour.

She'd kept her sense of humour when Dr Peck had as good as accused her of negligence. What that boiled down to was not being there when he wanted her, not immediately he wanted her. He'd wanted her at ten thirty-five – he expected her to be waiting for him when he got there. She didn't phone in until ten forty-five, answering her bleep, and she didn't get to the House until nearly eleven. It wasn't good enough. Taking thresholding profiles downstairs was fine, it showed praiseworthy concern, but he understood that she'd left the punishments officer by ten fifteen. That left three-quarters of an hour missing. It wasn't good enough.

Dr Landon let him finish. Then she nodded sympatheti-cally. It was very unfair, she said, that he should have missed his coffee break while she'd had hers. If he wanted to go off now she'd willingly hold the fort. The governor had been told, the police were on their way, there wasn't much else going on. She'd willingly hold the fort.

He hadn't gone, you bet. He might have missed the arrival of the police. He might have missed his moment, his moment as the doctor present at the scene of the crime, his fifteen

69

minutes of fame. With the inspector there he'd done a physical examination. Carole helped him. That was how she came to find the three hundred pounds — three hundred pounds in crisp twenties — in Beech's back trouser pocket. How he'd got that lot past Inductions was a pretty question. Heads would roll, surely . . .

In the nurses' room the telephone rings. Carole sighs and lowers her feet. The time is two twenty-five and rain lashes the windows. She answers the telephone.

'Punishment Building. Nurse Serote.'

'Outside call for you, Nurse. A Mr Freddy. Says you'll know.'

Carole frowns. 'Put him through.' She doesn't want to talk to Freddy. She never wants to talk to Freddy. It isn't even his name.

'Carole? Where've you been, pet? They couldn't find you.'

'I'm in the — ' She hesitates. 'I'm not in my room, Freddy.'

'Haven't they been telling me that? I said, end of the morning shift she's always in her room. No way, they say. It's not bloody answering.'

'So now you found me, Freddy.' She doesn't tell him where she is. It would raise too many questions. 'How're you keeping?'

'Hungry, pet. Bloody starving. Long time no hear.' Freddy's a stringer for a tabloid or two and she's his contact in Justice City. His inside track, he calls her.

'Things are quiet, Freddy. You know the way it goes . . .'

'Nothing brewing, then? Nothing you think I ought to know?'

He's after something. He's heard something. But how could he?

'There's talk of a hunger strike in one of the LTI blocks.' That's safe enough. 'Maybe I could find out — '

'Do me a favour, pet. A bloody hunger strike? Our readers would cheer the bastard on. Think what it'd save the poor bloody tax-payer if he snuffed it . . .' Freddy lowers his voice.

'Thing is, pet, the word goes you've taken delivery of a very fancy property. Or maybe it's just on its way . . .'

She's never wrong about Freddy. There are routine calls and there are specials. This one had *special* stamped on it right from the start.

'Fancy property, Freddy? I don't think so.'

She has her rules. There are things she'd tell Freddy and things she won't. Back at the beginning, when she'd bumped into him in the George on one of her visits home – a meeting he'd engineered, she now knew – back then there'd been talk of a prison officers' strike up in the City and all the media were giving out was what the governor handed them. The union side got nothing. So when Freddy suggested she set the record straight she was only too happy. She was bound by a confidentiality clause in her terms of employment, but the way things were she didn't let that worry her. Everything she told Freddy was common knowledge among City staff, not traceable to her, and the public deserved a balanced picture.

She was happier still when Freddy passed her a few fivers the following week. They hadn't been part of the deal but she needed the money – no, her Pa did.

'I *do* think so, pet. A very fancy property. Name of Beech. You know the name? Lucky to his friends – those sicko sods willing to come within a hundred miles of him.'

'Beech? Sure I know the name. What about him?'

'He's there, is he?'

'I didn't say so.'

'When he comes, then give us a bell. Anything about him – does he talk in his sleep – does he love his mother – does he bite his nails – the side he bloody dresses on . . . Anything at all.'

'Mr Beech arrived at Inductions this morning, Freddy.' She says this because he knows already. It stands out a mile.

'He did? Manchester moved fast then. And?'

'And nothing, Freddy.' That's as far as she's going. If anyone spreads Dr Landon's yarn about the injured inductee, it won't be her. She'd never dare. It's in-House information, she's too close to it, working in the place, and she'd lose her job. Freddy ought to know she can't talk about things so close to home. 'Mr Beech arrived at Inductions this morning. You can say he was very fit. And cheerful.' Probably the bastard was, down at Inductions, before he copped it. He was just the sort. At any rate, Freddy'll never know any different. 'Jokes all round. Very cheerful.'

'Give it a rest, pet. This is Freddy — remember? So less of the snow job. If Beech came in this morning he'll have been thresholded by now. So how was he? How did he make out? How many warders were needed to get him downstairs after? The great British public has a right to know these things.'

'Mr Beech has rights too, Freddy.'

'Crap. That murdering bastard? The only right he bloody has is to a rope and a hole in the ground . . .' Freddy pauses, turns on the wheedle. 'I can be generous, pet. You know that. You help me and I help you. You know that.'

She isn't tempted. She knows her Pa can do with the money, every penny she can send him, but she isn't tempted.

Pa ran a business once. A nice little metalware workshop under a railway arch where he made drawer slides and specialist hinges for the furniture trade. He lost it in the 90s recession: his customers faded away. He lost his and Ma's house too when he couldn't keep up the mortgage. It killed Ma more than the cancer, Carole thought, seeing Pa fail. They had their Jesus but he never paid the bills.

Pa was fifty-two, a young man, and he hasn't worked since. He lives in a bedsit on benefit and she sends him all the money she can. Maybe the saddest thing for her is the way he accepts it. She remembers him as a very proud man.

'I'm sorry, Freddy. Mr Beech was thresholded this morning. That's all I can say.'

'Now hang on there, pet.' The wheedle's gone now. 'Beech is the big one. I really don't think you should do this to me.'

'I said I'm sorry, Freddy.'

'So what's sorry? Maybe sorry says you've found yourself another buyer.'

'There's no other buyer, Freddy.'

'Look, pet. I don't like having to say this. I'm not a difficult man. Heart of gold — you know that. Time comes, though . . . What I'm saying, pet, is I don't reckon it'd play too good for you if the governor somehow got the name of Fleet Street's dicky bird up there in the City. Know what I mean? Governor Ransome would be — '

'Freddy? I've got to go, Freddy. Someone's calling.' Someone was. A man, out in the foyer. One man's voice, and then another's. 'I got to go. I'll call you tonight.' She starts to hang up. But there's something he needs telling. 'And Freddy? Don't ever you try to blackmail me. If you want to put me in the shit with the governor, then do it. Do it, Freddy . . . Just don't ever you try to blackmail me.'

She hangs up, waits till she is calm, then leaves the nurses' room and goes down the corridor to the foyer.

six

'The governor's expecting you, Chief Inspector.'

More than that, the governor had made sure that the most junior guard on the black steel gates to Justice City knew the registration number of Chief Inspector Duncan's blue Rover. The gates had opened as he and Sergeant Grove approached across the acres of windswept turn-around. By then the day's intermittent drizzle had settled to a steady downpour, mixed with sleet up on the high ground, that lashed the car, rocking it as Alec slowed to enter.

He parked by Reception and got out of the car, wincing as the gates closed silkily behind him and the air was suddenly still. He'd been there before, visiting the LTI blocks. Maybe he'd asked to see an inmate or maybe an inmate had asked to see him, but in either case deals (unofficially) had been offered and deals (unofficially) had been struck: usually information for remission. So he'd been there before and he should have been used to the stillness. But he wasn't: the granite walls dismayed him, the blank barred windows and the towering black riveted gates, and the stillness pressed itself against his skin.

The yard was cobbled, shining in the rain. Further double steel gates led the guilty through to Inductions, but for the innocent this yard was enough. Alec looked up at the sky, let the grey rain fall briefly on his face, then turned and went with Frank slowly through the heavy armoured door in to Reception, and across to the desk.

He had his warrant card ready but it wasn't needed. 'The governor's expecting you, Chief Inspector. I'll phone through, sir. Tell him you're here. Organize an escort.'

'Thank you, Officer.' The reception area was brightly lit, with Anti-AIDS posters on the walls, and had a feeling of the Liverpool nick. Alec shook off the yard's granite chill, leaned across the desk to read the man's lapel badge. 'Do that, Mr Jarman.' He rolled the 'r' in Jarman, Scots fashion. There was never any harm in playing up his Edinburgh roots. Scottishness was classless — Oxford-accented blacks in lounge suits put people's backs up. 'And you can tell the governor I'll be up once I've got things rolling.' He put his warrant card back in his wallet and stamped his feet briskly. He had a point to make. 'If that's all right, of course.'

The man looked doubtful. 'I believe the governor was hoping for a word, sir.'

'So was I, Mr Jarman. We need a wee talk. But in cases like this I like to get my sergeant started right off on an incident room — telephones, that sort of thing. It all takes time, ye ken. How many men can you spare me?'

Mr Jarman kept his head. 'I'm sure the governor has something in mind, Chief Inspector. I'll just call him . . .' With one hand he reached the telephone. With the other he pushed a glossy folder across the desk. 'And while you're waiting, Chief Inspector, we have a visitor's pack that — '

'You're very kind, Mr Jarman. Sergeant Grove . . .?' Alec gestured for Frank to pick up the folder. He himself was already on his way across the foyer to the barred gate leading out into Justice City. 'I'll be in the Punishments Building. Don't bother with an escort — I know the way.' The gate was electrically controlled from the desk. He tapped it lightly. 'Door, please.'

The desk officer looked up from his dialling. 'You and

your sergeant need City ID cards, Chief Inspector. You won't
get far without them.'

Alec returned to the desk. 'Thank you so much.' He held
out his hand impatiently. 'I'm sure you have the authoriza-
tion.' He had ground to regain – he shouldn't have forgotten
the electronic ID cards handled security codes throughout
the City. He smiled at the desk officer mercilessly. 'I don't
have to remind you, Mr Jarman, that this is an official police
inquiry.'

Jarman replaced the telephone receiver, pulled an open
book towards him, ran his finger down a column. Alec
looked up at the digital clock on the wall above the desk.
The time, not that it mattered, was two twenty-seven. He
clicked his fingers irritably.

The cards, complete with colour photographs, were ready
but Jarman wouldn't be hurried. He had his own point to
make. He stolidly entered the cards in the book, then offered
the pen for Alec, and then Frank, to sign in with.

'Thank you. Tell the governor I'll be with him in half an
hour.' Alec turned away, paused. 'Is Manchester here?'

'Been and gone, Chief Inspector. A whole raft of them.'

'Good. Good . . .' And it *was* good. Been and gone – he
was spared their size twelves.

He showed his card to the door slot and went out. Frank
followed him. Alec hoped he hadn't brought grief down on
the desk officer. Duels like that were pathetic, but in a place
like this he'd had to come on strong, his own man, a right
sod, beginning as he meant to continue, relying on the jungle
drums to spread the news.

They walked along a short corridor lined with closed
doors, out through a sliding grille, also card-controlled, and
found themselves at one corner of a grid of covered walkways. The winter sticks of rose bushes filled flowerbeds on
their right. Frank pointed beyond them.

'Isn't that the Punishments Building?'

'I've no idea. It's the LTI blocks I always go to.'

'They showed us a photograph on the course. Didn't it look like that?'

'I've no idea. I don't remember one.'

'Maybe you should have waited for that escort, Chief.'

'Maybe you should study the map in your visitor's pack, Sergeant.'

It probably was the Punishments Building. The map was small and the two twenty-eight light that day was very dim. They set off. Rain and sleet blew across the covered walk-ways. The flooring was plastic, slightly cushioned, wet but not slippery. They crossed a couple of junctions, both with sliding grilles, and went in through armoured glass double doors at the far end.

Alec sniffed. 'This smells right. Either that or it's the hospital.'

They were in a sage green, plastic-floored foyer, disin-fected, neon lit. Immediately to their left a small area was partitioned off, with a closed door and the label *Dispensary*. Ahead of them on the left an institutional staircase with a flat metal handrail led up to the next floor. Beside it a corridor angled away; straight in front of them were closed heavy double doors with glass portholes, and to the right of those was another door, also closed. Musak played. They might have been in a private, if cut-price, clinic. Even down to the bars on the windows.

Alec saw yellow adhesive police tape across the door to the right in front of him.

'We're in the right place . . . Hullo?' He raised his voice. 'Hullo?'

Sergeant Grove knocked on the door to the dispensary. 'Anyone there?'

A large black nurse came unhurriedly out along the corridor. 'This building is closed. Are you the police?'

Alec left his warrant in his pocket. 'Chief Inspector Duncan. Merseyside Police. I'm in charge of the inquiry.'

The nurse looked him up and down. 'We're expecting a Chief Inspector Duncan.'

Alec waited till her eyes met his. 'Now you've got him.' He didn't smile. 'This is Sergeant Grove. I'm to ask for a Margaret Landon.'

'Dr Landon's up in her office. We'll have to go up. I can't call her – the phone's through there.' Not looking away, she poked her thumb at the sealed door.

Alec nodded. 'Fine. Thank you, Nurse. That'll be fine.' He didn't move. A fact surfaced from his long ago telephone chat with the Super. 'You must be Nurse Serote. I think you found the body.'

'Found it was dead, you mean? Yessir.' She shifted, smiling and including Sergeant Grove. 'Nobody *found* the body. I mean, we all knew where Mr Beech was.'

Alec nodded again. 'There's another nurse?'

'On the morning shift? That's Jake de Carteret. He's in the nurses' room out back. Shall I . . .?'

'Later. Dr Landon first, I think.'

They went upstairs. Nurse Serote moved well, for her size. 'This looks a very small operation, Nurse. I'm surprised.'

'Six inductees in each batch, Chief Inspector. Two batches to a shift. That's maximum. Two shifts to a day. Twenty-four inductees. It's enough.'

'And a shift is?'

'Seven to two, morning. Two to nine, afternoon.'

'And now it's half past two and you ought to be off duty. I'll try to keep this short.'

He wouldn't. It would take as long as it had to take. But he was easing off. The disciplines of nursing staff were different. They could retire behind their skills. They needed wooing.

Dr Landon's door was ajar half-way down the upstairs corridor. Nurse Serote pushed it open. 'The police is come, Doctor.'

The note of parody told him a lot. Dr Landon and Nurse

Serote were on friendly terms. The place was well run (it had to be) but it wasn't a jail-style tyranny. And they weren't yet taking this murder seriously.

He went in.

Dr Landon was sitting at a government issue desk, unpleasantly cluttered. She was a young woman, quite pretty, with short dark hair and clever bright brown eyes. But she wore a bit too much make-up and her smile (too bright a red) was oddly fearless: the murder had occurred in her department and he'd have thought she had a lot to lose.

She got up and came round the desk to shake hands. She was smaller than he'd imagined: short in the leg so that the top of her head didn't quite reach his chin. Her dark hair was very shiny.

'Chief Inspector Duncan.' A strong hand, cool and dry. She smelt of some sort of flowery soap.

'Dr Landon.'

'Plain *Nurse*, Chief Inspector. My background is in psychotherapy . . . Take a seat.'

'Thank you, no. I'm on my way to the governor. But I'll need an incident room in this building and I'd like my sergeant here – Sergeant Grove – to set it up. I'm sure you can help him. He'll tell you what he needs.'

'You're planning to be here some time?'

'It's too soon to say. As long as it takes. Now – if you'll point me in the direction of the governor's office . . .?'

Nurse Landon frowned. 'The department's at a standstill, Chief Inspector. Your forensic people have come and gone. An inspector from Manchester too. There's a build-up of inductees in Inductions that can't be cleared while the thresholding rooms stay sealed. The afternoon shift's kicking its heels and the morning shift's been here since seven. I was hoping to be able to release them.'

'Of course you were. I'll do what I can.' Set a pace. Stick to it. 'I doubt the governor will keep me.'

He watched her sum him up and decide he couldn't be

pushed. An amenable man, he hoped, but not one to be pushed.

'I'll telephone Inductions, Chief Inspector. Tell them to keep everything on hold. There are pharmacological problems, of course . . .' She wanted him, as an amenable man, to understand her difficulties. Then she smiled. 'Nurse Serote will direct you to the governor. It isn't difficult.'

It wasn't. Alec half-remembered much of the route from earlier visits. Aggressively clean corridors, yellow brick and muted with the same rubbery flooring as the walkways, with a waist-high yellow plastic dado, TV cameras, area segregation gates needing his ID card, then a lift up to the third floor, carpeting, telephone noises, and the patter of keyboards.

His meeting with Nurse Landon had left him with confused impressions. Was she a suspect? It wouldn't be the first time the guilty party had had a pretty smile.

The governor sat him down in front of his desk. Governor Ransome's desk, modern and enormous, was unpleasantly clear: two telephones, one polished silver photogaph frame, one pen tray, one unmarked blotter, a great deal of blue Morocco leather. Behind it, and the governor in his big tweed swivel chair, a generous picture window filled much of the wall, the grey roofs outside it scarcely visible through driving sleet. Diffused ceiling panels lit the room, and a matt black halogen lamp by the governor's chair. Alec waited, kept waiting as the governor slowly took sheets of headed notepaper from a drawer, a pen from his breast pocket, squared the paper on the blotter in front of him, wrote a heading, and underlined it.

Digby Ransome was at the top of his profession, with an OBE, and now Justice City, to prove it. He was a heavy-jawed southerner, Bristol born, bulky and expensively tailored, with ginger hair and long colourless eyelashes over confrontational blue eyes. He tapped his pen thoughtfully on his blotter.

'I've had Reception on the phone, Chief Inspector. You twisted their tails, I gather.'

Alec was relieved: his lateness had received all the comment it was going to. He smiled and made a small twisting gesture with his hands. 'I asked for manpower, Mr Ransome.'

'So they said.' The governor was unamused. 'We run tight staffing ratios here, part of a special deal with the union. What did you have in mind?'

'Initially, two bodies to move furniture and set up screens. Your Nurse Landon is finding me a room.'

'Her department head's on his way back from the States. She was helpful?'

'Very.' Alec permitted himself this small overstatement. She was having a lot to put up with. 'Once I've got my room running I'll need, minimum, someone on the telephone. And for research. Someone computer literate. You realize, Mr Ransome, that Merseyside have sent me here with just my sergeant?'

'I'm sure they told you the reason.'

'The chief superintendent told me a lot of things. Frankly, Mr Ransome, I was on night duty and I've not had much sleep.'

The governor wrote something on his piece of paper. When he looked down, his eyelashes seemed to cover his eyes: they were incongruous against his broad, coarse face, like tiny paper fans. 'The Home Office is keeping this low profile, Alec. The fewer non-City staff involved, the better. You'll understand the reason.'

Alec was intimidated neither by the writing nor the *Alec*. 'May I ask how the hell Home Office got in on this so quickly?'

'You may ask.' The governor allowed an uncomfortably long silence, then laughed in mitigation. 'This isn't just any old murder,' he said matily. 'We're not telling the media. Not for the moment. When we do, we want to be able to announce – '

'Not telling the media?' Alec sat forward. 'How long?'

The governor shrugged lightly. 'Till Saturday.'

'You can't do that.'

'We fucking can.' All lightness, all matiness, was gone. 'We must. I'd wait longer if I thought we could keep the lid on. For your sake.'

'For my sake?'

'We need to announce the crime and its perpetrator at the same time.'

'Its perpetrator? By Saturday? You must be joking, Governor. Investigations don't work to deadlines.'

'This one does.'

Alec collected his thoughts. 'You're telling me you're prepared to keep the lid on a murder for three whole days? On the off-chance that by then I'll have given you the murderer?'

'This is a prison, Alec. Keeping lids on things is our business.'

'And the dead man's parents? His family? He must have some.'

'I'm saving them for Saturday too. A boon, surely? Three more days thinking their precious Albert is in the land of the living.'

And the week-end in which to grieve. Very funny. 'My presence here? The Manchester team? How will you explain all these coppers?'

'I've thought of that. We're letting it be known that – '

'I'm sorry, Governor . . .' Alec gestured hopelessly. 'I'm sorry, Governor – I'm going to have to confirm this with the chief constable.'

'Go ahead.' Governor Ransome nudged one of his telephones in Alec's direction. 'But you might like to read this first . . .' He produced typewritten sheets from a drawer.

'The first of your people up here was a detective inspector out from Manchester. They're supplying the forensics, of course. These are the inspector's preliminary findings . . . And this is the prison medical officer's report. It explains why I'm asking you to do this. We won't get post-mortem confirmation till tomorrow, but there really isn't any doubt.'

Alec took the sheets. He should have been given these sooner. Governor Ransome had been sounding him out. Suppression of information . . . three days to solve a murder . . . He'd told Frank this case was a career breaker and it surely was. He tried to focus on the PMO's typing.

'I'll sum it up for you, Alec.' The governor sat back in his chair, swung it from side to side, staring at the ceiling. 'The victim, Albert Beech, died of a thresholding overdose. Measured doses are prepared in disposable syringes. Beech received his first dose quite properly, from Charge Nurse Landon, and then, a short time later, while he was lying unconscious on the thresholding couch, he received a second injection. The evidence suggests that this was a further dose of the thresholding formula – you'll see why when you get to the inspector's findings. If it was, then it would certainly have killed him. The formula contains a paralytic and an overdose would have stopped his heart beating. The mark of a second injection is clearly visible on his arm. Beech was left on his own for ten or fifteen minutes after thresholding. Inductees usually are. There was plenty of opportunity. . .'

He stilled his chair, returned his gaze to Alex. 'You'll see now why we need a quick wrap-up. No time for speculation. No time for outrage . . . It's the use of the thresholding formula, Chief Inspector. The thresholding room, the thresholding formula, probably one of the thresholding staff . . . Politically the circumstances couldn't be worse.'

Worse for whom? Alec wondered, noticing that he was *Chief Inspector* again. 'What if Saturday comes and I'm nowhere?'

'We could lose the whole programme. Do-gooders like the Howard League dancing on its grave . . . and on mine.'

'You're asking a lot, Mr Ransome.'

'I'm trusting your chief constable. You're the man for the job.'

'I'm disposable, you mean.'

'I mean you're able and you have no friends, Chief Inspector.'

Very true.

His heart missed a beat, even so. No friends.

He felt bone weary. Pierced to the core. He had to hand it to the governor – Mr Ransome was a whizz at personnel management.

'The police watchers know that,' the governor went on smoothly. 'You're able and you owe no one any favours. You'll be believed. There'll be talk of a cover-up, of course, but you'll weather it.'

Alec had scarcely been listening. He dragged his attention back. 'I asked for men, Governor,' he said. 'I must have men.'

Pathetic. Rattling the bars of his cot. No friends? Morag loved him. So did his mother. May put up with him. Frank Grove hadn't asked for a move yet.

The governor glanced at his watch and stood. Until Alec failed him, until the do-gooders buried him, he was a busy man. 'I can spare you an officer for the telephone. Give me ten minutes, then contact LTI block C. Bodies you can scrounge on the spot.'

Alec stayed seated. 'Telephones? A computer link?'

'Call Engineering.'

'What if I tell my chief constable it can't be done?'

'You're entitled to your opinion. And it's not for me to pre-empt your chief constable. But I hope you won't do anything in a hurry. Have a chat with Charge Nurse Landon. Ask around. This Saturday deadline may be more realistic than you think.'

'There are things you're not telling me.'

'Like I said, have a chat with Charge Nurse Landon.' The governor offered his hand across the desk, and a merciless smile. 'We'll keep in touch, Alec. I have every confidence in you.'

Alec stood up and shook the hand. He'd used that smile himself at Inductions. It was a winner.

He went to the door. Mr Ransome spoke again, not raising his voice. 'Racism's ugly, Alec, but we'll never be rid of it. In this case, for once, I think it may work in your favour. At least it'll be one less thing they can accuse you of.'

Alec waited for him to go on, one hand on the doorknob, but nothing more came. He wasn't surprised – a sleepless night hadn't entirely dried out his brain and Mr Ransome had said a lot, too much, already. He left the governor's office and went down in the lift. Justice City had decided who it wanted as its murderer. Nurse Serote. Clickety-click. One nice black girl slashed and strangled by a white man; one nice black nurse with the white man at her mercy. Clickety-click: there could be expected, quite decidedly, to be a connection.

Alec laughed aloud, sadly, in the decent solitude of the lift. They'd got what they wanted. They'd got one nice black cop who, quite decidedly, couldn't quit.

seven

Granny Porter is lying low. Not hiding. Not exactly hiding.
He's not fucking stupid, he knows he'll have to talk to the
Blue sooner or later and he's got his story straight. But even
on the best of days there are times in his life of showing
willing when the effort catches up with him and he retires to
one of his hidey-holes for a drag. He's not a young man, for
fuck's sake. Sometimes, even on the best of days, he needs to
lie low.

Today is not one of the best of days. It's probably one of
the worst.

Luckily, since Missy Landon's told him not to leave the
building, one of his best hidey-holes is the staff toilet up on
the second floor. The whole place is used for storage and
nobody comes there. He can have a sit and a smoke in peace.
And a think.

He's sitting in one of the cubicles, door closed, hat on the
back of his head, roll-up held in the old lag's way, cupped in
his hand, invisible, the soggy end between his thumb and
fingertips. He doesn't expect to be interrupted but he fans
the smoke away just in case. He thinks.

For Granny Porter thinking is mostly a haphazard, unfo-
cused affair, a contented journey round his grievances.
Ginger snaps in the porters' lodge he can't get his teeth to.
Saturday afternoon shifts that make him miss the TV racing.
Floor cleaner that rots his fingers. A reassuring landscape. It

tells him he's put upon. It tells him he doesn't have to say fucking *thank you* all the time.

Today's thinking isn't like that. Fucking Beech has spoilt it. Ugliest time of his life, his months with Beech's outfit. Lucky Beech, they called him. Christ knows why. Too many people got cut, not only the girls. The man was a fucking maniac. He near as bugger-it got cut himself, the time he missed a pick-up. He was driving for Lucky Beech, back when Beech was only a lad but already a goer, driving round the clubs late at night for the takings, and he missed one out. Didn't think what he was doing. No fucking reason. Just missed it out of his round. The club manager said he didn't, of course, so there was a whole day's takings hopped it. Lucky saw him, personal, up in his office. In love with his razor, if ever a man was. Granny never found out why he believed him and not the club manager. He hadn't been going to – he had that look – but when push came to shove for some reason Lucky believed him . . . Only time in his life Granny pissed his fucking pants. Stood there in Lucky's fucking office and pissed his fucking pants.

It was the club manager who copped it. Nasty mess. But Granny'd stood there in Lucky's office and pissed his pants, and all Lucky's guys hanging round, laughing. You didn't like a man who did that to you. Maybe you were only fucking Granny, but you didn't forget.

He'd got out soon after – nine months in the Scrubs, if you want to know, for a spot of private enterprise – but he'd had dreams about Lucky ever since. Nightmares.

And then, this morning, there he'd been, fucking Lucky himself, in the fucking thresholding room, on the fucking bed.

The snout's burning Granny's fingers. He drops it between his legs, into the bowl with a tiny hiss, rolls another, and lights it. Luxury. Nobody's missing him. Normally he'd be over in Research by now, sweeping round – not them monkeys, he never touches them fucking monkeys – but

Missy Landon's phoned through to say he's been detained. *Detained* . . . All very hush-hush. Well, it fucking would be. He reckons Lucky Beech wasn't nobody's fucking favourite but it don't look good, him snuffing it. Granny sucks his teeth – the thing is, it was him found the body, found it was dead, that is. When he'd finished in the washroom – them bloody soap dispensers take for ever – he'd remembered the petals, them squashed fucking flower petals, and he'd gone to sweep them up. One look at Beech's lines told him, his green lines running flat across the screens. You get used to them jumping, the jumps and the pips. You notice straight off when they pack it in.

Granny hasn't said. Not that anybody's asked him straight out – the Blue's been up from Manchester but he's kept out of their way – and he won't if they do. Wouldn't look good. Asking for trouble. Why was he there, what was he doing, did he know the deceased, what was their relationship . . . What was my relationship, Officer? I hated the bleeder's guts, Officer. What was I doing? Kissing the bleeder goodbye . . .

Granny doesn't look for trouble. Never has. Show willing is his motto – show willing and be somewhere else when the shit flies. He was somewhere else today. Nobody can prove he wasn't. Missy Landon was coming out of Lucky Beech's room. She went down in the lift, the way she always does – he saw her but she never saw him. He was somewhere else.

Anywhere.

He draws on his fag . . . Anywhere isn't good enough: where was he? He considers. Cleaning the washroom over at Inductions.

All the time?

He grins at the trick question. All what time, Officer?

All the time from blah-blah to blah-blah.

It's a big washroom, Officer.

Would it surprise you, matey, to know that a reliable

88

witness used that washroom between fucking blah-blah and fucking blah-blah, and you wasn't fucking there?

Nothing would surprise me, Officer. Not when we're talking about fitting poor sods like me up with reliable witnesses.

Granny sighs and shakes his head. He was never much of a one for the old repartee. Maybe the washroom over at Induction's out. Where else, then?

Nurses' room? Yeah. Why not — with the poofter in the dispensary, and the fat blackie in the control room, should be safe enough. Yeah. Sweeping up the nurses' room. And if either of them looked in for a drag or whatever and he wasn't there, he'd just nipped out to the toilet. Yeah. He's an old man, when he got to go he got to go. Show us the evidence proves he didn't, Officer. Go on. Show us.

A poofter and a blackie . . . Christ on a crutch. Granny finishes his roll-up, sends the stub to join the first, flushes the toilet. Christ on a crutch, that's some duty shift, a poofter and a blackie. The worst part of the nick is the company you keep. He's shared with both in his time. Can't say which is worse — blackies all bounce and aggro, clever talk he don't get the half of, or poofters after his bum. He's never had no real trouble, mind. Not from neither. Keeps himself to himself and people respect that. People —

Granny stiffens. Someone's come into the toilet. Up here? No one ever comes into the toilet. Outraged, he listens to whoever it is. The geezer unzips, shuffles his feet, sighs as he starts peeing. Nobody ever comes into this toilet. Nobody ever comes up here at all, there's nothing up here but empty offices, junk.

Whoever it is finishes, zips up, sniffs. Sniffs again, not a snotty sniff, a smelt-something sniff. Granny holds his breath.

'Smoko time?'

Granny winces. The voice is big and cheerful. He doesn't recognize it but it sounds like a screw. Screws sound just like that. Big and cheerful. They fucking ought to – they own the fucking place.

'Smoko time over, friend.'

Granny doesn't make a sound. Friend? That's a laugh. He grabs the toilet seat beneath his skinny thighs with both his hands. He's caught, but he hangs on.

'How many of you are in there, for God's sake? A poker school? The air's so thick you could cut it with a knife.'

That's fucking screws for you. Two roll-ups, just two, and they turn it into a fucking orgy. The bastard bangs on the door. 'Time's up. Let's be having you.' He bangs again. 'You've just been volunteered, friend, so let's be having you.'

The catch doesn't hold and the door bursts open. Granny holds on where he is, he's never liked being volunteered, and pulls his bum down into the seat until it hurts. He looks up, sees this big cheerful bloke. Civvies, so he's not a screw. Big red hands and a shiny suit, so he's a copper. A CID fucker.

'You're not much, are you? Hardly worth the effort.' The copper looks him up and down, fanning the air. 'You'll have to do, though. Beggars can't be choosers ... Grove's the name. Sergeant Grove. Let's be having you.'

He steps back, hands on his hips, everybody's friendly fucking neighbourhood bobby. There's nothing for it – Granny lets go, fumbles his roll-up tin from his lap into his overall pocket, and stands. 'I can smoke here if I want,' he says.

'So you can, friend.' The copper leans forward, stooping, and reads his badge. 'So you can, Granny Porter. That is your right. Just as it's my right now to volunteer you for a nice little job.'

Granny's bold. 'I don't work for you,' he says, straightening his hat. 'I work for Mister Ransome.'

'Don't give us that,' Sergeant Grove says gently. 'Don't come the old acid with me. I'm the law, aren't I? You're a law-abiding citizen, aren't you? That being the way things are, if I ask you to help, Granny Porter, you help. That being the way things are.'

Granny hitches up his trousers. 'What was it you had in mind?'

'A little furniture removal. The lady downstairs sent me up here to look at a desk. A chair or two. She says they'll be dusty but I'm not to mind. They're surplus to requirements and I'm making a place for my gaffer . . . I reckon I'll need a little help on the stairs.'

'There's desks, all sorts . . .' Granny gestures along the passage. 'Heavy, though. I'm not a young man.'

'But you'll do what you can. No man can say more than that. So show me.'

Granny shuffles out. He's unsure of this Sergeant Grove's position. Maybe he'd be wise to show willing, and maybe not. One of the disused offices is stacked with furniture and he leads Grove to it. He shows willing.

eight

Alec checked in mid-stride. The foyer to the Punishments Building was deserted. The musak still played. He sniffed the antiseptic air. He had problems. Frank would be waiting for him upstairs, Nurse Landon too (*Charge Nurse* Landon, according the governor). Problems. An investigation that had to be cleared up by Saturday. A black suspect he could arrest without being accused of racism. Problems.

He remembered that the PMO's report was in his pocket and he still had to read it. He sat on the stairs and read it.

It contained little the governor hadn't already told him. Albert Beech had died of a massive overdose of a paralytic drug with a great many syllables. Of the two injection puncture marks in his arm, one was surrounded by bruising, which suggested that the drug had been clumsily administered, possibly when Beech was already unconscious. Alec was ignorant of thresholding procedures, but a plausible sequence of events presented itself: first the legitimate injection, part of the standard treatment, then the murderer returning to give the second injection some time later, in a hurry and perhaps unskilled. According to the governor, Beech had lain unattended for a while during or after his treatment, and accessible.

Alec turned to the report of the Manchester detective inspector. It had been written on a lap-top. *Upon arriving at the scene of the above-mentioned crime I . . .* Alec closed his eyes. Dear God, this year Manchester was giving lap-tops to *above-mentioneds*. He folded both reports and replaced them in his inside pocket. If the Manchester detective inspector said the second injection was of the same drug as the first, then the second injection was of the same drug as the first. *Above-mentioneds* got such things right. And if that was so, then . . .

Then nothing. Alec roused himself. He'd been nodding off. He knew nothing about this case, not a thing, and Frank was waiting for him upstairs. He got to his feet. He was about to force himself to climb the stairs when his eye was caught by the yellow tape still sealing the far door. Presumably the thresholding room where the victim died was on the other side of it.

He'd never seen a thresholding room. Did he want to? Sooner or later he'd have to.

He crossed the foyer and removed the tape. The door was unusually wide and beyond it he found an unusually wide corridor (for hospital trolleys?), with a barred window at the far end, six doors with portholes on the right, an elevator door on the left with a plain door on either side of it. Treading softly, he explored. Frankly, he was afraid of what he might find. What machinery.

The first room on the left startled him with its hi-tech dazzle: moulded plastic chairs ran on rails in front of screens and keyboards and banks of multi-track levers. The nearest thing to it he'd seen before was a recording studio. It was the sort of place, like a china shop, that made him aware of his size and his elbows. It also, in the context of the Punishments Building, confirmed his dread. No music entered its waiting circuits, none he wanted to hear. He wished he hadn't seen it.

There was a telephone. It reminded him that he had the governor's authority to arrange for a computer link and an assistant. He rang Engineering, as instructed, and then LTI block C. The block officer didn't welcome the call.

'It's a three-day assignment,' Alec told him. 'Not a minute longer. Guaranteed.'

The block officer wanted to know more but wasn't enlightened.

'Take it up with the governor,' Alec told him. 'And send me someone who's computer literate. I'll be expecting him within the hour. Thank you so much.'

He rang off. His telephone persona was masterful. Now, without it, he avoided the room's silent ranks of screens and levers, all nameless, that clamoured for his horrified attention, and backed out, closing the door in his own face. He leaned on it, looking sideways down the still, bright corridor.

He was wasting time. The pretty dark-haired Landon woman needed to get her people back to work. But he was drawn on, fascinated. He walked on his toes, scarcely breathing. After the elevator, the second left-hand door gave on to an elaborate washroom, toilets, baths, sinks and sluices, very white. Its cisterns hissed and the tiny scuffle of his shoes was magnified between the hard white walls and floor and ceiling. He returned to the corridor, the washroom door flapping shut behind him.

Nurse Serote had said, by implication, that there were six thresholding rooms. Presumably the six numbered doors on the other side of the corridor led into them. He crossed the wide corridor, bent his knees warily, and looked through number five's porthole.

'He won't bite you, Chief Inspector.' The voice was loud and Alec jumped. 'The fact is, they've taken him away.'

Alec turned. A young male nurse with a pony-tail was standing in the open door to the foyer.

'It *is* Herself's chief inspector, isn't it? There can't be many sexy black plain-clothes policemen in Justice City.'

Alec straightened his knees and strode back along the corridor, furious. 'This area's sealed. What the hell do you think you're doing?'

'And a chocolate voice to boot.' The nurse stood his

ground. 'The police tape was gone. I thought we were back in business.'

'You're the other nurse.'

'Not the most flattering description.'

'You're Nurse de Carteret.'

'It's a Channel Islands name, lovey. *Très exotique*. Most people call me Jake.'

Alec paused, adjusted his approach. He could deal with gays as camp as this. In his experience they made good witnesses. The agreeable thing about them was that they took most things seriously but never themselves.

'Now that you're here, Nurse de Carteret — '

'Jake?'

' — Now that you're here you can make yourself useful.'

'I can't wait. Is this an interrogation?'

'That comes later. For the moment what I need is a wee run-down on this thresholding. I went on a course but it left gaps. Maybe you could begin at the beginning.'

'Theory or practice?'

'Both.'

The nurse moved towards the nearest portholed door. 'May we?'

Alec nodded. De Carteret trotted in and perched on the bed, swinging his legs. 'Cosy, isn't it?'

Alec looked round. It wasn't what he'd expected. Even so, he'd been in motel rooms that were cosier. And there wasn't a window.

There wasn't a chair either, so he sat on the bed beside Jake de Carteret. He prompted him. 'This thresholding?'

'The theory's very simple.' De Carteret shuffled his buttocks back on the bed and hugged his knees. 'One: if sentencing is to be fair, and therefore credible, then the effects of the EAT need to be consistent. They shouldn't be greater for some than for others. Two: everybody's EAT thresholds are different. And so, three, we have to be able to measure an inmate's EAT thresholds in advance, simply and

95

reasonably pleasantly, so that we can then work out the levels of EAT to give him. Incidentally, for EAT read *punishment*. The public and the courts are happy with *punishment* – aka *retribution* – but we in here prefer the initials. We find them more . . . professional. OK?'

'EAT standing for Extreme Audio-frequency Treatment?'

'Exactly so.' He looked at Alec sideways. 'They're all euphemisms for *pain*, of course. We give the poor loveys pain . . . Measured to the last micro-dol. The same for each. All very scientific. No marks, no sweating warders. Just *pain*.'

Alec refused to be shocked. 'Pain thresholds – aye, everybody's heard of them.'

'And we discover each inmate's in here. On this bed and others.' He bounced up and down. 'It's stronger than it looks.'

Alec had already felt the metal frame concealed by the quilt beneath his thighs. 'You drug the inmates first?'

'New arrivals get tranquillized over in Inductions. After the PMO's had a look at them the inducting officer gives them a hot beverage stuffed with narcotics, mild euphorics, happy powder . . . Mostly they drink it down like the loveys they are. Then they're wheeled over here, dead to the world. The awkward ones walk it, and we persuade them to have what we call an immunization, which is the same thing. Dangle AIDS if they start asking questions. Then they're all laid out on these beds and wired up for the thresholding special. I mix it myself, a dash of this, a dash of that – hypnotics, paralytics, amnesiacs . . . And finally, when they're well and truly out, we zap them.'

'Zap them?'

'Hit them with increasing levels of EAT, and measure their autonomic responses. There's a monitoring room across the passage. All their signs are piped in there – blood pressure, pulse rate, skin conductivity, alpha waves, you name it. From these we compile an EAT profile, the levels at which they're dancing, and pass it on to the joyboys downstairs.' He suddenly ran out of perk. 'I'm not knocking the men in Punishments, lovey. I've worked down there myself. It's not the happiest job.'

He gestured awkwardly, offered a small triangular smile, and got down off the bed to fuss with the flowers in a vase on a table by the wall. This place, Alec thought, could make a man either very hard or very tender. 'EAT,' he said. 'On the course they told us it was sound waves.'

Jake studied the vase, his head on one side. 'So it is. Mostly not the ones you hear, though. Extreme Frequency — that means very high and very low.' He looked back over his shoulder. 'On this course of yours — did they try you with a sample?'

'No.'

'Useless bloody course, by the sound of it.' He gave the flowers a final tweak. 'Ah, what the fuck — they probably didn't have the equipment.'

He went over to one of the several large air-conditioning grilles set into the walls. It swung back like a cupboard door, revealing a bank of massive open metal mouths. 'These are exactly what the cells downstairs have, and they deliver the same effect. Everyone should try it. It gets to feel like your head's bursting.'

Seeing the mouths forced Alec to imagine it.

'You strap men down,' he said. He'd just found a buckle on the frame under the quilt. 'If they're unconscious, why is that necessary?'

'For their own protection. Stop the loveys hurting themselves if we got the mixture wrong. Know what I mean? If we went too easy on the paralytics. We never have.' He closed the grille and faced Alec squarely. 'Beech was deaded in this room. One of us three nurses deaded him. You know that, don't you?'

Alec swung himself down off the bed. 'I don't know anything. I've only just got here.' He went to the door.

'Thank you for the run-down. I'm releasing these rooms for the afternoon shift. Don't go far, though. I'm going to need another talk.'

He left the room, paused, looked back in. 'You mentioned injecting amnesiacs. Do they do what they sound as if they do?'

'They do indeedy.' Jake took a flower from the vase, a white chrysanthemum, and offered it. Alec saw it was plastic. 'They block the poor loveys' memories ... Isn't that a thought, Chief Inspector? What the loveys don't remember maybe didn't ever really happen. If they can't remember it, that's one problem less in a sad old world.'

Alec didn't answer. He went away upstairs to find Sergeant Grove. The nature of reality was not for a rainy afternoon in Justice City. He didn't accept the flower.

Sergeant Grove was in trouble. Beyond Nurse Landon's office a further staircase led up to the next floor and Frank was coming down it backwards, supporting the lower end of a substantial wooden desk and leaning backwards at an ugly angle. Alec went to help. Anxious grunts and cries, very obscene, came from someone out of sight above.

Alec took the weight, let his sergeant back down a couple of steps to gain a better purchase. They lifted and the desk slid jerkily down the stairs, its upper end dropping noisily from tread to tread. The racket attracted Nurse Landon.

She stood in her doorway. 'You shouldn't be doing that, Chief Inspector.'

Alec didn't answer. He agreed with her. Governor Ransome's debit account was mounting.

The desk was near the bottom of the stairs and behind it a crazy-looking old man in a straw hat had appeared, struggling with its other end and still swearing. Frank rested the desk on his knees. His face was a dangerous purple.

'It's heavier than it looked, Chief.'

Alec squeezed round to the other end of the desk and took

it from the old man. Incredibly, his badge identified him as one of the prison porters. Was this what the governor had meant by bodies he could scrounge on the spot? This man was ninety if he was a day. According to his badge his name was *Granny*. Governor Ransome's sense of humour? Did Governor Ransome *have* a sense of humour?

Led by Frank, they carried the desk into an office that already contained another, pushed to one side, a chair, and a couple of filing cabinets. Nurse Landon held the door open for them.

'Doctor Mellish and I share a part-time secretary, Chief Inspector. Daphne Tilder. This is her office – she's in tomorrow and she can come in with me.' She crossed to the window. 'Horrible view . . . Dr Mellish is my director. He's away in the States just now but he'll be back tomorrow.'

Alec settled the desk. 'I know. Governor Ransome told me.'

'Of course you do. I'm sorry.'

'No . . .' He was afraid he'd sounded abrupt. 'Always tell me things, Nurse Landon. I'd rather hear them twice than not at all.'

She nodded. Something caught her eye and she smiled. 'You'll need to wash your hands, Chief Inspector.'

He saw they were filthy from the desk. 'Aye . . . and a wee cloth . . .' He made scrubbing movements on the desk top.

'Granny'll see to all that . . . and meanwhile we can use my office.' She strode out past him. 'I think we need to talk.'

That should have been his line. Angry, but also amused, he went downstairs to the washroom opposite the thresholding rooms. There was no sign of the gay nurse, de Carteret. Presumably he and the black woman Serote had a room of their own somewhere in the building. He shed his jacket, rolled up his sleeves, and slipped off his watch. The time was three thirty. He washed his hands and up to his elbows, splashing cold water over his wrists, then over his face, trying to feel less gritty, trying to make his skin less grey. By now the two nurses had been on duty since seven that morning: eight and a half hours. Lucky them – he felt like he'd been on duty for weeks.

He dried his face and arms, replaced his watch and jacket. Sixty minutes in the place and already people were trying to take him over. The governor had chosen a guilty party, de Carteret was keen to narrow the field, and now the Landon girl had things she wanted to set him straight on. Out of her office a minute earlier and she'd have put herself in charge of moving the desk.

His tie was loose and crooked. He fiddled with it in the washroom mirror, screwing up his face, then thought *Ah, fuckit* and ripped it off, unbuttoning his top shirt button. His black neck emphasized the white open collar but he again thought *Ah, fuckit*. He went upstairs. He was the officer in charge. He could wear what he liked.

Nurse Landon, Charge Nurse Landon for sticklers like the governor, was behind her desk, waiting for him. He went in, closing the door behind himself. He ignored the desk ploy. He could afford to – at six foot plus he was taller than she, even in the lowish chair she offered.

'I told your Nurse de Carteret that I was releasing the thresholding rooms. You might like to call Inductions and tell them.'

'First I'll need to contact nurses' quarters, alert my afternoon shift. And I'll need to be free myself.'

'Then mebbe I'll not keep you. We can have our wee talk later.'

'You're a thoughtful man, Chief Inspector. But we'd better get it over with – the whole day's such a wreck already . . .' She shrugged.

Aye . . . she wanted her wee talk. He hid his smile in the business of setting out his recorder on her desk, explaining the routine, identifying time and place and interviewee for the tape. A belt and braces man, he then fumbled in his inside pocket for his notebook. With it he found the Manchester officer's report. Looking at it, he remembered that he'd never got past *the above-mentioned*. Too late now.

He returned the report to his pocket. 'Now then – '

'I've been thinking, Chief Inspector.' Her desk was tidier than it had been before, and her elbows were on it, her chin in them. 'There are several obvious facts about Beech's death that you need to know, Chief Inspector – obvious, that is, to anyone who's familiar with the workings of the department. Now, I can tell you them and risk you thinking me an interfering woman – ' she smiled disarmingly '– or I can leave you to find them out for yourself in your own good time.'

He'd been ready to tell her to get stuffed but her smile and her *interfering woman* outmanoeuvred him. Besides, she'd told Jake de Carteret he was sexy. 'My own good time is one thing I don't have, Nurse Landon. I think you know that.'

'Yes. Yes, I do . . .' She frowned. 'Mr Ransome's giving you till Saturday and he's imposing a news blackout. Even my own boss doesn't know why he's been sent for.'

'The governor's very thorough.'

'It seems a bit extreme . . . Dr Mellish will be on the plane by now, I gather, and he still hasn't been told what's happened.'

'News blackouts are a mite irregular. Do they worry you?'

'It's none of my business . . .' She caught his sceptical look. 'All right. Yes, I agree with you – maintaining freedom of information is everybody's business.' She paused and he watched her decide how much more she dared give. In the event, not much. 'Like everything else, it's a question of priorities. In this case there's a fairly good reason.'

He was disappointed. It made him combative. 'Your work might be interrupted. It might even be stopped. Obviously you believe in your work.'

'I believe in my work?' She raised her fine dark eyebrows. Suddenly there was a clear, almost unbearable tension in her. She sat back from the desk and crossed her plump, paisley-covered legs. 'We're getting very philosophical, Chief Inspector.'

'I'm sorry. We'll stick with the news blackout. Obviously Mr Ransome will want your support in it, and I can well understand that you – '

'No, Chief Inspector. We won't stick with the blackout. The question you asked deserves an answer.' She smiled coldly. 'It's the question most people want to ask.'

'It was still impertinent. This is a murder inquiry.' It was also, just then, a surprising exercise in police sensitivity. Could it be that he didn't want to hear her answer?

She arranged her arms carefully, hands together in her lap. 'I am not your traditional torturer, Chief Inspector. This is not your traditional torture chamber.'

The voice was quiet, almost casual, but the words stopped Alec dead. He looked away, lowering his gaze. There was a photograph on her desk, in a shabby leather frame. A middle-aged man, in a surburban garden, smoking a pipe . . . Outside in the passage Alec heard bangs as more furniture was moved.

Nurse Landon was answering an accusation he had not made.

'We hand out punishment,' she continued. 'Not torture – punishment. A better word is retribution. I don't hand it out personally, but I get the process going so I'm more responsible than many . . . But it isn't torture, Chief Inspector. It's retribution. There's a big difference. The difference is that I gain nothing from it.' Alec was still looking at the middle-aged man in the picture. Presumably he was her father. 'None of us on this side of the retribution interface here in the House gains anything from it. Not information, not revenge, not pleasure. We gain nothing . . .'

In the silence that followed more bangs were heard, and a sharp obscenity from Granny Porter. Alec looked up. The tension in her had ebbed.

She leaned forward. 'That's how punishment and torture

differ, Chief Inspector.' She hunted exaggeratedly in the junk on her desk, found matches and cigarettes, and lit one. Her hand trembled. 'Torture is inflicted for gain, punishment is not . . . I'm quoting from the handbook, of course, but I do happen to believe what I'm saying. I gain *nothing*.'

She thought about that. 'The sense of a job well done, perhaps. Pious things like service to the public . . . to the community . . . to people like you yourself, Chief Inspector. Nothing more.' She blew out smoke uninhaled, like a child smoking for a dare. 'So do I believe in my work? You have your answer.'

He did indeed. He needn't have feared to hear it. But he'd skimmed through the handbook himself, on his course, and he'd doubted then that department heads would be able to screen out the salacious or the vengeful. Now, talking to bold Nurse Landon, who was clearly neither salacious nor vengeful, he saw that it was possible. Why she'd wanted to join the prison service in the first place was another matter, but maybe it was lucky for everyone else that people like her sometimes did.

He squared his notebook on his knee, allowing a moment for the dust to settle. The solitary picture on her desk had intrigued him – a photograph of her father, no boy-friend. Yet he'd be willing to bet a month's salary she wasn't gay . . .

He cleared his throat, moved on. If she still wanted to brief him, why not? At the beginning of a case he was always groping. Maybe she'd give him a starting point.

'You mentioned obvious facts, Nurse Landon.'

For a moment she seemed not to understand him. She'd been away on some different trail. Then she nodded, remembering. 'I made a list while you were with the governor . . .' She parked her cigarette in a tin lid and referred to the back of a drug promotion leaflet. Alec made the comparison with Governor Ransome, who wrote his lists on headed notepaper. 'First fact – the murderer had inside knowledge of the workings of this department. He or she knew that prepared syringes are available on the medical trolley, and that a single additional dose would be fatal. Second – '

Alec raised a finger. 'Why not an opportunist crime?' He didn't believe it, but she needed interrupting. 'The sight of a syringe already filled, the hope that its contents would be fatal?'

'An unlikely idea for someone to have, Chief Inspector. Wouldn't you say?'

Alec shrugged. 'Maybe just the assumption that it would do Beech little good.'

'An accident you mean? No intent to kill, only to injure?'

'I can see a defence counsel arguing it that way. Could you refute him?'

'If the accused was a doctor or nurse, of course I could. If not . . . well, there were easier ways of hurting Beech. An unconscious man, strapped down – why not just knock him about a bit?'

'What about total accident, then? Couldn't one of your staff, even you yourself, have given Beech the second injection by mistake? Come to his bedside, not knowing about the first, and quite innocently have given him another?'

She shook her head. 'Not possible. The routine is strict, Chief Inspector. Only I give the injections. A mistake like that couldn't happen.'

'Are you really so infallible?'

'The routine is. A nurse prepares inductees, then two nurses are with me during the medication.' She paused, smiled at him sideways. 'In any case, I *am* infallible. In medical matters concerning this department I'm totally infallible.' She smiled again. 'Which I believe is a tautology.'

'As was my *so*.'

They shifted in their seats, sharing the very small joke.

Her cigarette was now mostly a drooping column of ash. She lifted it distastefully, knocked off the ash, then stubbed the remainder out in the tin lid. 'I'm sorry,' she said. 'I'm trying to take up smoking and I'm not very good at it.'

'Trying to take up smoking?' He'd never heard anything so crazy.

'Well, trying to look like a hardened smoker. It's for a play I'm in. Recording it for the City TV station. *Hedda Gabler.* The director thinks she's a sixty-a-day woman.'

It was an interesting idea, Hedda a heavy smoker in a time when women rarely smoked. Wasn't there a mention of cigarettes in the text somewhere...? Alec brought his thoughts back to Beech's murder. He liked the accident theory no more than she did.

'Any other facts for me?'

She looked at her list. 'They rather depend on the first. If the murderer knows the department's routine then he or she has to be one of this morning's shift. Put baldly, the murderer has to be Nurse de Carteret, Nurse Serote, or me.'

He frowned. He'd been told that already by de Carteret. He'd never known such people for condemning themselves. 'There's another shift. There are relief nurses. They all know the department – couldn't it be one of them?'

She considered. 'They couldn't risk being seen. This is a small department, they almost certainly would be, and it'd be too unusual. Too noticeable. We'd wonder why on earth they were here – they couldn't hope to get away with it.'

'You didn't see anybody, of course? No . . . but then, you probably weren't here all the time. So that still leaves the opportunist, someone coming in who just got lucky. I don't imagine anybody was watching Beech all the time, were they?'

'All what time, Chief Inspector?'

He stared at her. It was a good question. He vaguely remembered the governor saying something about a fifteen-minute gap . . . It would all be in the Manchester inspector's report, of course. The thing was, he'd approached this investigation arse backwards. Giving Nurse Landon her head had been a mistake. A tired man's folly.

'I reckon we'd better begin at the beginning.'

They did. She described how she had gone with Nurse de Carteret into Beech's thresholding room. Alec wanted to know how Beech had got there so she described the induction process – the hot beverage laced with barbiturates, the journey on a trolley from Inductions to the House, the transfer of the sedated inductee to a bed in a thresholding room, the straps to be attached and the electrodes, the final check on the inductee's vital signs, his fitness to undergo the thresholding process.

Back again in Beech's thresholding room, she described the shallowness of his stupor. 'He was moving his head, and his feet, and his eyes were open. I think they were focused.'

'The barbiturates hadn't worked?'

'Not fully. It does happen. Beech is – was a very large man. Very determined. Also, the officers over at Inductions aren't always all that careful. They have no medical training to speak of – they get the beverage/barbiturate mixes pre-packaged according to a simple bodyweight formula.'

'But you weren't in any danger? I mean, Beech was strapped down and so on?'

'No danger at all ... One funny thing, though. He said something. He looked round the room – I think he did – and he said something. One word. *Wishbone*. He said it twice. *Wishbone*.'

'*Wishbone?*'

'That's what it sounded like.'

'Did it mean anything to you?'

'Not a thing. That bit under the neck of a chicken ... nothing else. And then I injected him. Once. Only once. The first and only time.'

'Would he have said more if you hadn't injected him?'

'I've no idea. It's possible. I wasn't all that interested ... and besides, I was anxious to spare him distress.'

'Of course you were. What was his expression?'

'Expression?'

'The expression on his face. Was he angry ... sad ... frightened ...?'

'I think ...' She narrowed her eyes, remembering. 'As a matter of fact, I think he was smiling.'

'Smiling. So there was no real question of distress.'

'It's a medical phrase, Chief Inspector.' He was harrying her and she let her irritation show. 'We talk about sparing patients distress. Distress takes many forms ... In any case, I don't hold conversations with inductees. If they're awake I get them under as soon as possible. Thresholding runs to a very tight schedule.'

He eased off. 'And presumably Beech wouldn't have been making very much sense anyway.'

She seemed not to understand.

'He was heavily drugged, wasn't he?'

'That needn't stop him being lucid. Such people often are. You see it in hospital with post-operative patients. The family comes and talks to them and they're as bright as buttons. They're probably stoned out of their minds, and they won't remember a thing about it, but their relations never guess.'

Alec nodded, glancing through his notes. He wasn't sure why he was making such an issue out of Beech's lucidity. The behaviour was odd, though, a man who said *wishbone* for no apparent reason was very odd, and oddities could be fruitful.

'So what happened next?'

'I injected Beech and he immediately lost consciousness.'

'There was no other mark on his arm? You'd have noticed if there had been?'

'Certainly I would. There was nothing.'

'Bruises take time to come up, don't they? If there was just a puncture mark, perhaps you – '

'If you've read Dr Peck's notes' – she paused accusingly but he gave her nothing back – 'if you've read Dr Peck's notes you'll remember that the two marks are very close

107

together. I swabbed a wide area. I couldn't possibly have missed it.'

'Do you like Dr Peck?'

'What a strange question.' She stared at the back of one hand, considering. Her fingers were well-shaped, Alec saw: strong yet feminine. 'Not very much. He's lazy. He compensates by giving everyone a hard time. He's got that idiotic grin.'

'It was Peck who examined Beech over at Inductions, wasn't it?'

'I see where you're going . . . But that was early this morning. Far too long ago for – '

'How early?'

'Shortly after five. The duty PMO – that's the prison medical officer – the duty PMO examines all inductees on arrival. Beech came up from Manchester in this morning's first batch. They run a tight schedule. They have to.'

'Peck couldn't have got to him again?'

'Not without questions being asked. He goes for breakfast at six thirty and he doesn't exactly hurry back. It'll be easy to find out if he did.'

'I see.' Alec turned a page in his notebook. 'And what happened next?'

'Why all this interest in involving Dr Peck?'

'I asked you what happened next.'

Nice hands or not, she should be answering. In any case, there were no clear reasons for many of his questions. He was interested in Peck because he'd met the three main suspects so far and he wasn't impressed. Beech's murderer was more calculating, and surely more vindictive, than any of them. Maybe Peck would fit the description. He might even have a motive . . .

'You injected Beech and he lost consciousness – what happened next?'

'I prepared the other two.' She didn't like his sharp tone.

108

Her reply was minimal. 'We had four inductees this morning. Beech was the second man I got to.'

'Any reason for the order?'

'None at all. It was chance.'

'So no one could have foreseen it?'

'It wouldn't have mattered if they had.'

'Please answer the question.'

'I already have. It was chance. No one could have foreseen it.'

'Thank you.' He smiled. It was time for conciliation. 'I'm sure you see how important that is.'

'I'm afraid I don't. The order I treated the men in means nothing.'

'Why is that?'

'Because nothing could be done to any of them until after the thresholding. All through the thresholding procedure I monitor their condition from the control room across the passage. I'd have seen at once if Beech wasn't responding. I could probably have saved his life.'

'You do this monitoring on your own?'

The implication was clear and she gave him one of her sideways smiles. He gained the feeling, briefly, of a game being played between them. 'Nurse Serote was with me in the control room.'

'Is she always?'

'Someone is. It's too much to handle on your own.'

'And Nurse de Carteret?'

'Jake? I can't remember . . . Yes I can – he was working out in the dispensary. I'd asked him to sort the place out and do some stock-taking.'

'So that's located the three of you. And I'm sure Nurse Serote will confirm that Beech was alive and kicking at the end of the procedure.'

'Alive, Chief Inspector. Hardly kicking.'

'Of course. Now tell me – who knew that Beech was going to be here this morning?'

'Anybody in the City could have known. There's a roll goes up on the board over at Inductions.'

'When did you know?'

'Eightish this morning. When I got in to work. A file comes over with the inductees' particulars.'

'What did you feel when you saw that one of them was Beech?'

'What would anyone feel? Disgust? Anger?'

'His sentence was severe. Were you glad he was getting his come-uppance?'

'Not really . . . I have to admit I mostly felt sorry for the punishments officer, having to find space for Beech in his room schedule. I know how hectic it gets down there.'

He believed her. She was more the organization lady than he'd thought.

'And Nurse Serote? What did she feel?'

'I've no idea. You'd better ask her.'

'I'm asking you. You were with her for some time. Didn't she say anything?'

'Not a thing. It's busy in the control room.'

'All right.' Again the game – she knew why he was asking about Nurse Serote. Nurse Serote was black, Beech's victim had been black. 'So after the thresholding what then?'

'Inductees are left to themselves for fifteen, twenty minutes. They start resurfacing and then a nurse goes round, makes them ready for the men who take them downstairs.'

That would be the governor's 'fifteen minutes'. 'So what did you do then?'

'I printed out the profiles and took – '

'The profiles?'

'Read-outs of the men's thresholds.'

'Their pain thresholds.'

'Their pain thresholds.' She didn't blink. 'That way the punishments officer can programme each man's treatment – '

'Each man's punishment.'

'Can programme each man's punishment so that it's no more or less effective than the others.' She shook her head and corrected the euphemism before he could. 'No more or less painful ... I switched off in the control room and took the profiles down to the punishments officer. I usually do. I like to discuss them with him personally. Sometimes there's something special.'

'Was there anything special about Beech's profile?'

On her desk the telephone rang. She gestured apologetically and lifted the receiver.

'Charge Nurse Lan – '

The voice that interrupted her was male, and very loud. Alec couldn't make out the words, but they were angry. She waited for a while, her face turned away, looking out of the window.

'I'm sorry, Douglas ... Yes, I know that's not much help, but – ' The receiver protested and she waited again. 'Yes, there's been a hold-up ... Yes, a four-hour hold-up ... No. Look, why don't you call the governor? I said, why don't you call the – ' She distanced the receiver from her ear, turned back to Alec. 'It's Inductions,' she mouthed. Then, 'Not much longer, Douglas. No. I promise. Ten minutes.' She raised her eyebrows at Alec, who nodded. 'Ten minutes. Yes. That's a promise. Ten minutes. I'll be in touch.'

The receiver was still protesting as she put it down. 'I should have done what you said, Chief Inspector. Douglas is desperate. He's holding off Manchester but there's still this morning's second batch. They'll be coming to us cold, too ... Honestly, I hadn't realized how long this was going to take.'

Alec didn't apologize. 'I was asking if there was anything special about Beech's profile.'

'Beech's profile?' She gathered her thoughts. 'Not a thing. The four of them were very ordinary.'

'But you went down with the profiles all the same.'

'There are always final things to do in the control room.

Bits and pieces to be squared away. Programmes to be cleared. Preparations for the next batch. I leave those to my assistant.'

'And this morning your assistant was Nurse Serote . . . So you went downstairs to the punishments officer.'

'I went in the lift, actually. I wasn't with him very long – ten minutes at the outside. Then I took off for my quarters.'

'Leaving Nurse Serote upstairs in the control room and Nurse de Carteret in the dispensary.'

'It was ten o'clock. Somewhere around ten . . .' She spread her hands. 'Break time, Chief Inspector. Theirs too.'

'During which the four inductees, including Beech, were unattended. This is safe?'

'You mean medically? They're checked before the control room switches off, and then they surface gradually. There's no risk at all. They're still restrained, of course . . .'

'And that was the time during which Beech was murdered.'

'You have it. I gather Carole found him some twenty minutes later.' She saw he wasn't writing, and leaned forward. 'That's Carole Serote. And she found him dead.'

He still didn't write. She'd forgotten the recorder. After a while people did. 'And where was the medical wagon all this time?'

'The medical wagon?'

She looked at him blankly. 'I've no idea . . . In the passage somewhere. It needs to be available, in case there's trouble later, after the surfacing.'

'The surfacing's when inductees start coming round?' She nodded. 'So the wagon's always in the passage and anyone could get to it?' She nodded again. Alec sighed. 'You've been very helpful. Tell me one more thing – '

There was a knock on the door. It opened a foot or so and Frank Grove put his head round.

'Room for a word?'

'Room for several, Frank. Nurse Landon and I have just about finished.'

'We're in business, Chief. The computer's arrived, and now the bloke to work it. I said you'd want to see him.'

'Of course I do. I've even got something for him.' Alec looked at the word in his notes – *Wishbone*. Maybe the mainframe at the Yard would come up with something. He turned back to Nurse Landon. 'I was wondering . . . this time you spent back in your quarters. What were you doing? Did anyone see you?'

'I was learning my lines. Little and often. I do a bit every day – it seems to work.'

'Your lines? Ah . . . you mean Hedda. It's a big part.'

'Big enough . . . And nobody saw me. But if I murdered Beech I did it long before that, on my way past his room, going down to Punishments. It was the perfect opportunity.'

Alec stood up, closed his notebook irritably. 'What reason could a woman like you possibly have for murdering Albert Beech?'

'I've no idea.' She faltered. 'I'm sorry . . . all this is important and I've been sounding jokey. You're very patient . . .'

He looked down at her. *A woman like you* . . . he wondered what he'd meant.

He said, 'It's after four. I've got an office of my own now so I'll leave you. Sergeant Grove, Frank here, will be preparing a statement for you to sign, based on this interview.' He indicated the telephone. 'Douglas is expecting a call.'

He scooped up the recorder, joined Frank Grove at the door, turned.

'One last thing. I need a word with your two nurses. Where can I find them?'

Frank cleared his throat. 'Nurse Serote's waiting for you, Chief. There's a nurses' room downstairs. I parked the other one there till you need him.'

Alec smiled. *The other one* . . . Blacks Frank could manage. Gays, never. The two of them went out of the room, leaving Charge Nurse Landon to her Douglas.

113

nine

It's six o'clock now and Peggy Landon's finished for the day. *Not before time* she tells herself as she leans inside the lift on the way up from Punishments. Committing the perfect murder takes it out of you. So does dealing with the police afterwards.

That sudden blank over the wagon. Pretending she didn't know where Jake had left it. Why bother? She'd have noticed. Anyone would've noticed. It was hardly a startling admission. In fact she'd had to move it before she could get into the lift, so why pretend? She'd been up front over *Wishbone* – no alternative if Jake or Carole weren't to get in with it first, which would look suspicious – so why pretend about the wagon? The sexy black chief inspector was eating out of her hand, in any case, so why pretend? No, it had been bad thinking.

She'd have liked to quit at the end of her interview, she felt so battered, but there was still a full batch waiting to be thresholded. The conveyor belt didn't stop, just because one wretched man hadn't made it. Douglas wanted her to take the regular two afternoon batches but she told him no. She had her nurses to consider. The afternoon shift was understandably edgy ... late start, policemen underfoot. She hadn't been able to tell him *why* there were policemen underfoot – nobody was supposed to know but it hadn't helped. Douglas had bottleneck problems, he said ...

114

The lift doors open and she goes along to her office. In any case, six o'clock is late enough. Downstairs have their problems too. After six o'clock the punishments officer got into his evening mode. He wouldn't want to have to book in new inmates when his staff was supposed to be feeding round the existing ones. She'd told Douglas straight out no. If he didn't like it he could do the other thing. Ship his bottleneck back to Manchester for all she cared. Frayed edges were to be expected, she thought. She'd had a hard day.

She files the day's throughput by date in the cabinet behind the door, and cross-references the ten names. Six names in the afternoon, four in the morning.

Four names in the morning. One name. A name she'd never been told. Lucky – that was all she'd ever called him, just Lucky. And no beard, of course. All the same, going into his room, into Beech's room, she'd felt an immediate, over-powering sense of having known him before, in circumstances she couldn't remember. That, and the further suspicion that when she did remember she wouldn't like it.

And then he'd spoken. 'Wishbone?' he'd said.

He hadn't had her recognition problem. No wonder he smiled. Prepped out of his skull, but he remembered her well, even after eight years, nine was it? He had the advantage of her, of course – she hadn't grown a beard.

'Wishbone?'

Bloody silly name. It went with his, the first thing she'd thought of. He wasn't called Beech in those days – at least, not to the likes of her. 'Lucky'll fix you up,' she'd been told. 'Lucky's the guy you want. Try that pub down by the river.' So when he'd introduced himself in the Chandler, 'I'm Lucky,' and bought her a drink and asked her what they called her, she'd told him 'Wishbone' quick as a flash. He'd laughed, and it'd stuck.

He was clean-shaven then, a big blond man, soft-spoken, businesslike, not noticeably evil. She never tried to discover his real name and she made sure he never discovered hers. It wasn't necessary. More than that, it wasn't desirable.

Peggy takes off her white coat and hangs it on the back of the door. She looks at it, sees how grubby it is around the pockets. She'll need a fresh one tomorrow so she takes it down again and folds it over her arm. She's not an instinctively clean person – it's her nurse's conditioning that makes her do this.

If Beech hadn't been so prepped maybe he'd have kept his mouth shut. Realized how vulnerable he was and waited. Except that he couldn't have known she hadn't recognized him. But in any case she hadn't decided right away to kill him. That came later. She'd had plenty of time to think about it, three or four minutes, five even, while she was medicating the indecent exposure and the computer fiddle who was a Christian Scientist. No, her first priority, Jake and Carole and Granny Porter there in the room, had been to shut him up. With the thresholding syringe already in her hand, no problem. The decision to kill him came later.

Three or four minutes, five even . . . it isn't very long. And it isn't as if she doesn't value human life. She's a nurse, for heaven's sake. She has a vocation. She's been trained to be gentle and loving. She values human life very much.

Before her training, before her vocation, she'd valued her father's life. All through that last year, when she was hardly more than a kid, she'd talked him through his fears, his voices. She hadn't been able to save his life, but she'd sure as hell valued it.

She'd valued Albert Beech's life too. She values everybody's. The decision to kill him wasn't a matter of morality – that's why it was made so quickly. She didn't add up his sins and set them against hers and see that his were great while hers were rather little. The decision to kill him rested solely upon the answer to the question whether or not she could get away with killing him, and for that three or four minutes, five even, were plenty. Certainly she could.

116

She valued Albert Beech's life but she values her own more. It's *hers* and she values it more, and there's no way she was going to give it up for the sake of his which she valued less, and she could easily get away with killing him, so she did.

Peggy turns out the light in her office and goes downstairs. There are voices in the room she's given over to nice Inspector Duncan, and a light under the door, but she doesn't hang around. He'll be working late, with only till Saturday to find his murderer, and she feels bad about him. He's gentle, and quite big, and she'd never thought she'd find a black man so attractive.

She doesn't approve of murder. Murder's terrible, society would break down if too many people went around murdering other people, not to mention all the widows and orphans, and what about her with her nurse's vocation? But when push comes to shove you stay alive. It's as simple as that.

Admittedly there's a little melodrama here. An overstatement. Albert Beech couldn't actually have killed her, strapped to the thresholding bed, or downstairs, or in LTI, he could only have destroyed her career. But it comes to the same thing. Her career is all she has. She's worked hard to make it.

So the puzzle is, if her career was so precious – and it had been, even all those years ago – why had she ever endangered it? The money? She hadn't needed it. The urge to spit in society's eye? She hadn't felt it. The excitement? She'd suffered nervous diarrhoea from it. The stuff itself? She'd never used it.

Her first job in the prison service, junior nurse in the hospital, Wandsworth Prison. The charge nurse Patrick was leaving, and he'd been in-house supplier of illegal substances for the whole place. Patrick drew the line at LSD, bad trips attracted bad attention, but pot, coke, designers, heroin, he was the man everyone relied on. Now he was leaving (an unambitious guy, some said, retiring on his profits), and the torch needed handing on. And the thing was, he handed it on to *her*.

Two other nurses, any number of orderlies, porters, warders, cleaning staff, trustees, and he chose *her*. Looking back on it, Peggy saw that she couldn't have refused. She'd always been a push-over for pants that were filled in the right places. He'd handed the torch on to her, and taken his reward, which she'd have given him anyway. The money'd never been a consideration – it's in her building society now, a comforting sum but nothing to raise official eyebrows. One day, maybe, she'll think of something she wants to spend it on. Justice City satisfies most of her needs.

Downstairs in the foyer she pauses. She ought to go straight back to her quarters. She has a rehearsal this evening after supper, Act Three, and she ought to work on her lines. Her study period that morning had gone down well with the Inspector, but it hadn't happened. She'd like to see anyone settling down to learn lines fifteen minutes after committing murder. By the time she'd got through with the punishments officer she was on her knees. He probably noticed, but she doesn't mind: the best counsel in the world can't get a conviction on the basis of a few twitchy moments. Once back in her room she'd simply flaked out. She tried a cigarette, *à la* Hedda, the way twitchy people are supposed to, but it made her want to spew. So now she ought to go straight back to her quarters. She's edgy, though . . .

Patrick's torch led to Lucky, and Patrick set up the meeting. They met one November evening in a modern riverside pub, the Chandler, 'I'm Lucky. What do people call you?' then took the riverside walk, downstream towards Battersea Bridge. The path was modern too, in neat brown brickwork, with expensive big-windowed flats on one side and a brown brick parapet on the other, vandalized electric light globes at regular intervals on metal posts. Lucky stopped, and she leaned beside him on the parapet beneath a vandalized light. The wind came across the river from Chelsea Marina as if from the North Pole.

'What are you buying?' Lucky asked her.

'What Patrick buys.'

'The same conditions?'

'The same conditions.'

They exchanged Tesco shopping bags and parted. His contained Patrick's last order and hers contained the money for it. Business was regular between them from then on. Never anything more — he wasn't noticeably evil and his pants were nicely filled, but she must have known. Something must have warned her to keep her distance.

Ten months later the TV people arrived, and then the Home Office inquiry. It came close to fingering her, but it never did. She and Lucky ceased business by mutual agreement, and for a time the jail was clean and several of its inmates were crazy desperate. Then she left, posted to Justice City, taking her savings with her. She never thought of adding to them in her new job. She cared about her career and the risks weren't worth it.

It was all so long ago. Nine years. She couldn't allow her career to be destroyed by such a distant folly. She'd no idea what Beech would've done with it, but whatever he'd done would've been too much. The decision to kill him had made itself, once she'd seen how she could get away with it.

It wasn't as if he'd be missed.

Frankly, that was neither here nor there. Ten starving children, a destitute mother, and a wife with MND, and she'd still have given him the second injection, bruising the flesh so that she might have been Granny Porter. Jake, Carole, Granny Porter, they all had the opportunity and she might have been any of them. Her own opportunity came on her way down to Punishments with the profiles.

Peggy doesn't go back to her quarters. She's too wrought-up even to think of learning her lines. She decides to go and see Karl instead.

119

Dr Stanna – a real doctor, hugely qualified, with a Ph.D. in some arcane aspect of brain function – heads up the Research Centre, two grids to the north of the House in Justice City's pattern of covered walkways. Peggy goes to look for him there because that's where she knows he'll be. He has no conception of work as something separate from leisure – for him work *is* leisure. It's been dark now for a couple of hours and the clouds must have blown over, for there's frost about as the wind still rushes in from the moor, over the wall and down between the buildings. Peggy hurries, bent against it, tense with the effort not to shiver. She didn't dress warmly this morning so she's unprepared, but she doesn't bother with her grubby white coat: putting it on against such a wind would be ridiculous. She relies on speed getting her there before hypothermia takes over. With all the gates to get through, she only just makes it.

After dark Justice City loses none of its menace. Flood-lighting takes over, brighter than the January day just past, brighter than might be thought possible. It's inhuman, and it bleaches out what little colour there ever was. The grass is grey now, the sky invisible, the buildings roofed over by the shadowless glare. But Peggy doesn't mind the menace. She rather likes it. It's where she lives.

She shoulders her way in through the double doors to the Research Centre and across the foyer. Her face takes her past the armed guy at the desk (Research is given special protec-tion), and her ID takes her through into the restricted area beyond. The animal laboratory is out the back. Karl's workroom is on the right, with his operating theatre beside it. She knocks on the door.

'It's open,' he shouts.

If it wasn't, her ID would be useless. Sometimes his work is impossibly delicate – nobody in Justice City has a card that lets them just barge in. She turns the knob and enters.

Karl is at a huge high definition TV screen, rotating a 3-D projection she doesn't recognize. Coloured areas shaped like hands expand and contract, apparently at random. Karl freezes the picture.

'Pegsmegs my dear – it's good to see you.'

'I'm interrupting something.'

'Everybody always is. It can keep. Come – ' He swivels his chair to face her and holds out his arms.

She stays just inside the door. She's just realized that she urgently needs to get into his pants – that's why she's here – and it's all too hasty. Too incontinent.

She says, 'How's your day been?'

'Fine.' He tilts his head, working her out. 'And yours?'

'Fine.'

'That's fine . . .' He's worked her out now and his arms are still outstretched. 'I'm glad to hear it. Your day's been fine and so has mine. Good. Great. Now come and kiss me.'

She almost does. It's a habit of his to say kiss when he means fuck, and one of the advantages of the hours he works is the handsome day-bed he keeps in his workroom. It's narrow, but strong enough for two.

She snicks the door lock behind her and takes a step forward. She hangs her white coat over the back of a chair. 'Actually, that's not quite true.' She's decided to wait. 'My day's been horrible but I'm not supposed to tell.'

'Then I won't ask. Poor Magsbags.' He lowers his arms. He thought he knew where she was but now he's not sure. 'My day wasn't all that great either. None of my models fit.'

He's modelling electrical surface activity on the brain. He's got a dozen volunteer GBH LTIs as guinea-pigs. This much Peggy knows – if he could make patterns of excitement trigger the right chemicals he could make them self-modifying. Halve violent crime with a single implant.

'One of our inductees died on us,' she tells him. Bugger the governor. 'Ransome's keeping the lid on it till Saturday, till we find out why.'

'That's terrible.' He leans forward, really concerned. 'Who

was it? What did he die of? Who mixed the cocktail? Was it a mechanical failure?'

He led the team that developed EAT and he deserves to know it all, but for some reason she doesn't tell him. She doesn't, in fact, quite trust him.

'I'll tell you when I can, Karl. And till then . . .?'

'Till then – schtumm.' He has bright brown eyes and a wonderful grasp of the essentials. She'll tell him when she can. He sits back again and pats his knee. 'Now come and kiss me.'

She's waited long enough. She's across the room now and getting his zip down and he stands up to help her and there's contact between them and she gasps, her eyes wide. Now she does kiss him, mouths his lips, his rough six o'clock cheek, his ear. They fit together very well, standing up. They fit so well that he fucked her once in the lift going up to the governor's office, fucked her properly, bringing her off, a tribute to her as much as to him, in the four floors going up to the governor's office. The fun (there wasn't much) was in the risk.

Today they've got more time. Her brown paisley tights are down around her ankles, his green corduroy pants are down around his. They hobble across the room to the bed, laughing, and fall upon it. It groans but survives. They groan too, after a while, and survive. Across the room the 3-D projection above Karl's desk has been replaced by a procession of spectacularly collectable motor cars. They're what his computer does when he neglects it.

He stays on her, dwindling. She can never bear to let him go.

'Dear Meggity . . .'

'Shshsh.'

He can't leave her name alone. One night Meggity fondly became Maggity, and then Maggotty, which she hated. He likes word games and can't see the harm.

'Shshsh . . .'

122

Finally there's nothing left for her to hold on to. She sighs. 'I killed him, Karl.'

He stays above her, reassuringly heavy on the narrow bed. 'Nurses say that. Doctors too. They like to dramatize. Patients die, Maggity. It doesn't have to be our fault.'

He's giving her a chance to take back her confession and she wonders why she doesn't want to. Pillow talk? Post-coital tristesse? Because she wants to trust the man she's just welcomed into her body?

'Tell me, Karl.' Her subconscious, ever beavering away, has just come up with a nasty possibility. 'Tell me, Karl, would an official expert be able to find out who'd been wearing a particular pair of plastic gloves?'

Karl raises himself on his elbows and looks down at her. He's uneasy but for the moment he takes her question at its face value. 'From sloughed-off skin, you mean? Identifiable sweat?'

She nods. 'Anything like that.'

'You need to ask a forensics man. Myself, I'd say it depends who we're talking about. If it's doctors or nurses, they wash more than ordinary people. I doubt if they leave many residues . . . Sweat perhaps – if the gloves are on for long enough.'

'That's what I thought.' She'd worn hers for scarcely thirty seconds. 'Ta.'

He disengages now and gets up slowly. He's right about doctors' cleanly habits – now he's going to wash. He picks up his pants and walks away, slightly ludicrous now with his hairy bum showing beneath his shirt, and the wet end of his penis. Ordinary men would just stuff it all back in their briefs.

Suddenly she realizes that she doesn't know *what* ordinary men would do. She's never known an ordinary man. She came to nursing so young that the only men she's known have been doctors, student doctors, or male nurses.

Karl talks to her from the washroom next door. 'About

those gloves – I wouldn't rely on it, my dear. And in any case, it's always better to come forward.' He's putting two and two together. So far he's only made them three and a half. 'It looks so much better on your record – if there's ever an inquiry, I mean.'

She doesn't answer. There's only one thing she can trust about Karl, and that's his professional propriety. She's gone too far already. If he knew for certain that she'd done wrong, behaved unprofessionally, he'd throw her to the wolves – very gently, very regretfully, but he'd throw her. He's recorded this conversation word-for-word among his synapses, and if Inspector Duncan ever asks him for a replay he won't refuse.

She thinks back. Does it matter? No – her confession could be taken as a generalized nurse's *mea culpa*, the way he'd taken it, and her question about the gloves as the product of an innocent, quite natural curiosity. She hears Karl peeing. Both confession and question are suspicious, but the Inspector needs more than that, he needs proof, and there isn't any.

Karl appears in the open washroom doorway, zipping up his pants. 'Eating time. Let's blow ourselves to the City Bistro.'

She's pulled down her skirt. Now that he's finished in the washroom she can use it. Nurses are perfectly prepared to mop up other women's twats in public, but seldom their own. The City Bistro is an over-priced establishment with candles in bottles and red check tablecloths, franchised in from the private sector to keep senior staff in touch with the finer things of life. Montmartre come to Skagg Tor. Don't laugh – fifteen hundred feet up, twenty miles from the nearest human habitation, facing east, it doesn't do to be snobby.

Peggy gets up off the bed. Karl's given her his advice and, typically, he's moved on. She goes in to the washroom past him, kissing his cheek on the way, ashamed of having judged

124

him ungenerously but, she's sure, accurately. She closes the door behind her.

Her face is in the mirror. Murderers are supposed to stare, fearing to see traces of their crime, and vainly wash their blood-soaked hands. Peggy does neither. Her crime was so light and so easy that it can't have marked her, and she wore gloves. A thin film of plastic between her and it. A metaphor for her life? She cringes. Metaphor, schmetaphor.

She's brought her tights with her. She washes her twat and puts them on. Her shoes are out in the room somewhere, and so is her white coat with her lipstick in one of its pockets. Now that she does look at her face in the mirror she sees that her lips are slightly engorged with kissing. Not murder, just kissing. Frankly she wishes the effect would last: she looks better for it. She flicks at her hair and goes out to Karl.

'The Bistro's fancy,' she says. 'I ought to change.'

'You look fine, Pegs. They'll be lucky to get you.'

He's turned off his computer and tidied his desk. He's putting on his jacket. It's green corduroy and matches his pants. Only a very brilliant scientist would wear a corduroy suit. She finds her shoes and her coat, and renews her lipstick. She remembers she's got a rehearsal this evening and decides to cut it. There's plenty of Act Three they can get on with without her.

'The lab tech doesn't do his rounds till nine,' Karl says. 'I'll just check the boys and girls.'

She goes with him to visit his chimps. Sometimes she helps him, lets them out of their cages, plays with them, cheers them up. She's good with animals.

They're fine tonight, gone to bed in their straw. There's a blue light in the animal lab and they probably think it's the moon. She has a favourite, a young male called Joshua. Joshua came from the Channel Islands zoo and he's part of an important experiment. He's asleep in his cage now, an insignificant bundle of furry elbows and knees, but the time will come when he changes Chief Inspector Duncan's life. Peggy and Karl tiptoe round, then close the door softly.

The City Bistro occupies a unique location. It's within the walls of Justice City, but for security reasons it's separated from the City. There's absolutely no direct access from inside – you reach it down a corridor with Can-Can murals leading from Reception, outside all secure areas.

As they go through Reception Peggy sees Inspector Duncan in one of the public telephone booths. He knocks on the glass and waves at her but he doesn't look happy.

'Who's that black man?' Karl asks her.

'I've no idea,' she says, keeping things simple. 'He must think I'm someone else,' and they go on out, arm-in-arm, down the corridor past the pink Can-Can thighs and black suspenders.

ten

Alec Duncan had gone straight from Miss Landon to Nurse Serote. The move represented a change in style as well as content. What they shared in colour and experience made demands. They would watch each other, judge each other mercilessly. There'd be betrayals no white would notice. And times, plenty of them, for *Ah, fuckit*.

First, away to one side, there was the bloke Engineering had sent to answer phones and work their computer.

'Excuse me, Nurse Serote. I'll be with you in just a wee moment.'

'Waiting this long, Chief Inspector, another hour or two won't make no never mind.'

Fifteen all. Her Hackney versus his Edinburgh. He turned away and Frank introduced Engineering's bloke. Prison Officer Peter Padmore had been sent over from City Records. A small, ferrety young man with thick glasses, he looked suited to his work. Certainly, coming from Records, he should know his way round the computer. Alec leafed through his notebook, eyed the dead man's '*Wishbone*', and decided it was so outlandish he needed to check it first with another witness. Nurse Serote had been in the thresholding room, hadn't she?

He changed the cassette in his recorder and gave the Landon tape to Padmore. 'Look, I know you're not just a copy typist, Peter – that's all right, is it, *Peter*? – I know I shouldn't ask this, but if you'd key that in for a print-out I'd be very grateful.' He pressed the cassette into Padmore's hand. 'I've a terrible memory and we're strapped for time.'

A warm smile, then he backed off quickly. 'Frank? Is there any source of coffee in this place?'

'Haven't seen one, Chief.'

Nurse Serote cleared her throat. 'The nurses' room does instant.'

'Thank you, Nurse.' A cooler smile for her. 'Frank – coffee for four? Would you?'

He settled himself behind his desk and set up the recorder while Frank asked questions about milk and sugar, and went away. Then he opened his notebook, smoothed out the Manchester officer's report beside it, and looked across at Nurse Serote.

'From the beginning, I think. By which I mean from the first time you saw the victim. The first time you saw Beech.'

She thought about it. 'That's going right back. Fact is, I was the first to see him. Jake was in the dispensary – that's Nurse de Carteret – ' Alec nodded ' – and I was receiving. Granny Porter brings them over. You've seen Granny Porter. Mr Beech was number two.'

'You put him in number five? Room number five?'

'Granny did.'

'Presumably on your instructions.'

She explained patiently: 'We fill the rooms from the far end. Granny said there were only four inductees, Mr Beech was number two, so he ended up in number five.'

She watched him draw a row of boxes in his notebook, frown at them, then nod. He caught her eye and put down his pen. Her stiffness eased a shade.

'This Granny Porter's a bit of a character?'

'We're all God's children. This place has been the saving of him.' She tweaked at her nurse's cuffs. 'Sometimes, Chief Inspector, God's children could do with a bath.'

Alec nodded again. The man was probably an old lag.

Aye . . . jails could afford a lovable eccentric now and then. 'This *Granny* – it must be a nickname. What's his real name?'

'Lord knows. He was an inmate the last place I was at, before I came here to the House. A trustee. We called him Granny then.'

'The House? You mean this building?'

'That's what everybody calls it.'

'Did you recognize Beech?'

No transition, but she wasn't fazed. 'I'd seen the papers . . . They have name tags when they come over, name and number, but I surely did not need to read Mr Beech's.'

'How was he?'

'Fine. He was fine.'

'Granny Porter brings them over on trolleys. Sometimes they walk, I gather.'

'That's right. Mr Beech was trolley meat. Dead to the world. And weighty . . . I mean *a big man* . . .' She gestured with her hands, signifying his mass. 'Granny helped me transfer him to the bed.'

'Dead to the world, you say. Yet he came round later.'

'There's no rule. They sometimes do.'

The door behind her opened and Frank returned with mugs of coffee. It was a good punctuation point. Padmore had fixed himself up with an earpiece and a foot control for the cassette player. He was glad of an excuse not to start.

Frank handed round the mugs. 'De Carteret showed me where things were, Chief. He's not appreciating the wait.'

'I'm sorry.' Alec wasn't. Their earlier chat would have made Jake assume a special relationship. There wasn't one. He could take that as homophobia if it made him happy.

Alec tasted his coffee. It was instant of the foulest sort. He glanced up at the clock. Ten past four. Surely he'd been in this place longer than that? It felt like days. Outside the window the sky was dark.

'Nurse Serote, if you recognized Beech then you knew what he'd done. Do you always know that about inductees?'

129

She was drinking her coffee. 'I told you, they're tagged with just their name and number. Dr Landon has their details but she don't often pass 'em on.'

'Did she today?'

'There wasn't no need. I told you.'

'But did she?'

'*No.*'

It was a peevish sound. If she'd ever been wary of him she wasn't any more. He followed up fast. 'Don't you ever go and check the names of the next day's inductees on the board over at Inductions?'

'What for, man?'

'So you don't. And you didn't yesterday.'

'I don't and I didn't yesterday.'

'Knowing what he'd done, when you saw Beech, what did you feel?'

'Now wait.' She held up a large, traffic-stopping hand. 'That isn't easy. If you mean, did I feel I wanted to kill him for it, the answer's no. If you mean what did I *feel*, then I could fill a couple of them notebooks of yours with it.'

He glanced across at Frank. He liked her answers. Frank was at the other desk, drinking his coffee, paying attention but, as always, unintrusively. With no need to make notes, or to pretend to, Frank missed very little.

'So you dealt with Beech and moved on to the next.'

'Mr Beech was a bother. Two of the trodes wouldn't stick and I had to shave some body hair.'

'Trodes?'

'Contacts. Electrodes. For the monitors.'

Alec had guessed as he asked, and moved on. He was glancing through the Manchester officer's report. 'I see you wore plastic gloves?'

'You got it. Ever since AIDS. Myself, I don't like the things.'

'Where did you put them when you'd done?'

'Chucked 'em.'

'Where? In the bin on Nurse de Carteret's wagon?'

'In the bin in the washroom. Jake's wagon's always out in the foyer that early. See, he has to load it.'

Alec sat forward. 'There's a bin in the washroom?' He tapped the report. 'You didn't say that before.'

'Nobody asked me.'

He frowned at her. Was that a fair response? She wasn't stupid – she could see the importance of the gloves.

She shifted on her seat. It was a small chair, uncomfortable for someone her size, but it was all they had. She reached forward, put her empty mug down on the desk. 'All right, Chief Inspector. So I didn't think. That's no crime.'

Alec didn't contradict her. 'In the washroom, you said?' Someone would have to go and check. He tried to catch Padmore's eye but the young man had his earpiece in now and was pattering at the computer.

'Not any more, man. Not if Granny's done his job. It's been a long time.'

Frank had already half-risen. 'I'll make sure, Chief.'

Alec sighed. 'Would you?' He leafed through his notes so far. At this rate he'd still be on Nurse Serote come the Saturday deadline. 'You strapped Beech down and fixed the electrodes. When did you see him again?'

'After Petersen. When I went in with Dr Landon.'

'Petersen?'

'The guy in number six. We did him first. Then we went in to Beech.'

'Tell me exactly what happened then.'

She narrowed her eyes, thinking. 'First thing off, there's Granny in the way. Jake bashes into him, scatters the flowers.'

'In the way? Flowers? What d'you mean?'

'I mean Granny was standing just inside the door, holding the flowers, and Jake bashed into him with the wagon, and he dropped the flowers. The plastic flowers. All the rooms have them.'

That terrible old man again. 'What on earth was Granny Porter doing in the room?'

'Not much. Cleaning round, maybe.' She shrugged. 'He keeps hisself busy.'

Alec scratched the side of his nose. He skived off, more like. 'And Beech?'

'He was moving around. Dr Landon quickly gave him his medication.'

'She was wearing gloves? You were all wearing gloves?'

'We were all wearing gloves. I told you.'

'What next?'

'Mr Beech opened his eyes. He said a funny thing. He smiled. I guess he said it twice. *Wishbone.*'

'You're sure of that? *Wishbone?*'

'It's not a thing you could mistake.'

'What did you think he meant by it?'

'Not much. The man wasn't firing on more'n one in four.'

'Do they often say things? Men like him, inductees, before their medication?'

'Not often. Has been known. Rare, though.'

Yet she wanted him to believe she'd thought nothing of it. 'So Miss Landon gave him his medication. His injection. Did it work immediately?'

'Sooner'n that. Two heartbeats, maybe three.' She snapped her fingers. 'Then he was gone.'

'What happened next?'

'Nothing happened next. We moved on to the other two. I don't remember their names. Granny came with us. He'd picked up the flowers but there were still some petals.'

'So why didn't he stay and clear them up?'

'Dr Landon had a job for him. She doesn't like him hanging about.'

She didn't like him propping up the nearest quiet corner. 'So you medicated the other two and went to the control room.'

132

'I did. With Dr Landon. We started the EAT in the thresholding rooms. Jake went out to the dispensary. He – '

Frank came back into the room. He shook his head. 'The bin's been cleared.'

'And where's this Granny Porter now?'

'Don't know, Chief.'

'*Frank* . . .'

'Nobody said he was involved, Chief. I reckon he's buzzed off home.'

'Home being where?'

Frank's face was blank. Nurse Serote intervened. 'There's a hostel for civilian workers. The ride out from Manchester's too much for some . . . He won't run away, Chief Inspector. He does the early morning shift. You can pick him up tomorrow, come five thirty.'

Come five thirty tomorrow, Alec thought, with any luck I'll still be in my bed. But she'd come in on Frank's side and he was glad of that. He remembered his coffee, finished it in two unpleasant gulps.

Granny Porter was interesting. The Landon girl hadn't even mentioned him, yet he was always around. Like the postman in the famous murder story, the postman nobody saw because he was part of the landscape. Was Granny Porter part of the landscape?

Alec referred to his notes. Let's get on with it. 'You were with Miss Landon in the control room all through the thresholdings. Anything wrong with Beech and you'd have seen it on the screens. So he was fine when Miss Landon switched off and went downstairs.'

'You got it.'

'When was that? Accurate as you can.'

'Ten o'clock. Straight up. I remember because that's what it was. I looked at the clock and it was straight up ten.'

'So Beech was fine then. But he wasn't when you went to him twenty minutes later.'

'He was dead.'

133

Nurse Serote didn't waste words. It was risky, liking suspects, but he liked her. At this stage he was willing to bet Governor Ransome wouldn't get his easy solution.

'What did you do in those twenty minutes, Nurse Serote?'

'Squared things away in the control room. Then I took ten minutes out. Ten or so. Put my feet up.'

'In the nurses' room?'

'Nope. Stayed put.'

'So you didn't see anyone out in the passage?'

She shook her head. 'Didn't look.'

'Do you people at the House always take a break around ten?'

'Unless there's a hold-up.'

'And you never look in on the patients – the inductees – at that time?'

'They're strapped down, Chief Inspector. They ain't going anywhere.'

So anyone prowling would be safe as houses. But would an outsider know that? More to the point, would Granny Porter know that?

'This schedule of yours – how many people know it?'

'Anyone who's interested. It's like official. I mean, no one calls us then, not if they want an answer.'

Which wasn't, if he remembered right, what Peggy Landon had said. 'And where was Jake's medical wagon all this time?'

'In the passage. It's supposed to be a secure area. It was parked by the lift.'

'You're very certain.' More so than Peggy Landon.

'The passage ain't exactly crowded. 'Sides, I fetched it from there when I started surfacing.'

Which probably explained the difference. 'Ah yes, *surfacing* . . . You started at the end of the line?'

'That's right. Petersen. I removed his mouthguard and the trodes. He was doing fine.'

134

'And Beech was next. So when you got to Beech, and he was dead, what then?'

'I gave him standard resuss. Then I went and told Jake.'

'Jake? Why not Miss Landon?'

'She's never around is why. She goes down to Punishments with the profiles, then she might be anywhere.'

'And Jake did what?'

'He checked with the screens, then he rang Dr Peck.'

'Checked with the screens?'

'That's right. In the control room. And he looked in on Mr Beech after. *Then* he rang Dr Peck. I stayed with the body.'

'You told him an inductee was dead and he didn't try to do something?'

'Maybe he should of. But I'd told him Mr Beech was dead. I reckon he believed me.'

Alec heard the reprimand. She got on with people. 'And his wagon – all this time, where'd it been?'

'Out in the passage.'

'You'd dumped this pair of gloves in its bin?'

'The first pair. And then the second pair. After I'd found Mr Beech dead, the second pair.' She smiled. 'And then the third pair.'

'The third pair?'

'Life didn't stop just because Mr Beech's had. There were three other inductees to deliver to the guys from downstairs.'

'That's a lot of gloves.'

'We use 'em like Kleenex, Chief Inspector.'

'That's three pairs in the bin from you.' He reached for Manchester's report. 'One pair from Miss Landon?' She nodded. 'How many from Jake?'

'One for him too, I reckon. Unless he gloved up again when he came with me . . .'

'Did he?'

She paused, checking pictures in her head. 'No. No, he didn't.'

'One pair, then.' That made five pairs legitimately accounted for, and Manchester – surprise, surprise – had found six. 'Where are new gloves kept?'

'All over the place. They come in boxes.'

'So you said. Like Kleenex. But where are these boxes kept?'

'In the dispensary ... in the control room ... there's always one on the wagon ... mostly the thresholding rooms have them but I can't be sure about Mr Beech's.'

If they were on the wagon, that was all he needed to know. The disposable syringe used by the murderer came from the wagon too – four used legitimately on the inductees and Manchester'd found five. Fingerprints were out. He'd no idea what else forensics could come up with. Waste of time, probably.

'That looks like it, then.' He closed his notebook, leaned forward and stopped the recorder. 'You've been very helpful ...' He stretched and allowed himself a yawn. 'I expect Miss Landon's told you we're keeping this under wraps till Saturday. People will be curious and you'll have to stall them. Does that worry you?'

'Like Dr Landon said – not if it helps you guys catch who did it.'

'Mebbe ...' He was amused by Peggy Landon's gloss on the governor's instructions, presenting them as if they'd been thought up to help him with his investigation ... 'You *do* want the murderer caught, then? Even feeling the way you did about Beech?'

'I'd wanted Mr Beech caught, Chief Inspector, and I keep things simple. Thou shalt not kill ... It's the only way.'

He smiled. 'You'll be around if I need you again? There'll be a statement to sign, for one thing. We'll prepare it for you to approve, working from this interview. You'll be around?'

'I work here. Morning shift, six till noon, Mon to Fri.'

He stood up, took her to the door. 'What about weekends?' He was genuinely curious – what did people do here?

– and Nurse Serote and he had come far enough by now for him to dare. 'You'll no mind my asking?'

'I don't mind,' she said. 'I got a kid in the school here. It works out fine.'

'You go into town?'

'Manchester? Not if I can help it. There's facilities here. Mostly we stay in the City.'

'Where is your boy now? I've kept you very late. I'm sorry.'

'It's a girl, Rachel. I fixed it over the phone. She's with neighbours.'

Neighbours. She talked as if it was an estate here or a village. 'Well, I'll not keep you any longer. One thing, though – if you *do* think of anything, anything unusual, anything odd, I don't mind how tiny, if you *do* think of anything –'

'I'll pass it on.' She was standing up, Frank moving her chair back out of the way. 'Sure.'

'My trolley, lovey? Afterwards? Just across the passage. In front of the lift doors. Right up against them.'

'That's very exact.'

'I've thought about it.' De Carteret tossed his pony-tail. 'I knew you'd want to know. The trolley stays in the passage because it's needed for surfacing. Stimulants. Swabs. Gloves. A sterilized pot for the mouthguards. It's not all death-laden syringes.'

Alec nodded. He'd be getting to the gloves later. It was nearly six o'clock already, and Padmore was gone from his keyboard, back to wherever good little clock-watching prison officers come from. He himself was past tiredness. They'd been through the preliminaries, de Carteret's early morning chat with Miss Landon, the information (new to him, he claimed) that Beech was one of that day's inductees, the arrival by Beech's bed. Angry to have been kept waiting, de Carteret had started out unhelpful, but the luxury of Alec and Sergeant Grove's undivided attention, of anyone's undivided attention, had quickly thawed him. Guilty or not, he was giving the performance of his life. Sympathetic murder witness under ruthless police interrogation, take one.

Guilty or not . . . Alec rubbed his eyes wearily. He realized that he'd already decided that de Carteret was innocent. He didn't have cold murder in him. Some people didn't. Violence leading to death, yes. This morning's calculated termination of another man's life, no.

He'd ruled out Carole Serote too. For different reasons, but he'd ruled her out. Peggy Landon also, a woman like her . . . It was all such garbage. Soon he'd have no suspects left.

'So the trolley always stays in the passage. But not always in the same place?'

'Well . . . no. I'm a tiny bit disorganized on that. It stays where I leave it. Anywhere will do . . . And then of course there's always Granny P. Fussy old sod. He's perfectly capable of moving it.'

Aha. The porter again. 'But would he still have been around?'

'Course he would. He's always "around".'

'Always around? I thought he did other things.' Alec frowned. 'I mean, he doesn't only work for you people in the House, does he?'

'Of course not. The trouble with you, lovey, is you're *so* literal-minded . . .' De Carteret sighed theatrically. 'No, mine was a metaphor. A *façon de parler*. Like the people who say it always rains in Justice City. It doesn't, of course. It only seems that way . . . No, it's just that Granny P.'s a pervasive presence. A leaner-on at doorways. A picker-up of unconsidered trifles. Are you receiving me?'

Alec was indeed. He also didn't want to lose another suspect. 'But the porter did seem to have an interest in Beech?'

'He might have done . . .' De Carteret thought back elaborately. 'In fairness, though, I see him mostly fussing

138

with those bloody flowers. He'd got in the way of the door, remember and dropped them.'

'But he'd have known what was happening on the bed.'

'He's as old as God, Chief Inspector, but I don't think he's deaf or blind yet.' De Carteret looked at Alec sideways. 'You're very interested in Granny P. Do you see him as our perpetrator?'

'You don't, I gather.'

'I don't?'

'Last time we talked you said the murderer was one of you three nurses. You never mentioned Granny Porter.'

'I never thought of him. He's part of the furniture. Like I said, lovey, he's always there.'

Alec glanced across at Frank. Exactly so.

Frank took it as a cue. He saw where Alec was going and he was clearly dubious. 'What would an old lag like that know about giving injections?'

De Carteret tittered. 'In today's jails? What a beautiful world you live in, Sergeant . . . And in any case, whoever injected Beech made a real pig's ear of it. If he'd been half-way with us the poor lovey would've screamed the place down, stuck like that.'

'The bruising could've been done on purpose,' Frank said stodgily, 'to make it look like an amateur job.'

'There's shrewd . . . It could also just have been someone in a hurry. We're none of us perfect. I've ballsed up injections in my time. Even I.'

Alec cleared his throat. *Move along there*. The injection proved nothing. Like everything else in this case so far. Not a sodding thing. 'So the porter was there, and Beech regained consciousness, and I gather he said something.'

'Yes indeedy.' De Carteret sat back, crossed his legs, dusted the top knee. 'Very picturesque. A racehorse, I thought. The winner of the two o'clock at Aintree. I'm sure you're a betting man, Chief Inspector.'

An odd misjudgement. The Chief Inspector had never

placed a bet in his life. 'A racehorse, Nurse? Why a racehorse?'

'I couldn't think what else. *Wishbone?* . . . it could've been a greyhound. Something like that. Lucky for the punters – know what I mean?'

'So that's what Beech said? Just one word – *Wishbone?* Nothing else?'

'Nothing else. And not so prettily as you.' He gave the word a Cockney final ow-noise. '*Wishbown.*'

Alec took refuge in his notebook. The witness was flirting with him.

Wishbone – all the three people he'd talked to so far were agreed. Amazing. It said a lot for their hearing and for Beech's diction.

Beech's diction . . . 'You're sure you've got it right? He was heavily drugged, was he not?'

'Clear as a bell, Chief Inspector. I was right by his side. We all were – ' He looked up sharply. 'Do the girls say something different?'

Alec turned a page in his book. 'So Miss Landon medicated the patient. And then the other two inductees in their rooms.'

'That's right. Lovely word, isn't it? Not people – inductees. And then we give them EAT.'

Alec ignored him. They'd played that game before, down in the thresholding room. 'And then Miss Landon and Nurse Serote went to the control room. Am I right?' De Carteret tilted his head and one eyebrow, conceding. 'You were with them up to then. What did you do next?'

'Left my wagon by the lift and hied me to the dispensary. Herself had ordained a clear-up. The mess was as much the afternoon shift's as ours, but I didn't argue. Martyrdom becomes me.'

'And you were there until Nurse Serote found Beech dead and came and fetched you.'

'Never moved. That's how I knew it was one of us three nurses. Or Granny P., of course.'

'I'm sorry?'

'Geography. Nobody cometh unto the father but by me
... Oops.' He covered his mouth at the blasphemy, and
looked over his shoulder. 'La Serote'd skin me. A worthy
soul, but on the holy side.'

Alec grunted. 'You mean, as long as you were in the
dispensary nobody could have got into the building without
you seeing them?' He was going off de Carteret. 'You're
saying there's no other entrance?'

'Only the lift up from Punishments. And that wasn't used
until Herself went down in it. And then only the once.'

'How d'you know that?' Alec was dismayed. He hadn't
thought of someone coming up from Punishments. It opened
up daunting possibilities. 'The lift's in the passage on the
other side of the swing door out into the foyer – how d'you
know that nobody came up in it?'

'Because it pings, lovey. It pings.'

'And you can hear it out in the dispensary? Above the
musak?'

'Above the 1812, Chief Inspector. Believe me. It pings
when the doors open and it pings when they shut.' His voice
rose. 'It *pings*.'

Alec could have done without the imitation. Even so, it
closed the possibilities again. He'd have to check the lift
doors, of course, but de Carteret probably knew what he
was talking about. No outsider had entered the Punishments
Building.

'So while you were in the dispensary only Miss Landon or
Nurse Serote could have got to Beech without you seeing
them. Or the porter.'

'I could have got to him myself.' De Carteret sat back. He
observed the two policemen. 'You don't think I'm capable.
You think I'm a pussy-cat. You're wrong, you know. Where
some guys are concerned, just a few, I'm very capable. Look
– EAT's bloody, but it passes. Then it's LTI, Long Term
Incarceration, and believe me, for some guys that's the crime.

141

That's do-gooding gone crazy. Sun lamps and twenty-four-hour videos mayn't be your idea of heaven, Chief Inspector, but giving them to guys like Beech is crazy. You got him for one, but how many kids d'you think he really put an end to? Not to mention how. And he's rewarded with LTI? I didn't kill him, Chief Inspector, but I'm telling you I could have.' He paused. 'And I'll tell you something else. For once this crazy place lived up to its name. Beech got what he deserved. He got justice.'

Alec shifted his legs under the desk, wincing at their stiffness. He hadn't changed his mind. It was a good speech, but nothing more than that. De Carteret was no cold murderer. He didn't have it in him. Some people didn't. Alec set store by his judgement in these matters.

'So Nurse Serote came out to the dispensary and told you Beech was dead. What then?'

'I went with her. Checked Beech's screens. She was quite right.'

'You checked Beech's screens. Not Beech. You checked his screens.'

'I'm a screens person, Chief Inspector.' He leaned confidentially forward across the desk. 'I expect it's all this S and M porno we gays love to watch. Screens are so much more *real*.'

Alec bored on. 'But in this case you had to look at the actual Beech eventually.'

'So what do you want me to say? He had a hairy chest. I hate hairy chests.' He glared accusingly at Sergeant Grove's shirt front. Alec wondered how he'd guessed that only Frank's winter vest kept the hairs from sprouting between his buttons. 'I didn't try the old resuss, if that's what you mean. I was glad to see him dead. Heaven forfend I should bring him back.'

Alec wondered why Jake had suddenly got so shrill. The business of the screens? He didn't like himself? 'In any case, you'd have been far too late.'

'In any case, I'd have been far too late.'

He didn't like himself.

'So you sent for Dr Peck.'

'And I paged Herself. Miss Landon.'

'Leaving Nurse Serote with the body.'

'Leaving Nurse Serote with the body.'

Alec considered. He'd lost this witness. He'd started out liking Jake de Carteret. They'd started out liking each other. They didn't any more, and it showed, and – on his side, certainly, and at this stage – it shouldn't. He had to get through to Jake again.

'I want you to go back to when you first saw the dead body. The bed, the whole room . . . was there anything odd? Anything out of the ordinary? Take your time. Think about it . . .'

De Carteret screwed up his eyes. Witnesses liked to be told they could take their time. It bestowed importance on their recollections. On them.

Jake shook his head. 'Not a thing . . . The corpse was odd, of course. We don't often – '

'You knew at once that it *was* a corpse?'

'The screens – ' he corrected himself ' – Nurse Serote had already told me. And then there were the eyes. I hadn't noticed before how blue they were . . . Blue. And blind, of course.' Suddenly, quite unexpectedly, his voice broke. His fussy twitches stilled. 'I've seen a lot of dead men, Chief Inspector. I haven't always been in the prison service. I've seen a lot of dead men's eyes. Blue. Brown. Hazel. All sorts . . .' He lowered his head, covered his own eyes with a hand.

Alec waited. He didn't know enough about the people in this case. A lot of dead men? He didn't know anything. But he did know that if Jake de Carteret was a screens person, then something had made him that way. Something that maybe had a relevance to this murder.

Eventually. 'But you didn't close them?' He prompted gently.

143

'My goodness, no.' De Carteret removed his hand, essayed a titter. 'La Serote neither. We didn't touch a thing. We were saving the sod for Dr Peck.'

'But you saw the second injection.'

'That's your literal mind again, Chief Inspector. Yes, of course we touched him. We just didn't *alter* anything.'

He was recovered now. His usual perky self.

'One thing more, Jake. Gloves. You nurses all wear plastic gloves.'

'You bettee. On account of *you-know-what*. It's standard.'

'A different pair for each inductee?'

'Of course . . . No, I lie – not when I'm only assisting La Landon. Trundling the wagon, handing out this and that. One pair does me then.'

'And when you went to Beech the second time? After Nurse Serote had called you?'

'You know, I don't think I gloved up at all. I was *so* surprised . . . In any case, we weren't exactly going to be exchanging bodily fluids. I leave that to the necros.'

Alec referred to his notebook. He wondered why de Carteret bothered. He'd heard worse. Any policeman had.

One pair of gloves for the first visit. None for the second. Nurse Serote had a good memory. And that left one unattributed pair for forensics in Manchester to play with. One pair in Manchester for unattributed forensics to . . . one unattributed Manchester for pairs in forensics . . . one Manchester pair for . . . Alec jerked his head upright. Incredible. He'd been fast asleep.

He sat forward, gathered his resources. It was time to wind things up. He had a question for such moments. It sometimes worked.

'Jake – it's late and I'm bushed. You too, I'm sure. We'll get out a statement for you to sign later. But you know these people, so just tell me something. Before we call it a day just tell me something. If you didn't kill Beech, who did?'

*

144

'Two of them are his colleagues, Chief. The other one's a joke. What could he say?'

'A joke, Frank? Granny Porter? We haven't even talked to him.'

'I have. You get to know someone, moving furniture. He's a joke.'

Alec didn't argue. It required an effort. Anything required an effort. His feet were on Miss Landon's secretary's desk, his chair tilted steeply. Going home required an effort.

By all outward appearances, certainly, it was hard to take Granny Porter seriously. But the real problem here was that it was hard to take the crime seriously. It was non-abhorrent. In the outside world, if a villain got topped (tidily, no spill-over, no vendettas), police inquiries tended to be less than zealous. As for Beech, most people would say he was better dead. All three witnesses so far were agreed on that point. And he'd slipped away painlessly, so one couldn't even get exercised about the method. As a policeman he might believe that Beech hadn't been killed for what he did to that black girl, but to his witnesses the point might well be academic. A killer had died. Been killed. The crime was non-abhorrent.

He had four suspects. Four possible suspects. Four very marginal suspects. Three of them were nice, decent, ordinary people. Three of them – although not necessarily the same three – were also, as Frank had pointed out, colleagues. What hope did he have that one of them would knowingly shop another?

He smothered a yawn. 'What's really interesting, Frank, is what de Carteret *didn't* say. He's a clever wee laddie. He'd spotted the way my mind was working – he could have encouraged me, told me what I wanted to hear, pointed me in the direction of the porter. But he didn't. Not at all . . . And I think that's because he's an honest wee laddie, and he doesn't believe the old man's guilty.'

'To be fair, Chief, he didn't point you in any direction.'

'Except maybe his own. Did you notice that? And d'you want to know why I think that was?'

Frank heavily examined his watch. Thresholding was over downstairs and the building was quiet. It was a good two hours' drive back to Liverpool.

'I think it was because he's innocent, Frank, and he's afraid that one of the women isn't. Probably Nurse Landon.'

'And I think you're talking in your sleep, Chief.' Frank got to his feet. 'I think we both are.'

'You don't want to know why I said, probably Nurse Landon?'

'We'll know more when we've spoken to the porter.'

Alec stirred himself as Frank's earlier remark got through. He was running on residual brain electricity, like a frog that twitches long after it's dead. He heaved his feet off the desk and stood. 'Which of us is fit to drive, Sergeant Grove?'

Frank went to the window, cupped his hands against the glass. 'There's a good moon.'

'Nevertheless, Frank, I shall flex my muscle. My one, very small muscle.' He picked up the City telephone directory from the desk, looked up the motor pool, and pressed the buttons. 'This is Chief Inspector Duncan, Merseyside Police. I'm here on special assignment to Governor Ransome – you'll have been notified, I'm sure – and I'd like a car and a driver for myself and my sergeant. Immediately. The journey is to the Liverpool area, and we'll need a pick-up in the morning.'

There was a muttered consultation at the other end, after which the dispatch clerk agreed. Alec was mildly surprised. He rang off and he and Sergeant Grove left the office. He paused outside, went back, wrote a note to Padmore for the morning, and propped it against his computer screen: LOOK FOR WISHBONE. ANY MENTION. Then he rejoined his sergeant and the two men went downstairs.

The foyer doors were locked and needed his ID card. They

traversed the covered walkways to Reception, gates at every junction. Gates made sense in ordinary prisons, where you might actually see a prisoner, but why here? Maybe prison officers liked them. The night was windy and wild, Frank's moon invisible above relentless banks of floodlights. Alec had to shield his eyes against the glare.

In Reception he spotted a public telephone booth against the wall opposite the desk. He wouldn't be home till nearly nine, which would wreck another of May's evenings. He decided to ring her, and sent Sergeant Grove on to wait in the car.

'May? It's Alec.'

'Alec? Good. Excellent . . . I'm glad you called, Alec. I – '

'May? You're home, then. Good. The thing is, May – '

'That's excellent, Alec. I'm glad you called. That's really excellent.'

He shook his head. She sounded strange. Perhaps she wasn't hearing him. He raised his voice. 'The thing is, May – '

'The thing is, Alec, I don't run a hostel for social inadequates.'

'May? What – '

'Or maybe I did, and you were it, but I don't any more.'

Hell. He didn't need this. 'Look, May, would you kindly tell me . . . I've had a hard day. Would you kindly tell me – '

'You gave that oaf my clothes, Alec.'

Clothes? He rested his forehead on the cool glass of the booth and closed his eyes. Clothes?

'And you left his under the kitchen table. You couldn't even be bothered to – '

Clothes? He remembered now. The morning's druggie. He'd said his name was Humphrey. It was all so long ago. *Clothes . . .*

'Not exactly clothes, May.' He laughed. 'I gave him that old pair of gardening jeans. He – '

'I don't have your sense of humour, Alec. I – '

'For God's sake, May, what was I supposed to do? Mine were way too big and he wasna' even decent.'

'I'd have said decency was the least of his problems. You ask me what you were supposed to do. I can tell you one thing. You weren't supposed to – '

'Where's your sense of proportion, May? I mean, when did you last wear those – '

'You weren't supposed to poke around in my cupboards, to poke around in *my* cupboards and hand out my clothes to total strangers without a by-your-leave. And don't you dare talk to me about proportion. What about – '

'All right. All right, May. I'm sorry. I really am.' He gestured with the edge of his hand. This was bad. This was more than just a pair of jeans. This was bad. 'I'm sorry I gave that addict your clothes. I should have asked you. Of course I should. And I'm sorry I laughed.'

'And now I suppose you're calling to say you're sorry but I'll be eating alone again. Well, I'm sorry too, Alec. It – '

'Now wait, May.' He had to stop her. 'You're upset. You – '

'It just isn't good enough. And of course I'm upset. You take my things for granted, you take me for granted and it just goes on and on.'

Dear God . . . He turned his head away from her voice. Outside in the foyer Peggy Landon was walking past with some man in a green corduroy suit. She'd taken off her white nurse's coat and she looked quite dumpy. He tapped on the glass and waved at her. God knows why. Luckily she didn't seem to notice. She went out with the man through doors marked CITY BISTRO.

'Alec? Are you still there?'

'I'm still here, May.'

She was quiet now. Not angry any more. Sorrowful. Like him. Full of sorrow. 'I expect this sounds to you like just another policeman's woman bitching on at him about his hours.'

'No, May. No, it – '

'I'm afraid it's more than that. This morning was crazy. You need to get yourself sorted out, Alec.'

He stared at the telephone buttons. Don't we all? 'I'll take myself over to Morag's, then.'

'It's not that I don't love you, Alec.'

Ah, come on . . . 'I'll be in touch.' He kept it brisk. He'd his own place in Liverpool of course, a tiny flat on the waterfront, in a converted warehouse, but he'd never face that now and she knew it. 'And thanks.'

He waited. The line stayed silent. 'I must go now, May. Frank's waiting.'

The silence continued. Then, faintly, '*I'm so very sorry* . . .'

That made two of them. He rang off. 'And I love you too,' he said, making the words bearable by pressing a telephone button, any button, for each.

He left the booth, nodded to the man behind the reception desk, and went out to Frank. Their car from the motor pool was just backing up in the cobbled yard beneath the black steel gates. No wind blew here and frost was forming on the cobbles.

wednesday

eleven

Getting up on a workday morning is boring. Descriptions in books of getting up on a workday morning are boring. Even the glimpses of frowsty nakedness that books are permitted in their descriptions of getting up on a workday morning are boring. Particularly the glimpses of frowsty nakedness. Accordingly this story doesn't join Peggy Landon on Wednesday morning until she's leaving her quarters, properly bathed and dressed and breakfasted.

At her administrative level in Justice City Peggy gets a little sitting-room and her own kitchenette, as well as the usual bed and toilet-with-shower, so she's spared the canteen and this is her first interface of the day with the outside world. The hour is smallish – seven forty – but the corridors of staff quarters are already peopled. Basically Justice City never sleeps. The LTI inmates may sleep, when they can tear themselves away from their computer games and their videos, but the City itself remains awake and watchful, and seven thirty to eight is a major shift change-over time. Peggy expects to meet all sorts – colleagues, acquaintances, even friends – in the brightly lit corridors, and she presents herself accordingly.

Good morning.

Hi there.

Happy Wednesday.

The crisp white coat is new on today, the tights sport

black-and-yellow zig-zags, the hair shines, the lipstick dazzles. She is, in short, her usual look-the-world-in-the-eye self. There's no resemblance at all to a murderer on the morning after. This isn't the result of any great effort – it's just that she ate well at the City Bistro last night, she's slept well since, she's breakfasted sensibly, and now she's ready for, even looking forward to, whatever the new day has to offer. Happy Wednesday, hi there, good morning.

Outside staff quarters there's a black snap in the pre-dawn air. It checks her, but only briefly. *Hedda*'s director has justifiably left expletives concerning the missed rehearsal on her answerphone, and she wishes she hadn't lied to Chief Inspector Duncan about the medical trolley, also justifiably, but neither's going to spoil her day. She strides out, more alive than she's been for years. She does a little two-step shuffle on the cushioned plastic flooring under the covered walkway. She's in fine form. Yesterday morning she came closer than close to total disaster, and today she's safe again. Yesterday morning she near as dammit lost her career, her livelihood, everything she's ever worked for. She thought fast, on her feet, three minutes maybe four, and today she's safe again. She comes to a gate, offers her card with a flourish, goes through, does another shuffle-hop, is stared at by a prison officer coming the other way.

'Lovely morning for the race, Jim.'

What race? The human race. But he's already gone, catching the gate while it's still open, and he doesn't ask her.

She strides out again, feeling free. It's like being given a reprieve. Terminal case one minute – oops love, it's non-malignant, they mixed the slides, the next. And only herself to thank. All her own work. A thirty-second stop-off on the way down to Punishments, and whammo – Albert Beech has joined the Great Majority.

The Great Majority? Wasn't that what her dad called it? Joining the Great Majority? He made dying sound really quite respectable. Like voting Conservative. His end was crass, and messy beyond belief, when he came to it, bouncing from bollard to bollard, but she reckoned they welcomed him all the same. Winston Churchill and the rest. Augmented now by one Beech, Albert.

She reaches the House. She has her ID card ready but the doors are already unlocked. Granny Porter must have got in early. She prances in, does a turn round the nicely warm foyer, then takes to the stairs. Nobody's switched on the musak yet. Granny Porter can't be in. Someone else, then – maybe Jake.

She hums her own tune instead, reaches the upstairs corridor. She's safe again. Her job is safe. Her life in Justice City. Her future. If she minds her ps and qs (Dad again), one day she'll have her own department. The Herr Direktor won't stay in the House for ever. One day he'll –

He's waiting in her office. He's back from Chicago. Dr Mellish is sitting at her desk. Happy Wednesday.

'At least you get in to work on time, Margaret.'

She skids to a halt. The clock says she's ten minutes early, but she's more concerned with that 'at least'. It promises more to come.

'Good morning, Director. I hope you had a good flight.'

'Bloody awful. Chicago to New York, New York to Manchester. Disgusting food. Unspeakable movie. Hardly a wink of sleep. Only just got here.' This explains his pre-dawn presence, and his worse-than-usual temper. And his slept-in (if only intermittently) suit. 'What the hell's going on, Margaret? Nobody I've spoken to so far seems to know a bloody thing.'

'They wouldn't, Director. Mr Ransome's imposed a news blackout. Hardly anybody knows.'

'So?' He glares at her, jet-lagged and red-eyed. 'I've only been gone four days. What the hell's happened? It sounds bad.'

She sits down, uninvited, and tells him. It *is* bad.

'An inductee murdered?' He pounds her cluttered desk. 'For Christ's sake, woman, how *could* you?'

His question might be misunderstood by someone with a guilty conscience, but she understands it perfectly. He's concerned for his position. So is she. 'We've never anticipated such a thing, Director,' she says. 'Here, inside the City – why should we?'

The 'we' is hit hard. He rejects it. 'You're on the ground, Margaret. This is the age of the homicidal nut. Everybody knows that. You should have taken precautions.'

Peggy wonders what it is that has put her *on* the ground and him in some miraculous fashion *off* it. This is not a profitable thought. Instead, 'I don't want to pass the buck, Dr Mellish' – *ho-ho* – 'but isn't security the governor's responsibility?'

'Security is everyone's responsibility.' City staff handbook, chap 1, para 1. But he likes her thinking. 'Even so, Margaret, I do take your point. It's a question of the budget, really – we can only do so much. After that it's up to Mr Ransome.'

She's glad to hear the 'we' creep back in again, and moves on. 'In any case, Director, this really is nothing to do with poor security. This isn't an outsider, a homicidal nut. This murderer's one of us. One of the morning shift.'

'Explain.'

She explains.

He sucks a breath in through his teeth, hissing. 'It's hard to believe. And the morning shift was who?'

'De Carteret and Serote.'

'So which of them did it?'

'I find it hard to believe,' she says truthfully, 'that either of them did.'

'Well, one thing's for certain. I'm bloody sure you didn't.' She inclines her head taking this as read. 'So the local plod's got something wrong. It's as simple as that.'

'Not so much of a plod, actually. They've sent someone over from Liverpool. A chief inspector. I was quite impressed.' She omits his colour. 'He's set up shop next door. I gave him Daphne's office – she can share with me.'

'You've warned him not to interrupt the work here?'

She smiles. 'I'm afraid we may have to put up with *some* interruption . . . The governor's demanding quick results. He believes he can keep Beech's death quiet until Saturday, by which time he's hoping to be able to announce both the murder *and* the murderer. He wants – '

'Saturday? You must be joking.'

'He wants to pre-empt public opinion. Mr Ransome is concerned for this department's future. He's very anxious that the reform lobby shouldn't have an excuse to – '

'Ha. Is that what he's saying?' Dr Mellish flings back his chair, leaps up, strides about the room. He's big and personable. Every morning the mirror tells him he's a born leader. 'This department's safe as houses – he knows that as well as you or I do. We satisfy a public demand. The public demands revenge, and we deliver it. We deliver what the public wants and the public loves us. For God's sake, if they thought there was a chance that they'd hear the inmates' screams they'd be out there in their thousands' – he gestures fiercely – 'with their ears against the walls.'

He settles by a filing cabinet, hangs an arm over its square metal top to calm himself. 'Things have changed, Margaret. These days revenge is respectable. My God, you should hear the people I talk to in the States. They've got it pat. Revenge is gratitude's twin. Opposite and equal, yin and yang. It's – '

'It's not doing much for the crime rate.' She can't resist it.

'Crime? What's crime got to do with it?' His fervour mounts again, irresistibly. He *believes*. 'There's always been crime and there always will be. That's not what we're here for. We're talking basic morality, Margaret. People expect virtue to be rewarded and evil punished. *Punished*. It's a word that went out of fashion a few years back. And we know what happened – people got pissed off, paying for a system that didn't punish evil. That didn't deliver justice.

Now it does. The reformers don't stand a chance. You and I know that, and so does the governor.'

In the doorway behind Peggy someone clears his throat. Dr Mellish looks past her. 'Well? What is it?' But he can't yet stop. He's been caught, as it were, in mid-climax. 'I'll tell you something else, Margaret,' he rushes on, 'Mr Ransome is no fool. The public has an instinct for justice, and justice is revenge legitimized. He knows that. It's revenge made legal. He knows that. And this department – more than any other, this is the department that feeds the public *justice*. Which Mr Ransome knows also.'

He subsides, quite spent, and glares at the man in the doorway. 'Well? Don't just stand there.'

Peggy has screwed round in her chair. 'It's the messenger from Inductions, Director. He's got the first batch of inductee files for me.'

'So hand them over, man. Hand them over.'

The messenger gives Peggy the files. There are six of them, a full batch. After yesterday's missed intake it's only to be expected. She signs the chitty and the messenger goes.

Dr Mellish returns to the desk and collapses. His course is run. 'No, between you and me, Margaret, if Mr Ransome's worried it's for other reasons. You said it yourself – security is his responsibility. He's not going to come out of this well. He needs a quick result. He . . .'

Peggy's glancing through the files. Suddenly she's struck with the thought that someone else from her past might return to haunt her. Who? For a start, any one of a dozen or more of her Wandsworth customers. Granny Porter had been a trustie at the time but he was never, thank God, one of them. He's done stupid things in his life, but never drugs. But it's still a miracle that so far only Lucky Beech has resurfaced from her Wandsworth years.

She sorts through the file polaroids and recognizes none of them. No – in any case the real miracle is malign, that the first man from her past who's seriously able to hurt her should have turned up awake for thresholding. They simply never do. If they see her it's later, when they're having their nervous breakdowns down in Punishments, and she could always duck out of that. But Lucky Beech had to be awake and *compos mentis*. That's life, of course.

Dr Mellish is rumbling on. She leans forward, finds a space for the files on her side of the desk, and uses the extension of her wrist from her sleeve to glance at her watch. The time is eight o'clock.

'. . . But he'll do what he can, of course. Poor sod. You said he came over as intelligent?'

Dr Mellish seems to have reached her black chief inspector. She nods. 'Very. He asks good questions and he listens to the answers.'

'I'm sorry for him, then. Solving this case by Saturday sounds like a ball-breaker. Especially if it's an inside job. You said it yourself – neither de Carteret nor Serote are half-way probable.'

Maybe that's why she's nice about her chief inspector. He's on to a loser here and she's sorry for him . . . *Her* chief inspector? Heavens – why *her* chief inspector?

'I tell you one thing, Margaret. It'd better not be either of those two. Homicidal nurses are bad for all of us. It's a relationship built on trust. What happens to that if people get the idea that the next nurse along is going to dot them one?'

Peggy's got work to do. She gets up and stands by her desk, hinting.

'And in any case, what about that bloody porter? He's always under everybody's feet. And he's the one with the record, for God's sake. Couldn't he have done it?'

Peggy's amazed. Granny Porter. She's never given him a thought. She does so now . . . His record isn't violent. At least, she doesn't think it is.

'That's it then.' Dr Mellish stands up too. 'Simple process of elimination. Can't be them, so it must be him. Courts need proof, of course.' He stares at the blank black glass of the window, hissing through his teeth, then turns back to her. 'I don't need to say this, Margaret. You'll help all you can?'

She nods. 'I spent a long time with him and his sergeant yesterday. They'll be back again today.'

'Not here yet, of course.'

'They have to come from Liverpool.'

'All the same . . .'

She frowns. What the hell does he expect? It's a two-hour drive. But she lets it ride. More than anyone she knows, Chief Inspector Duncan is not a man who needs to be stuck up for.

'Is it all right, Director, if I start checking these files?' Yesterday morning she hated her desk. This morning she loves it. It's part of the life she nearly lost.

Dr Mellish moves to one side. 'I'm in the way. Rabbiting on . . .' He goes to the door, looks up at the clock. 'Need to see the governor. Can't expect him till nine, nine thirty. At the earliest . . . Christ, I feel like death warmed up.' He turns. 'I'll be in my office if anyone needs me. Unconscious.'

He goes out, returns immediately. 'The man this chief inspector needs to concentrate on is that bloody porter. I expect he knows that already. If he's as bright as you say he is.'

He goes again, stays gone, and Peggy hears his door along the passage open and close. She sits down at her desk.

It's odd that she hasn't thought of Granny Porter as a suspect. He's the obvious one. So obvious that he's crying out for a stitch-up. Thinking about that, she realizes how lucky she is that Chief Inspector Duncan isn't the stitch-up type. She wonders what she'd do if Granny Porter were tried for her crime and found guilty, and she honestly doesn't know.

For Granny Porter getting up on a workday morning isn't boring. Too many joints and organs need to be got back into working order. And then there's his BM. To others, however, the boringness would be total. Accordingly this story doesn't look in on Granny Porter until he's leaving the hostel canteen, shaved and dressed and full of well-sugared tea. At his administrative level in the City he gets a bed-and-chest-sized cubicle, finis, so by now his day's interface with the world has already included the hostel washroom and the queue at the canteen tea dispenser.

Move over, cunt.

Piss off.

Fuck you, mate.

His outfit this morning is much the same as it was yesterday. In fact, right down to the skin, it's identical, and it'll stay that way until Saturday. He's his usual aggrieved and anxious self, hurrying a little but not too much. He likes to show willing.

He spent yesterday evening at the City movies. He can't remember what he saw, he dozes a lot, except that there was gunfire and some brave old guy in a cowboy hat with a pretty daughter. Granny doesn't have a daughter. He doesn't have anyfuckingbody.

He arrives at Inductions, breezes in through the double doors, rubbing his hands and puffing. 'Morning, boys. It's bloody cold out there.'

The three inductions officers don't look round. Their six inductees are out cold, the chief's through in the hospitality room with Dr Peck, and they're enjoying a fag and a natter. One of them has his newspaper open at the tits and bums. Fuck you, mate.

'I tell you one thing,' Granny says. 'It's bloody cold out there.'

He picks up his worksheet. Then he goes to the first of the inductees, reads his label, and checks it against his worksheet. He moves the inductee's trolley away from the wall.

'I'll be off then.' He leans on the trolley handles. 'I'll be off then.'

One of the officers, Kevin, turns. 'Granny! How yer doin'?'

161

'I said, it' bloody cold out there.'

'Yer right, squire. Sodding brass monkey weather.'

They grin at each other.

'I'll be going then.' He reads the inductee's label again, checks it again against his worksheet, looks along the line of trolleys. 'You've been busy. Full house this morning. Didn't have no trouble?'

'Drunk up their cocoa good as fucking gold.'

'Makes a change. I'll be going then.'

Another of the officers, Wilf, looks up from the paper. 'Talk of sodding trouble – what happened yesterday? Talk of sodding trouble, we missed a whole sodding intake. Had to send them back to sodding Manchester.'

Granny knows he should have expected this and pushed off when he could. When will he fucking learn? He leans on the trolley handles. 'Yes. Thing is, we had a little spot of bother.'

'A little spot of bother? That you must of. What sort of bother, for fuck's sake?'

Granny's torn. This ought to be his moment of fame. He's the only one of them who knows about Lucky Beech's one-way ticket and it's worth a fag or two, a thing like that. But that sodding Sergeant Grove'd put the mockers on him proper if he so much as breathed a word. That sodding Sergeant Grove had sorted him out while they were shifting furniture. An old man like him, shifting sodding great desks. *The governor says this and the governor says that, and if the word gets out about Lucky Beech's sodding one-way ticket then the governor's going to be pissed as hell off, and he'll know who sodding done it because it won't be one of us. OK, friend? OK?*

Granny Porter temporizes. 'Like I said, Wilf. Just a spot of bother. Broken syringe. You know the sort of thing.'

'Broken syringe? *Broken syringe?* Coppers crawling all over the place, a whole intake missed, and you tell us broken syringe?'

He never expected it'd hold them. But he panics. When in doubt, horse it up. He leans forward, peers round furtively, lowers his voice. 'The thing is, boys, don't spread it round, for fuck's sake . . .' they lean too, wanting to be thrilled '. . . don't spread it round or you'll have me fucking skinned, but we're bringing back the fucking death penalty. Unilaterally. We topped a guy yesterday, we topped a whole fucking intake and the blue's shitting bricks, and the Queen's sending Charlie to pin fucking medals on us.'

For a moment you could hear that pin if it dropped. Then pandemonium breaks out as the officers throw clipboards, cushions, tin ashtrays, and Granny makes his escape, clutching his boater, out through the doors and along the covered walkway. His inductee smiles and lurches with the ride he's getting, but sleeps on peacefully.

Over a short distance Granny's fine, likewise his story. Ten steps, though, and both are in a bad way. He's leaning on the trolley handles, gasping, and behind him the boys are pissed off and will ask again when he goes back the next time, and they'll expect an answer. He's clowned his way out of a lot in his life, but never anything that mattered . . . He moves on very slowly, shuffling his sneakers. He has his ID card clipped to his pocket but he doesn't need it – someone's unlocked the doors of the Punishments Building and turned on the lights. He goes in, still breathless, and across the foyer. The blackie nurse is coming along the corridor from the nurses' room. She holds the door open for him, following him through into thresholding.

'Did I hear *Good morning, Nurse Serote*? And *Good morning* to you, Granny Porter.'

It's as quiet as the grave in here. Gives him the creeps. He pauses, hawks phlegm which he swallows, and flaps a bony hand at his inductee. 'Simpson, six eleven.'

He takes Simpson into the room at the far end of the passage. Carole Serote follows him. She has a worksheet too. She checks it. 'Simpson, six eleven.'

She aligns Simpson's trolley and transfers him on to the bed. The worksheet tells her he suffers from high blood pressure and will need a special mix. That's Jake's job. She gloves up, listens to Simpson's pulse, then sits him up to remove his shirt. Granny Porter is leaning against the table under the mirror, fanning himself with his hat.

'Bloody idjits.' In Nurse Serote's presence, sometimes, on account of she's a woman even though a blackie, he moderates his language. 'Them in Induction. Bloody idjits. Always taking the piss.'

There's a hook for Simpson's shirt on the wall by the bedhead. Carole Serote says thoughtfully, 'Folk give you a hard time, I reckon.'

It's a general observation, for her own satisfaction, but she doesn't expect Granny Porter to take it that way and he doesn't.

'A hard time? You wouldn't chuckle. It's this bloody murder – what'm I supposed to say?'

She's had the same problem, not half an hour ago, when she took Rachel round to her neighbour. Mrs Patel is a married woman, with her husband in Catering, and yesterday he had to deliver six hot lunches to inductees before they were sent back to Manchester. And one of Mrs Patel's friends has seen uniformed police around, in and out of where Mrs Serote works. According to Mrs Patel, everybody's saying there's been a hoo-ha in the Punishments Building. An inductee's run amok. Some say he got a weapon in past Inductions and they're in big trouble. Mrs Serote works in Punishments – what Mrs Patel wants to know is, was the weapon a shotgun like some people are saying?

Carole Serote remembers that Granny Porter wasn't there yesterday morning when Dr Landon gave Jake and her the governor's instructions, and told them the cover story. Not that she was happy, asking them to lie, but the rumours would get out of hand if they didn't say *something*, and it was for the department's good . . . Forgetting Granny Porter was a bad mistake – not knowing about Frank Grove's dire warnings, Carole reckons they're lucky Granny Porter hasn't already spread the murder all over the City.

She slips Simpson's wrists into the straps and tightens the buckles. Dr Landon's story worked on Mrs Patel, it'll do for Granny's yobbos over at Inductions.

'The murder? Dr Landon's told us what we should say about the murder.' She goes to the foot of the bed and straps down Simpson's ankles. 'We have to say an inductee fell and hurt hisself. He hurt hisself and now he's suing Justice City. We're trying to get him to change his mind . . . It explains the hold-up, and the police, and why we're not even releasing his name.'

She puts Simpson's shoes on the floor under the foot of the bed. 'You think you can remember that, old man? You want me to go over it again?'

He sniffs, he's not a fucking idjit, and puts on his hat. 'I'll be off then. Give us the bloody trolley.'

'An inductee fell.' He's sure to make a mess of it. 'He fell. You don't have to say how. You wasn't there. And you don't know his name.'

She opens the doors in front of the screens above the bed and reels out the cables for Simpson's trodes. His chest is thin and hairless. She pauses, looks across at Granny Porter – why *isn't* the murder all over the City? Suddenly she sees Granny as something more than just a smelly old man. She sees him, funny clothes and all, as a murderer. He's feeble, sure, but injecting Beech didn't take any great muscle, and he's mean enough. Why isn't the murder all over the City? If he didn't do it, why hasn't he gabbed it around? Maybe he's scared. He's always everywhere and nobody notices him – now even that seems sinister.

For Carole Serote the time-lag between thought and action can be measured in nanoseconds. 'Granny Porter – did you murder Mr Beech?'

She has to ask. The reasoning stinks but it chimes with her

wishes. She's been awake all night, worrying. If Dr Landon or Jake had done it she wouldn't blame them. Beech was a terrible man. A terrible fellow. But she could never look at them the same again. She'd have to leave. It didn't matter which of them – Dr Landon was a nice woman, decent, very clever, and Jake had a good heart too – but if either of them had killed a man, an inductee, a *patient*, she couldn't go on working there. She'd have to leave. Ask for a transfer.

'Did you? Did you murder Mr Beech?'

Granny Porter gapes at her. 'Piss off. Who d'you think I am? Piss off. What'd I want to do a stupid thing like that for?'

She'd asked him a stupid question. He'll never admit it. So what next? She fingers the bundle of cables in her hand, thinking. He's got a point there – why *should* he do it? The way he talks about blacks when he thinks she can't hear, he'd have held Beech's coat for him and bought him a drink after . . . Not quite that maybe. But this is a crime that needs outrage and she doesn't think he's a man to feel it. Not for some black girl he's never met. So he's a poor bet for the murder.

She bends over the cables, sorting them according to their colour coding. She's ashamed. She'd have liked Granny Porter to be guilty, and it makes her ashamed to have wished such a sin on any son of Jesus.

'What about you?' he says, scragging his neck at her. 'You blackies stick up for your own, don't you? If anybody bloody done it, why wasn't it you?'

He advances. Indignation is what he does best. 'Fat black cow, what bloody right d'you think you got, flinging accusations? I know your sort. Just come down out of the jungle and you think you're bloody something. We had Magna Charta while you was still pissing into coconuts. Why d'you come here? I'll tell you why – because it's so bloody horrible back home. And now you – '

'Old man, you better quit that talk.' She straightens up. She's deserved his anger, but not this. 'I'm sorry I said what

I did, and I really mean that, but that's all you're getting. I don't take no name-calling shit from you, not from anybody. So quit it.'

She's formidable. Big. She points at the empty trolley. 'We got work to do. So you take that with you and go right on back out to Inductions. And if they give you a hard time just tell them a guy fell and hurt hisself and now he's suing Justice City. OK? You got that?'

Granny Porter is small. He lacks resources. He was never a big man, and now he's really small. He takes the trolley, shouting *Know-all fucking blackie* in his head, and pushes it out of the thresholding room.

Out in the corridor, the door shut behind him, he stops to kick the wheels and curse. The telephone in the control room starts ringing. He walks straight past it, out into the foyer. Answering telephones isn't what he's paid for. That'll fucking teach 'em.

Jake de Carteret has just arrived from the men's quarters and he's on his way into the nurses' room to hang up his quilted jacket. Jake never walks round the City in white, looking like a nurse. He likes to be seen as a person, not as a functionary.

He dodges Granny's trolley. 'Greeting, fair Titania.'

Granny pauses, glaring. 'It's as quiet as the fucking grave in here. Don't anyone but me like fucking music?' But he doesn't turn it on.

He shuffles on out through the double glass doors, taking the empty trolley with him. On the covered walkway he bumps into another blackie. The blackie copper who's up from Scousland to solve this murder. He won't if Granny Porter has anything to do with it. The genius who topped Lucky Beech did the world a fucking good turn.

Jake looks out at them, the tall black policeman and the shrimp of a porter in his concert party hat. The foyer is indeed quiet. Jake hears the telephone ringing in the control room and goes through to answer it.

167

'Punishments Building.'

'Nurse Serote, please.'

Jake sees his reflection in a blank black screen and smoothes one eyebrow. If Granny Porter's leaving with an empty trolley, then La Serote's already working on a lovey.

'I'm afraid she's busy just at present.'

'I was told to ask for her.'

'She's tied up, love. I'm sorry.'

'It's important.'

'So is what she's doing.' He's losing patience. 'Can she call you back?'

It's a man on the other end, trying for posh but not succeeding. Leeds Polytechnic. Jake has an ear for these things. The man hesitates.

'Perhaps you could help me. My name is Gorton. I'm Albert Beech's solicitor.'

Crikey. Jake widens his eyes at his reflection. 'Albert who?'

'Don't pretend you don't know who I'm talking about, young man. Mr Beech was sent to your place yesterday. And now this has happened, I want an explanation.'

So much for the governor trying to keep a lid on things. The City's as leaky as a Catholic condom. 'What *has* happened, Mr Gorton?'

'I was hoping you could tell me.'

'Perhaps if I were to put you through to the governor's office, then – '

'And don't give me that either. The governor's office? At this hour of the morning?'

'Then I really don't see how I can help you, Mr – '

'Who's this I'm talking to?'

It's an old trick, and it's wrong for Jake. He isn't intimidated. 'De Carteret, love. Jake de Carteret. Shall I spell that? It's a Channel Islands name. *Très exotique.*'

'All I want is to know what has been done to my client. I want to speak to him. I know my rights.'

Which are nil in here, love. Noddings. Zilch. Jake's

168

smelling a rat. Solicitors try things on, it's their job, but this sounds way over the top. 'You say your client has been sent here, Mr Gorton. When would that have been exactly?'

'Look, his sister's very worried. You can see that, can't you? Anything you told me would be treated in the strictest – '

'Which firm of solicitors did you say you represented, Mr Gorton?'

There's a tiny pause and then the line goes dead. Jake stares at the receiver thoughtfully, shakes it, then hangs it back on its hook. That's no solicitor. A hundred to one he's a newsman. He's picked up Herself's story somewhere. He's worked out that Beech arrived yesterday, he's tied it in with the story, and he's flying a kite.

Up to now Jake's had no need to tell the tale. He saw only Davey last night and Davey gets the truth. Always. They discussed the murder. Davey works in the motor pool but he knows all the main characters. Davey sees Herself as the murderer. No reason, it's just a feeling he has. Jake goes for Granny Porter – at least, he did until this morning's phone call. There's something going on. Why did the newsman ask for La Serote? Maybe he wasn't a newsman. Maybe they've got something cooking.

Jake frowns. This isn't a game. But he sidles down the corridor, playing it, to the end thresholding room. Inside it Carole Serote is finishing up Simpson six eleven. She's done the electrodes, and the mouthguard. Simpson has a full top denture and it's in the plastic jar clipped unobtrusively to the bedhead for the purpose.

'Morning, Jake,' she says. 'You slept well, I hope?'

'Tip-top, love. And you?'

'Fine.' She nods, smiling. Life should always have time for these little courtesies. Today they calm the jangling left by Granny Porter.

'I've just had the oddest phone call,' Jake tells her. 'Fellow asking for you. Then he tried to pump me about Beech. Said he was Beech's solicitor.'

169

Carole finishes what she's doing. Problems, problems. If the man asked for her, he wasn't no solicitor. He sounds like Freddy. And if Freddy's already got hold of Dr Landon's story, she can't be the only snitch in the City. 'You didn't tell him nothing?'

'What d'you think? He was a reporter. Must have been. And if he's heard something's up, then they all have.'

'Job for the press officer. No comment, no comment . . . You put him through?'

'He rang off. Didn't give me a chance.' Jake looks at Simpson's label. 'Why did he ask for you, though?'

She shrugs. 'Maybe they do that. Find out names first. Man answers and they ask for a woman. Woman answers and they ask for a man. Makes them sound like they know what they're doing.' She shoos him out into the corridor. 'What we should do is get the exchange to stop all calls. I'll tell Dr Landon.'

She pauses by the door to the next room along, turns back to Jake and taps her watch: the time is eight thirty. 'You need to get changed, man. The director's in and so's Dr Landon. I heard them upstairs when I was coming in.'

She goes into the thresholding room and perches on the bed, waiting for Granny to bring the next inductee. She's got to get rid of Freddy. He doesn't know when to stop. One day he'll bring her real trouble.

twelve

Was this murder clever or lucky? Planned or impulsive?
Brave or cowardly . . . a man's or a woman's . . . for gain or
for passion . . . big or small . . . hot or cold . . . merciful,
indifferent or enjoyed . . .? The questions were classroom
stuff but Alec used them with Frank that morning as the City
limo took them on to the M62 out of Liverpool. It was
supposedly a way of building up a character profile of the
criminal.

He'd asked for the pick-up at six thirty. He'd hoped to get
out of the house without disturbing anyone but there wasn't
a chance. Jamie was four and woke early, and with Uncle
Alec clattering about downstairs – he'd knocked the bread-
bin off the counter and it'd gone clanging across the floor
like a Trinidad steel band – there'd been no way of persuad-
ing the wee lad that it was still the middle of the night. So
Iain and Morag came down to the kitchen in their dressing-
gowns with him, and the four of them sat around in that
overlit no-place, no-time that the most familiar room
becomes when it's visited out of hours.

Alec perched Jamie on his knee and they shared his
cornflakes. Iain sat across the table from them, drinking
double-strength instant coffee, and Morag smoked a cigarette. It was six fifteen and chat didn't come easily. Alec had
told them very little about his break with May. It was their
first split and he didn't know if it was for good, but he

171

thought it probably was. He and May had been together upwards of three years, which was long enough to make serious connections, and anyway he reckoned they were rather serious people, not lightly given to tiffs and reconciliations. He knew that Iain and Morag weren't all that keen on May, but they didn't say much – the period before her, after the end of his marriage, didn't bear remembering. Last night he'd wolfed down the meal Morag had kept hot for him and fallen into bed half an hour later. They knew he'd been up all the previous night and now he was working on a case out at Justice City, but nothing more.

Iain thought Justice City obscene and he never pretended otherwise. And although Morag looked for mitigations – it was an improvement on the many overcrowded Victorian jails still in use – Alec knew it wasn't an easy topic for either of them. Not in his presence.

Now they sat and watched him eat cornflakes.

After a while he put Jamie down in front of the last of his cereal, went to the cooker, fried himself an egg. Iain and Morag watched him.

Iain shifted on his chair. 'I don't envy you this case, Alec. Is that place as bad as they say it is?'

Alec shrugged. 'I've been there before. The people do their best.'

Morag came to his rescue. 'A lot of policemen don't like jails, Iain. They don't all leave the Force. Look at you – you're not happy with everything that happens in the education system.'

Iain opened his mouth to speak, then closed it again. He drank his coffee.

Smoke was rising from the pan and Alec turned down the gas. Iain hadn't said so, but he wrote letters, spoke at meetings, fought the system constantly. The police force was different: loyalty wasn't merely advisable, it was demanded. Even so, Alec was grateful for Iain's tact. He cut bread and buttered it.

172

Jamie shovelled in cornflakes and looked up at his big shiny uncle. He kicked his legs in their pink pyjamas. This was Alec's family and he loved them very much. He flipped his egg over, then transferred it on to the bread on his plate.

'It's good of you lot to take me in. I'll get my own place going again in a day or two. It's just that at the moment I – '

'Nonsense,' Morag said. 'You're always welcome. You know you are.'

'It's what spare rooms are for,' Iain said.

Still Alec needed to explain. 'It's just that I'll need to get in supplies, things like that, and I'll be working late at the City, and then there's the drive – '

'I told you, Alec, you're – '

'But it's only till Saturday. I'll be finished then.' Finished? Briefly the word stopped him. Finished in more ways than one, maybe. 'So if you'll just – '

'A fixed term contract?' Iain said. 'That's unusual, isn't it?'

'Very.' Alec broke his egg-yolk on to his bread. 'Very unusual.'

And then the limo had arrived, and he'd hugged Jamie and thanked them again, and told them he'd be back around seven thirty, and Morag had suddenly wanted him to wait while she packed him some lunch, and he'd told her no, not to bother, there was a fine canteen out at the City, and she'd said it wasn't a bother, he should save his pennies, and Iain had said, only just amused, that she sounded like a Jewish mother from Central Casting, and he'd backed away down the path, and now Frank and he were trying to fit a character profile to Beech's killer.

His family ... Frank too? No, at nudging seven on a January morning Frank was the friend Governor Ransome had said he didn't have. Even that was pushing things. At nudging seven on a January morning Frank smelt of Imperial Leather and seemed, from the sounds in the dark, to be sucking large breakfast fragments from between his teeth.

Character profiles were classroom stuff. Alec knew that,

173

so did Frank. But the case read like a bad exam question: they had four suspects – four exactly – all with exactly equal opportunity, all with exactly no evidence implicating any one of them, and all with exactly no convincing motive. Perhaps a character profile would help.

The back of the Justice City limo smelt of stale cigar smoke, the ill-fitting side windows were noisy at speeds above twenty, and the central armrest sagged. But there was a reading spotlight on a flexible gooseneck which he'd been able to adjust until it shone on his notes.

'An impulse crime,' he said, 'yet calculated.'

Frank smothered an early morning yawn. 'Hard to put together, Chief. As impulses go, matey's must've been a bloody strong one. Murder's a risky business.'

'Aye. Especially for someone as calculating as this particular matey.'

'So what's next on the list? Brave or cowardly? I'd say neither. Careful, more like. Someone who susses things proper, then makes the decision.'

'Mebbe it only looks like that. Mebbe the deed was done, and everything just slipped into place after. Not clever at all – just lucky.'

The car leaned slightly, pouring round a gentle curve at ninety-plus. Alec could claim privilege if stopped. He was on his way to a case.

'None of this quite fits, chief. We've been talking about an impulse crime – fact is, all our suspects first saw Beech at least twenty minutes before they could hope to get back to him. Alone, like. With no one else around. So whoever it was had plenty of time to think about it. To work it out.'

'Plenty of time? Be realistic, Frank. You say *work it out* – what they do out there's a team job. Needs concentration. Their twenty minutes would've been pretty full. Fat chance they had of working anything out. No, I see this as a sort of instant revelation. Either that or pure luck.'

'Can't say I go for the luck, Chief. Syringes, gloves, wagon

... it's all too neat. And if it's the other then we're looking at someone pretty bright.'

'You're right. Unless of course . . .' Alec sorted through his notes. He speeded up, suddenly enthusiastic. 'Unless our man's the porter. As far as I can see, after the business with the plastic flowers he didn't do a damn thing. He just dropped out of sight. I agree he's not exactly Einstein, but . . . and in any case, he'll have seen Beech long before the others, over at Inductions. Maybe he sat in a loo somewhere, thinking things over.'

'That's where I found him, Chief. Having a drag.'

'There you are, then.'

'That was later.'

'Of course it was bloody later . . . Still, I'm looking forward to our talk with Granny Porter – which reminds me, Frank, what the hell's his real name? It's ridiculous, calling an old man like that Granny.'

'Wilks, Chief. I got Padmore to check with Records. Timothy Wilks . . .' Frank stretched his legs smugly and eased his waistband up over his belly. 'Can't fancy him, though. Seeing as we're talking character, his is wrong. I mean, I know he might've been able to do the injection, but would he have thought of it? Wouldn't injections come more natural to the others? I mean, being nurses?'

Which was true. 'Let's get back to the profile,' Alec said, not wanting to lose his best suspect. 'About the crime – is it a man's or a woman's?'

'Don't see as that matters.' Frank sniffed. 'Leaving out Wilks, what we've basically got is three women.'

The darkness hid Alec's smile. 'We're not leaving out Wilks, Frank. Not yet. Are we?' Frank remained rebelliously silent. 'But I agree with you – the crime is certainly more a nurse's than a porter's. So we'll move on to reasons, gain or passion, and admit that we've no idea. The black nurse obviously hated Beech . . . but enough to kill him?'

Frank again offered silence. Alec looked thoughtfully over

the driver's shoulder, at the road rushing at them in the car's headlights. Dawn was beginning to brighten the sky ahead. The driver had his radio on very softly, giving sports results.

'Enough to risk trial and conviction?'

'Comes back to the time-lag, Chief. She's no dummy. I reckon she's bright enough to see there wasn't no risk.'

Frank's money was on Nurse Serote. Alec had believed in her fierce moral tone. Also he didn't want the governor to be right. He sighed. 'No risk, Frank?' he said, manoeuvring sideways. 'You don't think we'll clear this one up?'

A lot of road streamed under the car while Frank thought about that. Finally, 'Do you, Chief?'

Alec was ready for him. He'd had time. 'I'm pinning my faith on Wishbone.'

'Wishbone?'

'It's got to mean something.'

'Why?'

'Why not?'

'Beech was stoned, Chief. Making no sense. I mean – look at it. *Wishbone* . . . He thought it was Christmas.'

'Aye . . . Well, I don't agree.' He couldn't afford to. 'What if Beech . . . Remember, Frank, Beech was a crook. Drugs, banks, you name it. And Wishbone sounds to me like the name of a job. A heist, mebbe. A code name. And somebody in that room recognized it.'

'So they killed him? For naming a job?'

'They were afraid he'd betray it. Betray them.'

'One of our lot, Chief? In on a job with a big-time London villain?'

'He gets around . . .' Alec sighed. It was thin to the point of invisibility. 'Wishbone must mean something, Frank. It's all we've got.'

His sergeant peered out of the side window. 'Where the hell are we? . . . If we're calling this a clever one, your Miss Landon's the cleverest.'

Alec let ride the description of Peggy Landon as 'his'. 'She

176

hasn't the capacity, Frank. It isn't in her. Believe me.' But he knew Frank wouldn't.

Frank didn't. Frank had been a policeman for thirty-five years, and he believed that murder was in everybody. But his circle of acquaintance was different from Alec's. He changed the subject. 'Had you thought of a conspiracy, Chief? All of them? On account of what Beech did?'

Alec frowned. 'We might as well go home, then . . . I can see a conspiracy *after* the event. Unspoken. More a cover-up. They work together. They've known each other a long time. I can imagine one of them – '

The car twitched as a quiet oath came from the driver.

'The bastards . . . Bloody hell. Listen to this, Chief Inspector.'

He turned up the radio. It was a news broadcast. In Belfast there was a hospital with a surgical team specializing in the reconstruction of shattered knee joints, the results of terrorist knee-cappings. It had developed new and successful procedures. Men who would have been crippled a few years ago were walking again. Now a woman claiming to be the grateful wife of an ex-patient had left the team a packet, a pound or so of Semtex, a bomb disguised as a thank-you box of chocolates. It had blown a hand off the nurse who opened it. Three other members of the team were seriously injured. The police were releasing an artist's impression of the woman who delivered it. The Secretary of State for Northern Ireland had denounced this latest atrocity. So had the Prime Minister. And the Archbishop of –

The driver switched off angrily. 'Bloody IRA,' he said. 'We got IRA banged up in the City. Lucky for them they're shut away in bloody LTI. I wouldn't give much for their chances in any other sodding nick.'

Alec grunted, shifted in his seat, slipping lower. Men in LTI were isolated, safe from their fellows. And from the staff. He thought that the decision to release details such as the blown-off hand was questionable. Intended by the British authorities to damage Noraid's fund-raising work in the USA, it would also stir up hatred here in Britain, and there was enough of that already. More than enough. And in any case, Irish Americans simply blamed the Brits — there was a war on, and it was the way of wars that innocent people got hurt.

'Will people never bloody learn?' Frank said. 'Accepting packets . . . opening packets . . . will they never bloody learn?'

Alec closed his eyes. 'A woman with a box of chocolates, Frank — what sort of life would it be, trusting nobody?'

The car rushed on, faster still. Soon the motorway merged with the Manchester/Huddersfield tollroute and the booth operator waved them through.

At Justice City Alec thanked the driver and told him he wouldn't be needed again. He asked him to thank the motor pool commander for the use of the limo. They'd had their own car there last night but they'd been at the end of a thirty-six-hour duty and not in a fit state to drive. It was a recap of the story but Alec thought it would do no harm. It had been only the deputy motor pool commander he'd spoken to last time round and lines of communication easily got crossed. He could have spoken to the motor pool commander at the time but he'd wanted to keep his distance. The same now, going through the driver. Courteous but remote.

It was the way he treated all the Justice City authorities. Not only now. Always. He'd never examined his reasons and he still didn't. The granite courtyard was cold and silent.

At Reception the duty officer had an envelope for him from Manchester. He leaned against the counter, leafed through the contents. Preliminary post-mortem report on Albert Beech, preliminary findings from forensics on the gloves and syringes. No surprise. Well, one surprise . . . There were traces of other than City drugs in Beech. Some designer compound, a new molecular grouping, not yet

178

identified. A euphoric, probably, but in very small quantities, a residue from some earlier high, definitely non-fatal. Substantial amounts of the paralytic used in the thresholding procedure were present also. Beech had died of heart failure, and for the moment a connection could safely be assumed. No other abnormalities had been discovered. Investigations were proceeding. Beech was not HIV positive.

Alec passed the report to Frank, drawing his eye to the one surprise. Designer drugs in a man who'd been in police custody since forever. The Home Office wasn't going to like that.

Frank glared at the report. 'This thing's bloody useless. "Very small quantities" . . . why can't they say how much and at least give a hint of how long ago?'

'If they could I'm sure they would, Frank. Sometimes these nightmare brews are gone quicker than the high. No hangover − it's a big selling point . . . Looks as if it's not what Beech died of, though, so it's not our problem.'

They left Reception and made their way over to the House. The time was eight twenty-five, broad daylight, and Granny Porter was leaving with an empty trolley.

Alec detained him. 'Mr Wilks?'

The old man was miles away, muttering angrily: '*Fucking morgue . . . Don't anyone but me like fucking music . . .?*'

'Mr Wilks?'

He pulled up short, peering. 'Who wants him? Fucking hell, you dug a long way to find that one.'

'Can we talk, Mr Wilks?'

'Takes me back. Haven't been called that one, oh, in fucking donkey's years.'

'Can we talk?'

'All right with me, Inspector. Don't know what Inductions'll say. I'm running late. They still got five more over there for Missy Landon.'

Alec considered. He'd caused enough disruption yesterday. And he knew the routine now. 'Bring them over, Wilks,' he said briskly. 'I'll see you afterwards. Come up to my office when you've done. Nine or soon after.'

He was sounding like a schoolmaster. A revealing thought – there was much of the schoolboy in Wilks. In Granny Porter. And then there was Alec's need to call him Wilks. Promotion was making him pompous.

He softened his tone. 'I'll be in my room. You'll mind where that is. Nine or soon after, now.'

The difficulty, seeing Granny Wilks Porter now, was to believe in him as a serious suspect, as a serious anything. He made a laugh of the profile. Thinking things over? Working out the risks? Do me a favour – if he sat on a loo it'd be to have a shit. Period. Or, as when Frank'd found him, a drag. Thinking just wasn't in his line. He was sloping off now with the empty trolley, muttering under his breath, his sneakers loose on his feet, slapping at the ground, laces trailing. Alec avoided Frank's eye, walked on into the House's foyer. At this early stage, he told himself, it was as dangerous to write suspects off as to assume them guilty.

The gay nurse, Jake de Carteret, was in his dispensary, fussing with his wagon. 'Morning, Chief Inspector. You're looking better today. That's nice.'

'Better? Aye. Well . . .' He walked on.

'I felt for you last night. You looked quite horribly exhausted.'

Alec didn't need it, not at this hour of the morning. He went on by. Gays would always tend to feel for other men, of course. He paused. No, that wasn't accurate – gays felt for other people. No, that neither. Ah, the traps. Gays weren't a faceless block – they *were* other people. Just the way blacks were. Alec retraced his steps.

'So this is what you do, is it?' He looked down at the wagon, swabs, disinfectant, tubes of gunk, instruments, syringes in their rack. 'I don't suppose you've thought of anything else I ought to know? Anything about yesterday, anything out of the ordinary?'

'Not a sausage.' Jake blew into a plastic liner and slid it down into the waste bin. 'I've thought and thought.'

Alec lingered. Frank went on past him and up the stairs. In the car they'd talked about conspiracy . . .

'I know how you felt about Beech, Jake. I asked you yesterday and you told me . . . I don't think I got round to asking how you felt about whoever it was who killed him.'

De Carteret gave one of his sideways triangular grins. 'You mean, would I lie to protect them? You know, Chief Inspector, I don't think I would.' He tucked a box of plastic gloves into its holder on the wagon. 'No, I'm sure I wouldn't . . . I've not the faintest idea why.'

'Mebbe it's to do with your nurse's oath.' Alec believed him. 'You do have an oath? Like doctors?'

'Actually we don't. But the principle's the same. We – '

There were voices on the stairs. Frank, going up, had met Peggy Landon coming down. She was wishing him a happy Wednesday. It was an affectation but Alec thought she got away with it. They passed and she continued on down the stairs, clipboard under her arm. She looked very crisp and neat today. He wondered who the man had been, going with her to the City Bistro.

'Good morning, Chief Inspector. You're an early bird.'

He was tempted to ask if she had any worms for him. 'I've a lot to do, Miss Landon. You're well, I hope?'

'Very well. *Very* well . . .' She smiled at him, smart as a button. Was it a cause for shame, after the news from Belfast, that she made him feel . . . optimistic?

'I need to have a word with the punishments officer,' he said. 'Will that be a problem?'

'The punishments officer?' She raised strong, well-shaped eyebrows. 'Oh, of course – you need to check my story. When I went down to him with the profiles . . . No, no problem. Give him ten minutes or so.' She looked up at the foyer clock. 'His men'll be feeding round then. You'll find him in his office.'

'Thanks. I'll do that.' *Feeding round* – the allusion was agricultural. Farmers with cattle fed round . . .

He was eyeing the doors to the lower floor and she noticed. 'You need to take the lift, Chief Inspector. The doors are on a special lock. They're only for emergencies.'

'Emergencies? Fire, you mean?'

'I mean anything that calls for a quick get-away. Fire. Riot. Nuclear holocaust.'

She was laughing at him. Either she'd detected his prickliness or it was so usual among visitors to Punishments that she was simply assuming it. She was right, of course, and right to laugh – most of his working life was spent delivering villains to one version or another of this building, and yet now, already, he'd felt a need to defend himself against it. The reality, here, was so unequivocal. His mental picture of the doors, he realized, had been of a river bursting out through them, a torrent of human pain, overriding the special lock.

It wasn't something he wanted to tell her about. In any case, she'd guessed the general picture. He walked past her up the stairs, then turned. 'One other thing. The porter was in the room when you injected Beech. You gave him a job to do. Can you remember what it was?'

'Checking the soap dispensers, I think . . . Yes, the soap dispensers above the basins in the washroom. They squirt out pink gloop. The day before I'd noticed one was empty.'

'A big job?'

'Ten minutes or so.'

'Did he do it?'

'You know, Chief Inspector, I really haven't checked.'

She was laughing at him again, and he took the point. Since then she'd had other things on her mind. 'Aye. Well, I'll not keep you . . .'

'How's the investigation? Any break-throughs?'

His turn to smile. 'You wouldn't expect me to tell you that, Miss Landon.'

She flipped papers on the clipboard, unamused. 'I don't like my nurses being under suspicion, Chief Inspector. And now Dr Mellish is back from America.'

It was a curious *non sequitur*. 'He'll be wanting a word, then.'

'Several.' She relented, put a hand on his arm. 'Later, though. He's in his office, sleeping off jet-lag. I'm to wake him around nine thirty. He wants to see the governor.'

'I'll tread softly, then.'

They hadn't lowered their voices. Even so, the hand on his arm made it almost a conspiracy. He disengaged, and went on up the stairs. At the top he paused, looked back. Miss Landon was busy, talking to Jake, consulting her clipboard.

Frank was in their improvised incident room. So was young Padmore. He didn't seem to have been there long: he was staring at the instructions Alec had left him.

'Wishbone, Chief Inspector? What's the file?'

'The file?'

'The *file*, sir. In the *menu* . . . The context, sir.'

'The context, lad? Albert Beech is the context.'

Padmore put on a patient expression, tapped his screen. 'First I have to access the Scotland Yard mainframe, Chief Inspector. Well, I've fixed that. I've already been on to Manchester and they've given me the codes.' He paused for applause. None came. 'So next I'll call up a menu. A menu isn't just a list of criminals' names, sir. I'll need a file. And – '

'Don't you bloody lecture me, young man. I was hacking computers before you were born – ' Alec checked himself. Padmore wasn't CID. He wasn't a bright young detective constable who'd rather be out feeling collars. He was a prison officer, clerical grade, sent up (as a great favour) from City Records. 'I'm sorry, Mr Padmore. Wrong side of the bed and all that . . .' He sat down, put his elbows on his desk, covered his eyes with his palms. 'Just find us a menu, lad, and we'll see what's on it. OK?'

His palms felt pleasantly cool against his eyes. It was a fine morning and the sun was well up now, wintry but brighter than he needed. He listened to Padmore at his keyboard. Downstairs the foyer double doors banged open very faintly, then shut again. Granny Porter, with another inductee on a trolley? Alec considered soap dispensers. If Granny Porter'd been in the washroom filling soap dispensers he could have nipped out and done Beech easy . . .

Frank was dithering by the door. 'Coffee, Chief?'

Alec opened his eyes. He remembered the previous day's instant. 'I suppose I must.'

Frank went out. For a man with a wife who cared about coffee he was incredibly undiscriminating.

Padmore tapped more keys. 'Menu, Chief Inspector.'

Alec got up, looked over his shoulder. 'Work in from charge sheets, Mr Padmore. Beech'll be under several headings, all cross-referenced. Start with murder. Evidence, depositions, interrogations, court proceedings, you'll need to search the lot. Any mention of Wishbone, any at all.'

He went back to his desk, sat down, drummed his fingers. What now? He'd talked himself out with Frank in the car, amazingly no one upstairs was asking him for daily reports, his backlog of paperwork was in Liverpool, and until he could get down to the punishments officer he had nothing else on. Nothing else on. He smoothed his already smooth black frizz. What the hell was he to do about him and May?

She liked his piano playing. The flat in Sefton Park had a piano in a front bay window, a big black beast kept in tune for her Grieg, the easy pieces. It was far too grand for his sort of music but she never minded. Last year, at a gig he'd done in a pub to help out old friends, trumpet and bass, like when he was young, she'd gone along and liked it. Quite liked it. Usually, because players couldn't depend on his turning up, he did solo spots in easy-going places.

What else did she like? What was it she called him, last night, on the phone? She said she'd been running a hostel for social inadequates, meaning him. True or not, it left him little room for manoeuvre. Ah, but you shouldn't go too much on what people *said*, not in the heat of the . . . in the cold of the moment.

He reached for the telephone, meaning to call her, and remembered Padmore just across the room, and remembered the time. By eight thirty-five on a Wednesday morning she'd be on her way to work. He'd ring her office later. But wasn't Wednesday one of her days in court?

Oh May, May, what opportunities for failure are packed into living with, into caring for. Into loving.

Frank returned. Alec sipped his coffee, shuddered, left it. Padmore was into search mode and gaining momentum. The ten-minute delay Peggy Landon had recommended was up. Thank God for that.

'Hold the fort, Frank. I'm off down for a word with the punishments officer.'

He went downstairs, past Miss Landon and Jake still by the dispensary, and through into the corridor outside the thresholding rooms. He called the lift. Nurse Serote came out of one of the rooms behind him and wished him good morning. The lift arrived, pinged loudly, and as he went down in it he realized he hadn't answered her.

The doors opened again before he had time to regret this, and he walked out into Punishments' central area.

The place was like a work station in a big modern hospital. Bright lights, brisk footsteps, telephones ringing, a large circular desk in the middle with seats at its centre, looking out at banks of screens. And around the outer wall of the area wood-veneered doors and openings into passages. Just now all the seats inside the desk were empty save one, in which a bored duty nurse sat nibbling the rim of his polystyrene drinks machine beaker. Clearly the rest of the staff were feeding round.

The nurse saw Alec and put down his beaker. 'Yes?'

Alec showed his ID. 'I'm here for a chat with the punishments officer.' The nurse looked from the ID to Alec and back again, clearly reluctant to believe the connection. 'Please call him up and see if it's convenient.'

The nurse returned Alec's card and pointed with one finger, as if pressing a button, 'Over there.'

What happened to old-fashioned manners? Nurses were a step up on warders . . . was that the point he was making?

Alec turned, saw a glass door with a window beside it, both obscured with slatted blinds. A prison officer emerged from a passage, wheeling a tall trolley stacked high with plastic breakfast trays. He went on by, eyed Alec with open curiosity. Alec didn't altogether blame him: a stranger . . . civilian clothes . . . black skin. He crossed to the glass door and knocked.

'Enter.'

The punishments officer was bloodless, with round, wire-rimmed spectacles. He got up from his desk and held out his hand. 'My name is Wilson. You must be the policeman.' He smiled minutely. 'Charge Nurse Landon mentioned you.'

Alec shook the hand. It was thin and dry. 'Chief Inspector Duncan. Mebbe you can spare me a moment. Nurse Landon suggested this might be a good time.'

'About the only good time. Sit down, Chief Inspector. You catch me at my break.' He indicated a picnic thermos flask on his desk, its plastic cup full and steaming. 'The machine out there purveys muck. Muck. I've told the governor about it. I've told him repeatedly . . .' He didn't bother to finish. 'And what can I do for you? Hm?'

Alec didn't know what he'd expected, but it hadn't been this. It probably should have been. A timetables man was what the job needed. A man whose job satisfaction came from making things work. It didn't matter what.

'You'll be aware, Mr Wilson, that I've an investigation going on upstairs.'

'Yes indeed. I do get told things, Chief Inspector, even down here in my oubliette.' Another vestige of a smile. 'And besides, that man Beech never made it into my schedule. I gather he's over in the hospital. And he's suing someone for assault. Or is it neglect? In either case, I find that ironic. In a rapist and murderer, I mean. Don't you?'

Alec gestured evasively. He hated being obliged to lie, even for the sake of Governor Ransome's cover story. 'I'm here collecting evidence, Mr Wilson. That's all. And . . .'

'A chief inspector? On some trumped-up assault charge? It seems a bit over the top.'

'It's likely to be a high profile case, sir . . . And now, if you don't mind, just a few questions?'

'Willingly. I didn't hear anything, if that's what you're hoping. We're soundproofed down here' – he picked up the plastic cup and drank from it – 'for obvious reasons.'

Alec got out his notebook. He had only the one question, but he was going to dress it up. He didn't want to appear to be doubting Peggy Landon's word. He riffled notebook pages impressively.

'When your men went upstairs yesterday morning to bring down the inductees after thresholding, they were turned away, I believe.'

'Correct. On Dr Peck's orders. Conveyed by that de Carteret. I'm sure you know who I mean.'

Alec detected a whiff of homophobia and the invitation to share it, man-to-man. 'When would that have been, Mr Wilson? As near as you can say?'

'I can say exactly, Chief Inspector. We run things here by the clock. We have to – scheduling's very tight. My men go up for the early morning batch at ten thirty. Yesterday that de Carteret turned them away. They reported back to me at ten thirty-four.'

'Was Nurse Landon with you at that time?'

'She was not. De Carteret had already called me, looking for her. The profiles were straightforward and she'd been gone for quite a while. I had to contact Dr Peck instead. It was most inconvenient. I finally reached him at . . .' he put down his cup and consulted his desk diary '. . . at ten fifty-two. There were three other inductees upstairs at that time, Marsden, Petersen and Carter. Beech might be incommunicado, but there was no reason why I shouldn't have *them* . . .'

'Aye. I can see that. And did Dr Peck let you?'

'He couldn't stop me. They'd surfaced, I had their papers, there was nowhere else for them to go.' He indicated the wall chart behind his desk. 'Although in Carter's case I'm not sure why I bothered. An indecent exposure, given only four hours . . . tell me, Chief Inspector, do the judges out there ever think about the paperwork they cause? In one day and out the next – do they ever wonder if it's worth it?'

Alec remembered he was a policeman. 'It's the deterrent effect, Mr Wilson.'

'Ha! And we all know what that amounts to.'

Alec took refuge in his notebook. 'So Nurse Landon had left you by ten twenty . . .' He hesitated, hard up against the only question that mattered. 'When did she arrive?'

'Ten ten.'

He felt a chill. Carole Serote said Peggy Landon had left the control room at ten, straight up and down. Three paces to the lift doors, one floor down in the lift – there was no way she could have come straight here and taken ten minutes.

'Ten past ten . . . you're sure of that?'

The punishments officer gave him an old-fashioned look. They'd been through this already. 'If she's telling you something else I fear she's mistaken.'

'Not at all,' Alec quickly assured him. 'I have to confirm these times, that's all . . . The fact is, I haven't yet asked her.' Which was true. Back when he'd talked to her the exact timing hadn't seemed important.

Mr Wilson nodded sharply, like a bird pecking. 'Good. Good . . . Charge Nurse Landon is a reliable person, Chief Inspector. Most reliable. If someone assaulted Beech I'm sure it was not she.'

Which, grammar and all, gave Alec the perfect lead-in. 'So everything was perfectly normal? She wasn't flustered? Not agitated in any way?'

'Not at all ... Although in fairness, Chief Inspector, if you've talked to Nurse Landon you'll know that she wouldn't be one to fluster easily.'

No. No, she wouldn't.

Alec sorted through his notes. 'Thank you. I think that's all, then.'

'Excellent.' Mr Wilson emptied his teacup and stood. 'I have to admit I'm not sorry Beech has been delayed for a while. These long-term punishment men cause all sorts of problems. I've been given new EAT rooms recently, but it's still no picnic. Everything's always at such short notice. Nobody ever *thinks*, do they? The appeal courts turn them out and they're here the next day. The public loves it, obviously, but they tie up a room for weeks and there's others who have to be held over.' He turned to his wall chart. 'With Beech in abeyance, as it were, I can make proper arrangements ... You've no idea how long he will be, I suppose?'

Alec cleared his throat. 'That's not for me to say ... I'm grateful for your time, Mr Wilson. I'll be on my way now.'

He went to the door. Mr Wilson followed him. 'You'd like a look round, perhaps? See how we do things? The officers are feeding round at present, so – '

'It's good of you to offer, Mr Wilson, but – '

'We have only minimum contact with subjects, of course. It's easier on both sides.' He led Alec out past the central desk. 'It spares my officers accusations of bad behaviour ...'

Alec followed him, ashamed of his reluctance.

'Food gets delivered via sealed rotaries. You'll have seen them over in the LTI blocks, I expect. The cameras pick it up if there's anything seriously amiss. There's always a nurse on duty.'

There was indeed. Curt, but undeniably on duty.

'And of course there's Charge Nurse Landon on call, in case one of our chaps really gets into difficulties with the treatment. She's a trained psychotherapist, you know. Quite excellent.'

They were walking down a corridor, past a succession of closed doors. Near each a rotary was set into the wall, a vertical drum large enough to accommodate a food tray, which could then be rotated into the EAT room beyond. Above the door a TV screen showed the interior. Each room contained a man in prison uniform, sitting, standing, walking, as they went past. The rooms were surprisingly ordinary. No sharp corners, presumably bolted-down furniture, but no visible padding. Possibly the men took their punishment like men. Possibly.

'You'll see we don't have spy-holes, Chief Inspector. Inmates find them demeaning, you know. They much prefer camera surveillance.'

Alec listened to the silence, and remembered the iron mouths Jake had showed him in the thresholding room upstairs. EAT began at eleven. Even then, out here, it would still be silent.

The corridor curved. He wondered how many rooms there were, but didn't ask. A prison officer came towards them, pushing an empty food trolley. As he passed them Mr Wilson smiled and said, 'Good morning, Sam. Any problems?'

'No problems, sir.'

'Excellent. Well done . . .'

Alec had visited many big conventional penal institutions. He was used to them. They were noisy, cruel, stinking, violent. They punished randomly, and at length. It was nonsensical to find this place worse.

The corridor returned the two of them to the central area. Mr Wilson spoke to the duty nurse. 'May I?' He spun one of the desk screens on its mounting. It repeated one of the above-door pictures. A prisoner was eating his breakfast. 'The EAT rooms are self-contained, you see. No slopping out. We'd have preferred greater separation for each room's toilet facilities, but it would have interfered with surveillance. As in all prisons, suicide is a constant worry. We've never had one yet, I'm proud to say.' He leaned on the desk. 'We keep good care of the men you send us, Chief Inspector.'

Alec met his gaze. 'I'm impressed.' It was a better record than that of any conventional UK nick.

Mr Wilson pointed. 'LTI blocks are down that corridor. Kitchens down that one. Also Holding Block, otherwise known as Limbo.' This prompted one of his small smiles. 'Frankly, I'm glad you had an excuse to come and talk to me, Chief Inspector. In my opinion we don't get to see you people often enough.'

Alec looked for responsible-sounding formulae. 'I'm sure you're right, Mr Wilson. After all, we're part of the same process . . . But there just aren't enough hours in the day. We both know what our masters in Whitehall would say if I suggested a week's work study here for every member of the Force.'

They shared a professional chuckle. Alec thanked him again, they shook hands, and Alec made his way to the lift.

Part of the same process? His job was catching villains. Wilson's was ensuring that justice was seen to be done. They united, arguably, in protecting the public. Then again, arguably, they didn't. Long Term Incarceration protected the public. What Extreme Audio-frequency Treatment did was keep the public happy. It was a useful job, but hardly the same.

The lift doors opened, Alec went in, and they closed behind him.

thirteen

It's nine-ish and Granny Porter's enjoying a cuppa with his mates over at Inductions. This is the big back room, where inductees are brought to wait after their hot beverage, before he takes them over for thresholding, and it's clear at the moment. The trolleys are empty, lined up along one wall, ready for the next batch. It's a cloudy day outside, but fine in between: just now there's even a little sunlight coming in, brighter than the neon overhead tubes. The radio's on, giving the Wednesday racing news, and Granny's scrounged a morning paper. He's perched on a radiator under a window, warming his bum, the paper open at the sports page and folded into a narrow strip two inches from his nose.

He peers. He needs glasses for reading but he's always breaking them. There's a nice little two-mile handicap at Aintree this afternoon, three o'clock, and he's got his eye on a little darling. Porky's Lass has had a terrible season and she's not carrying anything you'd care to mention, but Granny reckons her trainer's been holding off and today's the fucking day. The only other half-way decent nag's got the cough and won't be running, says the man on the radio, so she'll walk it. Twenty to one, in the paper. Twenty to one, Granny tells his mates, if they get a move on.

'Half that come the fucking start,' he tells them. 'Once the word gets round it'll be tens. Fives. Bound to.'

His mates, sitting round the radio, are more interested in

the paper's front page. There's a headline OUCH, THAT HURT! above a stupid story about a prisoner in an unnamed jail who's fallen and twisted himself. Granny's already read it: it's a lot of nothing. And he heard the story about the swindler who twisted himself back when he was at the Bethnal Green secondary modern.

'It isn't often the bookies drop a fucking clanger,' he tells his mates. 'Twenties here in the paper, and she's a little darling.'

Nobody hears him. He scratches the stubbly hair under one side of his boater, pushing it crooked. Christ, what he'd give to be able to tell them the truth about that feller in the paper. They'd listen to him then. But he fucking can't, and there's an end to it. He raises his voice.

'Porky's Lass,' he says. 'Don't look at her form, for fuck's sake. It's like I said – she's been saved up for today. Nah – look at the bloodline. Bloke with a tenner on Porky's Lass is looking at a safe two hundred.' He peers at his paper. It's already scrunched and blurry. 'A safe two hundred. I'll tell you that for nothing . . . fucking don't then. Please your fucking selves.'

One of his mates looks up from their paper. 'You what?'

'I said, any of you lot got a spare fiver you'd give me a lend of?'

'Drink your tea.'

'Porky's Lass in the three o'clock. She's a cert.' Justice City runs to a nifty betting shop, but it doesn't give credit. 'Just a fiver? Three quid, then?'

'Drink your tea.'

His mates have moved on now. They're looking at the page three tits. Granny drinks his tea. They're nice boys, and the tea's a freebie. It comes out of a kitty, along with the biscuits – digestives, not like the tooth-breakers over in the porters' lodge – and they all put into it except Granny. They're nice boys.

He shifts his bum, enjoying the radiator. Beside him are

the doors out to the front, where the new batch from Manchester is being booked in and examined by the doctor. Cough please and how's your arsehole. He can hear the voices. Soon they'll have their hot beverage and they'll start arriving from the cubicles. He'll be gone by then. Any minute now he's got his date with the blackie copper.

Christ on a crutch . . . He finishes his tea, puts the mug down on a windowsill, wipes his chin, starts to roll a fag. Christ on a crutch – a blackie copper . . .

He runs over his story. It's straight enough and he'll keep it that way. No last-minute improvements. He was sweeping up the nurses' room. Saw nothing, heard nothing. No improvements . . . He's sat across too many tables from too many coppers in too many nicks, and hanged himself with fucking improvements.

Know your story and fucking stick to it. Bloke he's shared a cell with once had a motto: Keep It Simple, Stupid. KISS. A genius with the wallpaper, that bloke was, with the fake cheques, but he'd never done more than a month or two. Told a simple story and stuck to it. No last minute improvements. Keep it simple, stupid.

Last night, in his pisser in the civilian workers' hostel, Granny'd had a revelation. It was Missy Landon who'd done for Lucky Beech. It must have been – he'd seen her coming out of Lucky's room, hadn't he? Watched her take the lift down to Punishments. Five minutes later, when he went to sweep up the petals, Lucky'd fucking snuffed it. She'd done for him, all right.

He didn't wonder why. Lucky being Lucky was reason enough for someone to do for him. He'd've done the job himself if he'd been thirty years younger. Missy Landon had done the world a favour. Good fucking luck to her.

All the more reason, seeing what he'd seen, that he'd been somewhere else. In the nurses' room. Sweeping up. He lights his fag. Keep it simple, stupid.

Sweeping up, Officer. Just sweeping up.

All the time?

Again the trick question. All what time, Officer? Chief Inspector? Blackie Chief Inspector? All what time?

All the time from blah-blah to —

Voices approach the doors beside him. The doors burst open and the Inductions boss, Captain Carey, hurries through. He's closely followed by the governor. Fucking hell. Granny unprops himself from the radiator and nips out his fag. Fucking hell – the governor.

'Look in, lads.' The inductions officer stands in front of the still flapping doors. 'Look in. Mr Ransome's got something to say. Something to ask you.'

The others have scrambled to their feet. One of them turns off the radio. A teaspoon falls off the table, noisily on to the tiled floor.

'Sit down. At ease, you people.' The governor comes forward. He always calls his staff *people* – it covers him with the women officers, of which, here in Inductions, there are none. 'I've a question to ask you all about yesterday morning. I've been talking to the officers out front, and the duty MO, and Douglas, Mr Carey here, and now it's your turn.'

He gazes round. His pale eyes are fearsomely direct, and Granny cringes. Governor Ransome is no blackie chief inspector. Governor Ransome knows Granny's most secret thoughts. Governor Ransome is Granny Porter's god.

'You'll have heard,' the governor continues, 'that we had a bit of trouble yesterday with one of the inductees. Now, I want you to think back to that morning. I need an honest answer, and I promise you here and now that there'll be no disciplinary action, whatever that answer is. So think back, all of you – were the inductees ever alone in here? I'm talking about the first batch. It was a short batch, only four. Was one of them, or were all of them, ever left untended? Even for a moment? They shouldn't have been, I know that, but that's not the point. Were they?'

The officers round the table eye each other. They think theatrically and shake their heads.

'I'm not talking about very long, you understand. And I'll be frank with you — there's a possibility of drug abuse here. What I need to know is if one of the inductees got to be on his own — went to the toilet, maybe — for even a minute or so. And I need an honest answer.'

A pause. One of the officers, Granny's mate Kevin, elects himself to answer. 'Not a chance, Mr Ransome. They were out for the count, sir. Never stirred.'

Governor Ransome looks from him to the others, one by one. 'Fine, fine . . . But bear with me. We're all of us only human. Faced with a row of stiffs, it's a temptation to slope off for a smoke or a pee or whatever. And then again' — he rides over their denials — 'then again, once in a while, for some reason or another, an inductee resurfaces — or may have been faking his unconsciousness in the first place. So I'll ask my question just once more. Was one, or were all of the inductees in yesterday morning's batch left alone in here? I know they shouldn't have been, but were they?'

The governor folds his arms, waits. The officers deny it. Granny Porter's puzzled — it's as if Governor Ransome *wants* them to have left Lucky . . . but even if they had, where could the sod've gone? There's nowhere back here, not so much as a tin foot locker. Not to mention where he'd've got the fixings. Shooting up takes fixings. Blokes shoot up in the City, all over the place, Granny's seen it, but not till they get settled. Not out here. Not —

'Not left alone ever?' Governor Ransome insists. 'You're sure of that?' He crosses to the far doors, looks out along the covered walkway, turns. 'I meant what I said, remember. No disciplinary action. No matter what. So none of you need fear landing the others in the shit. Right?'

He looks round again. Granny's sure now — he really wants Lucky to have had a chance to stick himself. Why? Suicide would get them all off the hook, but Lucky'd never

196

have done it. He'd reckon on putting together some sort of deal, even in Justice City. So what else – a straight OD? Lucky wasn't that stupid . . .

Governor Ransome waits a long time. Captain Carey's looking down at his shoes. He likes to think he runs a tight team here, and Granny knows he'll be pissed rigid if they've let him down. But they haven't. No one says a word.

The governor returns to the middle of the room. 'Right. Well done. I'm grateful.' He doesn't look grateful. He looks pissed rigid. 'And I'm sorry I had to ask what I did. It was insulting and I'm sorry. It's just that in a matter like this we have to be certain.'

In a matter like this . . . Granny notices the way Governor Ransome's keeping things vague. Lucky's death can't be hushed up for ever and this way he's distancing himself from the pack of lies he's got everyone up in Punishments telling.

The governor turns to Captain Carey. 'Your people do a fine job. The smooth running of this City depends on them, and they do a fine job. I really appreciate it. Well done.'

The two men return to the front reception area. As the doors close behind them one of Granny's mates blows a wet fart raspberry. Granny doesn't like it. Governor Ransome's a good man. He hands out pious shit from time to time, but that's what bosses do. They fucking have to. It comes with the job. His mates are young, still wet behind the ears, and they don't fucking know this, but if they ever get to be bosses they'll do the fucking same. He's seen it.

Not that Granny tells them this. Instead he gives the doors that have just closed behind Governor Ransome two fingers. 'Bleedin' tosser.' And a second time, to be sure he's noticed. 'Bleedin' tosser.' He smoothes out the fag-end he's been hiding in his palm and parks it jauntily behind his ear. 'Yes sir, no sir, two bags fucking full, sir.'

He ambles over to the far doors. It's coming up to nine fifteen, time for his trip to the blackie copper. The others are talking among themselves and waving their arms about. 'I'll be off then,' he tells them, and goes out briskly.

On the walkway his pace slows. The morning's cold and he folds his arms protectively round his skinny chest. 'I was in the nurses' room,' he mutters. Keep it simple, stupid. 'In the nurses' room, sweeping up . . .'

As he enters the House foyer Sergeant Grove is coming down the stairs. The fat sergeant sees him, checks, and beckons with one finger. Granny tips his boater and does a devil-may-care soft shoe shuffle.

It's an hour and a quarter later, around ten thirty: Peggy Landon is downstairs in Punishments with the profiles and Jake and Carole are resurfacing the first of the mornings batch. The man stirs as Jake removes the mouthguard. He'll be conscious at any moment.

Carole watches him. She's already tidied away the electrodes and their cables. Inductees react badly enough to the holding straps, without seeing all that other stuff.

'Dr Peck surely knows his way around,' she says. 'He could've got in somehow to that Beech.'

'Past me?' Jake says, dropping the mouthguard into the jar of disinfectant on the wagon. 'No way. I was out there in the dispensary the whole time.'

The inductee opens his eyes. Carole points to the corridor outside the room and whispers across him, '*In through the window?*'

Jake laughs. 'In broad daylight, lovey? On the risky side, wouldn't you say?'

The inductee, coming round and seeing two nurses, is bewildered. Inductees usually are. 'Here,' he says. 'What's going on?' He discovers the straps on his wrists and cringes. 'Christ. What're you going to do to me?'

Carole moves to the foot of the bed. Often inductees fight their straps and shout at this point. She reads the label on his ankle. 'We're not doing nothing, Mr Fraser,' she says.

'You've had some tests done, is all. Minute or two and the guards'll be coming to fix you up. All you got to do is stay cool, wait till they get here, Mr Fraser. Think you can manage that?'

It's her standard routine, on the edge of nigger talk, soothing for whites who want to be soothed. Blacks get something whiter. Fighters and shouters get nothing at all.

'We'll be going off now,' she tells him. 'Anything you want, Mr Fraser, just you ask the guards. They'll be here any minute.'

She turns to go.

'Hey.' Mr Fraser's been testing his straps. 'Hey – I'm tied down here. I can't get up.'

'Like I said, Mr Fraser, the guards'll be round any minute. They'll see you right.'

She leaves the thresholding room and Mr Fraser's plaintive cries. Jake follows her with his trolley and they pause in the corridor. They've got to talk about the murder and it's difficult to fit it in.

'The window's got bars,' Jake tells her, checking it. 'They all do. No, lovey, if the good doctor saw to Beech it was before he got here. Back at Inductions – it's not impossible.'

Carole frowns. 'I'd have seen the bruise while I was prepping him.'

'Not necessarily. Bruising can take time to show.'

'How long are we talking? At least half an hour. Maybe longer. God knows when Granny brought him over. I don't think he – '

They hear the lift approaching, bringing the guards up from Punishments, and they duck into the next thresholding room. They've got to keep ahead, and so far they've only processed four-four-three Fraser.

There'd been talking time earlier, on their rounds with Peggy Landon and in the control room, but in her presence they'd felt inhibited. They've not discussed this, but it may be that they both subconsciously believe she's the guilty

199

party. Jake knows his Davey does. Jake began the morning thinking it was Granny Porter; now he's switched to La Serote, which is not a solution he relishes. Hence his efforts on Dr Peck.

Carole, after her brief go at Granny, had been refusing to speculate. Then, in their break at ten, Jake had discreetly raised the possibility that the murderer might be an outsider. She warmed to the idea – and if an outsider, then why not Dr Peck? None was more plausible, or more satisfactory. Nobody liked Dr Peck. He rarely visited the House, and then only on sufferance. He was of a complaining, idle disposition.

Knowing about Beech's arrival long before them, he'd have had plenty of time to make his plans. His motive, behind that mindless smile, was as strong, or as weak, as anyone's. His method, though, was still a problem. If he was responsible for the injection that had caused the bruising, when had he performed it?

The next inductee is already excessively awake. He's spat out his mouthguard and his screaming hits them the moment they open his door. It checks when he sees them, then intensifies. Not all people are reassured when nurses in white coats come towards them.

Carole removes the electrodes, wipes off the jelly, and winds up the cables. Jake closes the doors to the monitors above the bed. He finds the mouthguard on the pillow by the screaming inductee's head and puts it into the disinfectant jar on his trolley. He waits for a gap in the screaming.

'There's nothing to be afraid of,' he says quietly, and smiles. 'Nobody's going to hurt you.'

This is what he always tells the screamers, and it's a lie. There's EAT to be afraid of, and Mr Wilson downstairs is going to hurt them. But this screamer believes him, like many, and stops. He twists his head from side to side and his eyes roll. His wrists strain against the straps.

Carole pats his ankle. 'You'll be fine, Mr Goldsteen. Just fine.'

'Goldstein,' he tells her. 'The name is Goldstein.'

'Right.' She checks his label. 'Right . . . My mistake, Mr Goldstein.'

If she remembers his particulars right, five-three-six Goldstein is a hit-and-run driver.

They leave him. Outside in the corridor Mr Wilson's two officers are just going in to four-four-three Fraser.

'Bruising can take hours,' Jake mutters. 'And it's the only answer. Beech was already injected when you prepped him. You simply didn't see the puncture.'

Carole considers this possibility, thoughtfully smoothing the thin plastic gloves on her broad black hands. 'I *might* have missed it . . .'

Jake leans forward. 'You'll say you could have missed it?'

She snaps the plastic. 'If Beech was hit all that time before, how come he was awake when Dr Landon got to him?'

'You'll tell the chief inspector you could have missed it?'

'I'll tell him. But I still don't see how – '

'We'll leave what Peck gave him to the experts. Chances are they've found it in the post-mortem.'

'All this needs for Dr Landon to have missed the puncture too.'

'No problem, lovey. If you did, why not her?'

The two officers come back out into the corridor, bringing four-four-three Fraser with them. It never takes them long, getting inductees off their beds and downstairs and into their EAT rooms. Four-four-three Fraser has his shirt on and he's carrying his socks and shoes. Technically, with his thresholding over, he isn't an inductee any more, he's an inmate.

Carole remembers the man they've just left. 'Get back soon for five-three-six Goldstein,' she tells the officers. 'He's not happy.'

She and Jake go into the next thresholding room, where the man on the bed is still unconscious, but his signs on the screens are good. He stays that way as they carry out the necessary procedures. Before she leaves Carole feels his pulse.

His screens have been disconnected now, and closed off, and she likes to be certain.

His heartbeat's strong and steady. She leaves it to the officers to wake him. Usually a word or two does it, but once in a while they have to call Dr Landon. Carole doesn't like waking inmates, not for what they're on their way to downstairs. The principle, with which she agrees, is one thing, the practice quite another.

'Peck got here very quickly, don't you think?' Jake asks her outside the thresholding room. 'When I rang for him – as if he was expecting it?'

Carole sighs. For Jake this is all a game. She doesn't think he killed Beech but he might have, and in any case he doesn't blame who did. He'll work with them, shake their hand. She isn't like that . . . She thinks back, remembering Beech's hairy arms. She wants to have been wrong about the injection, but could she have been? And Dr Landon too? Could they both have missed it?

fourteen

By the time Alec had got back from his tour of Punishments the secretary, Daphne Tilder, had arrived and, presumably moved on by Frank, was settling at a makeshift desk in Nurse Landon's office. He leaned in through the open door, observed her indignant banging at drawers and papers, introduced himself, and apologized for having taken over her room. She was an elderly woman in a woolly lavender suit, very proper and put-upon by the disruption, with fluffy blue-white hair and gold-rimmed half-glasses, not at all his idea of a Daphne. He made what peace he could and went down the passage.

Frank was busy typing up his tape of Nurse Serote's interview. Padmore looked up from the computer screen.

'How far back should I go, Chief Inspector?'

'As far as it takes. You're our best hope, laddie. Just remember that.'

He sat down at his desk. The mug of coffee Frank had brought him was still there, cold now and scummy. He looked for somewhere to put it but nothing seemed suitable so he left it where it was. Not that the desk was exactly cluttered – a telephone, a plastic holder for pens and paper-clips left over from the secretary, a lamp, a writing pad, a small, depressingly small stack of papers relating to the case. Alec sorted through them. Dr Peck's report, the Manchester officer's report, young Padmore's typed-up version of the

Peggy Landon interview, this morning's report from forensics, and the Beech post-mortem. It wasn't much.

His empty desk reminded him of the mess on Peggy Landon's. That photograph of her father in a leather frame. The ophthalmoscope. The swimming cap . . . She hadn't said she swam. Presumably there was a pool somewhere in the City. They hadn't talked about it, but why should they? He imagined her swimming and thought she might be good at it. Her legs were thick, but not enough to matter. He imagined her short dark hair slicked close to her head and her face with the make-up washed off.

A photo of a father, but none of a boyfriend. Since she wasn't gay that usually meant no boyfriend, or else too many to register. She didn't look easy, but they often didn't. He didn't think she was, though. Still, there was the acting and actresses were easy. Were supposed to be easy. He flicked through her interview, read random answers. This wasn't a woman who was easy.

He frowned. They hadn't talked about her father, either, and they should have. There wasn't a decent motive in this case yet, and relatives were important. The photo wasn't recent so the father was gone away or dead. A wild thought – maybe Beech had in some way been responsible?

Peggy Landon a murderer? He'd told Frank she didn't have it in her. Didn't have the capacity. She was, in the best sense, ordinary. Not all that virtuous, but not evil either. Tough – she was working here, for God's sake – but not uncaring. Serious, but with a sense of humour. It all added up to a professional: her job would be too important to her for her to risk it. He stared at the interview typescript, his eyes unfocused. Murder was excessive, and Peggy Landon was moderate. Ordinary. He used the word again, ordinary, and didn't like it.

He knew what the trouble was: she hadn't been worried enough. An ordinary person being interviewed about a murder is anxious. She'd been too confident, as if she knew something. Maybe she knew who the murderer was . . . He flung down the thin sheaf of papers. This was ridiculous – he hadn't even interviewed all the suspects yet.

'Frank?' It was well after nine now. 'Frank, go and have a look for that porter, will you? Wilks, or whatever. Hurry him along for me.'

As Frank pushed back his chair there was a knock on the door. He grunted.

'Talk of the devil . . .' He raised his voice. 'Don't just stand there. Let's be having you.'

The door opened, revealing Daphne Tilder, clearly unamused by her summons.

Alec stood. Basically he didn't care how unamused she was, but he didn't need enemies. For the second time, he apologized. 'I'm sorry. We were expecting someone else. Can I help you?'

She fingered her pearls. 'The director will see you now, Chief Inspector.'

Angered at this office boy treatment, he decided not to understand, and tilted his head as if favouring a good ear. 'The director?'

'Dr Mellish.' In a who else, for heaven's sake? tone of voice. 'He's ready to see you now.'

'Ah.' How bloody nice of him. 'Aye, well . . . will you thank Dr Mellish very kindly and tell him I'll be in to see him in a wee while? I'll try not to keep him waiting, but there's a thing or two I have to see to first. I – '

'Dr Mellish is just back from the USA. He has a very crowded diary. He'd be with the governor at this minute if Mr Ransome hadn't suddenly been called away.'

A second choice for the nine fifteen slot, Alec was unrepentant. 'Oh, I expect he'll fit me in,' he said easily.

Defeated, Daphne turned to go. Then she remembered something, a small retaliation. 'Typing paper, Chief Inspector. If you'd be so good? In the top drawer of your desk?'

Her desk, really. Oh, the inconvenience . . .

'Of course.'

She came forward, they discussed how much she wanted, and she ended up taking the whole box. Meanwhile Frank, behind her, escaped down the passage in search of Granny Porter. She clasped the box to her chest, gasping discreetly at its weight. Daphne Tilder played frail and was steel with phosphor-bronze bearings.

Alec humoured her to the door, closing it thankfully behind her. Padmore looked up from his keyboard.

'I'm back three years, Chief Inspector. This man has a busy record.'

'I knew he would.'

'His name crops up in dozens of investigations, but he's never been inside.'

'Aye. There's always villains like that.'

Padmore pushed his spectacles up the bridge of his nose. 'And now he never will be.'

This worried him. He peered at the screen, frowning. A man who'd broken every rule in the book . . . Alec went back to his desk. Clearly Padmore felt that by getting himself murdered Beech had cheated justice. It was another of his crimes.

Frank, who'd been gone hardly two minutes, returned with Granny Porter. The old man was panting from the stairs. He sat down, uninvited, in front of Alec's desk, took the grey dog-end from behind his ear, eyed Alec, and put it back.

'I was in the fucking nurses' room,' he said. 'I was sweeping up. I didn't see nothing.'

Alec switched on his recorder, spoke the lead-in, took out his pen, opened his notebook. 'Let's take it from the beginning, shall we?'

They took it from the beginning, by which Alec meant Granny's very first sight of Beech, over at Inductions.

'Tell me, Granny Porter . . .' He'd decided on the nickname, for its lack of side. The interview was in its early, friendly stages. '. . . Tell me, Granny Porter, did you recognize Beech? Did you know who he was?'

Granny was startled. The question was clearly unexpected. He took off his boater and considered its frayed rim while he waited for the safe answer to occur to him. It finally did. 'His name was on the list, wasn't it?'

'You always read the list?'

'I get give me own. It's me job, innit?'

'So you knew who he was.'

'I told you, his name was on the list. Can't be many Albert fucking Beeches.' He looked up. 'Wouldn't of recognized him, though. Not under all them fucking whiskers.'

'You'd known him, then? Met him before?'

Granny returned to his boater. He'd said too much. Alec watched his lips move silently as he cursed himself.

'Worked for him, mebbe?' Alec prompted.

Crinkles of straw were being pulled from the rim. 'In a manner of speaking.'

'I'm afraid I didn't hear that.'

'I fucking said, in a manner of fucking speaking.'

'Worked for him? When would that have been?'

'Years ago. Down in the Smoke. Ten years, at least. More like twenty. Look – I know you sods. Why're you doing this? You've got all this on your fucking computer.'

Alec nodded. They did indeed, but their computer was otherwise engaged. 'Tell me about Wishbone,' he said.

He liked these switches but this one didn't work. Granny's confusion was genuine. Either that or he'd missed a dazzling career in the movies.

'What sort of fucking question's that?' he demanded. 'Tell you about a fucking wishbone? What sort of question's that?'

'Not *a* wishbone,' Alec persisted. 'Just Wishbone.'

'And that's supposed to be better?'

'Could it be a racehorse?'

'Could it be a racehorse? You tell me, mate. Wouldn't put

207

tuppence on it, if it was. Supposed to grant your wish, aren't they? Never did for me. Not fucking once. As a kid, that is. Never tried since.'

Alec was intrigued. These replies had implications. 'It was the word Beech said, wasn't it?'

'When was this, then? Lucky said all sorts of things.'

Alec noticed the *Lucky*, let it pass. 'In the thresholding room. Just before Nurse Landon injected him.'

'New one on me. Why would he say a thing like that?'

Alec sighed. Either the other three suspects were lying or Granny Porter was deaf, and he knew which of those he'd choose. But it did mean that if Granny Porter was the murderer, and if he was deaf, then Wishbone was irrelevant.

Over by his typewriter, Frank murmured, 'Cup of coffee, Mr Wilks?'

Granny, his eyes still on Alec, didn't answer. Alec sighed again and drew boxes on his page. If Wishbone was irrelevant, Padmore was wasting his time. He should be searching Granny's career for the Beech connection. But Wishbone was all they had. Wishbone *couldn't* be irrelevant.

'Just now you called Beech *Lucky*. Why was that?'

'It's his fucking name. It was his name. Everybody called him it.'

'What exactly was this work you did for him?'

'I was his bag-man. On the legit side. I collected from his clubs. Every night I collected from his clubs.'

'Nothing else?'

'Nothing else.'

'You've served a lot of porridge, Granny – '

'Too fucking right, I have. Never from my work with Lucky, though. If I'd stayed on with Lucky, maybe I'd of done a bit fucking better.'

'Why didn't you? Why didn't you stay on with Lucky?'

'We . . . had a disagreement.' Granny shut down, retreated to his boater. 'We had a disagreement.'

Alec tapped his pencil thoughtfully. The question had been

208

too abrupt. Sailing along, and now this – they'd get no more this time round on the subject of Beech and Granny Porter's 'disagreement'. He glanced at Frank, who shook his head dubiously. Admittedly the motive here was thin – ten years ago or twenty, according to the old man (couldn't be twenty; Beech wasn't old enough) – but perhaps he should put Padmore on to this 'disagreement'.

'You brought Beech over from Inductions,' he said, 'and you helped Nurse Serote transfer him to the bed in number five thresholding room. What did you do then?'

'Fetched the next. And the fucking next.'

'So when did you see Beech again?'

'I was cleaning up his room. Then that fucking poofter bashed into me and – '

'Wait a minute. Cleaning up his room – what does that mean? Do you always clean up inductees' rooms?'

'Clean them. Bit of dusting.' He looked up. 'Like I said, it's me job, innit?'

'So you weren't there for any other reason?'

'I was cleaning his fucking room. Same thing with them all. Look – I didn't even do him first . . . And I can prove it. Feller next door, there's an acorn on his table. A fucking acorn. And how did that get there? Ask around, Guv'nor. And how do I know if I didn't fucking find it? I was there. An acorn, for Christ's sake.'

Alec wrote the word in his notebook. It didn't help. First Wishbone, and now an acorn. It sounded genuine enough, but it didn't help.

'So you were in Beech's room when Nurse Landon gave him his thresholding injection. Did anything happen? Anything unusual?'

'He woke up.'

'But he didn't say anything.'

'Nah. Missy Landon stuck him too fucking quick.'

'I see. What then?'

'She moved on to the next room along.'

'And you?'

'I buggered off.' He put on his hat, tapped it down. He was oddly jaunty. 'I was in the nurses' room. I was sweeping up.'

'Didn't Charge Nurse Landon tell you to see to the soap dispensers in the washroom?'

'Maybe she did.'

Alec waited but nothing else came. He might have ignored her. Granny Porter was an independent soul. 'So you were in the nurses' room all the time?'

'All what time?'

'From then until Dr Peck was called.'

'I was sweeping up.'

'That's over an hour.'

'I was sweeping up.' Granny's confidence faltered. 'Maybe I sat down a bit. Parked me bum.'

Alec could imagine it. 'But you didn't leave the nurses' room.'

'Nah. I was there, Guv'nor. I was there. All the time.'

He seemed needlessly positive. Alec wondered where he'd really been, then decided that was wishful thinking. Sometimes people were positive because they were positive. Granny could well not know that by locating himself in the nurses' room, with Jake de Carteret outside in the dispensary, he'd given himself the perfect alibi.

'Have you ever taken drugs, Granny Porter?'

'What sort of question's that?' The old man looked at him sideways. 'Sniffed a bit of coke, once. Gave me the trots.'

'I mean heroin. Something like that.'

'You mean shot up? Fuck me, you're as bad as Mr Ransome. No, I never shot up, and no more did Lucky. He'd got more sense. He sold the stuff, didn't he? He saw what it did.'

Alec was puzzled. 'The governor's accused you of taking heroin?'

'Not me. Lucky. Just now, over at Inductions. Me, I can't

210

abide fucking needles. Can't look. Fainted dead away, one time, back in me army days, and that was from seeing the feller in front.'

Alec closed his notebook. A roundabout approach, but he'd got his answer. If Beech had been killed by means of a hypodermic syringe, then someone with a needle phobia was an unlikely culprit . . . It was possible, of course, that the entire Granny Porter persona was a performance – it was overdone enough – but Alec wasn't counting on it. All in all, his favourite suspect had turned out to be less than satisfactory.

And as for what Mr Ransome had been up to, over in Inductions . . . an investigation of his own, for God's sake?

Frank Grove cleared his throat noisily. 'Would you say this Wishbone sounds like a code-name for a job, Mr Wilks?'

Granny heard, but kept his eyes on the Chief Inspector. 'A code-name?' He was an old hand – these side questions were meant to confuse you.

'That's right,' Frank said. 'The sort of thing a villain like Beech might come up with. For a criminal enterprise, you understand.'

'Why's he asking me, Inspector? The stuff I done for Lucky was legit. I told you. Bag-man, that sort of thing. What'd I want with fucking code-names?'

'That wasn't what I asked you, Mr Wilks.' Frank yawned menacingly, tilted his chair and stretched his beefy arms. 'It's just that, working for him like you say you did, I thought you might have heard something. Might want to help. As a law-abiding citizen.'

Granny was indignant. 'Course I worked for him,' he told Alec. 'Is your sergeant calling me a liar?' Alec observed him mildly, not answering. Eventually Granny conceded. 'Can't remember no fucking code-names. Lucky wasn't like that. He called things what they were. Called a spade a bloody shovel.'

Alec pushed his chair back. Frank had clasped his hands

behind his head and was staring at the ceiling, unbothered. The code-name idea had never been more than a straw to clutch at.

'Thank you for your time, Mr Wilks. You've been a great help.' Which, in a negative sense, was true. 'I won't keep you any longer.'

The old man untangled his feet from the legs of his chair. 'I can go, then?'

'You may. Not too far, though. I may need another word. Not outside Justice City.'

'Do me a favour.' He got up stiffly, in stages. 'What the fuck would I want with Outside?'

Get yourself a shave and some decent clothes, Alec thought. 'Close the door behind you,' he told Granny Porter.

After Granny Porter had left a silence ensued, broken only by Padmore at his keyboard. Alec glared at his notebook, at the boxes and *acorn*. The theatricality of this case offended him. It was all tricks. Only four suspects, and none of them had done it. And if Wishbone wasn't a code-word, what the hell was it?

'Time I got the director over with,' he said.

At least Granny Porter had worked for Beech, which was half-way to a motive. On his way out he paused, came close to cancelling Wishbone and putting young Padmore on to Granny Porter's past, and his and the dead man's disagreement. That he didn't was mostly Frank's fault. He couldn't face Frank's silent pity.

He went along the corridor to Daphne Tilder. If a man had a secretary it was sensible to use her.

'I'd like to see Dr Mellish now, if that's convenient.'

Daphne picked up the telephone. He was surprised to see Peggy Landon in the room, stooping over her desk. He had a question for her, but he'd expected her to be tied up downstairs with the thresholding till after ten.

'Nurse Landon – a word, if you please?'

She straightened. 'I really can't stop. I was missing one of my report sheets.' She had it in her hand. 'Jake and Carole are waiting for me.'

'Just one question.' He needed to know. 'It won't take a moment.'

She leaned against her desk, irritated. He said, 'Yesterday morning, after the first batch of inductees, when you left Nurse Serote in the control room, you went straight down to Captain Wilson?'

'More or less.'

'More or less?'

She glanced impatiently at her watch. 'I stopped off to go to the toilet, if you must know.'

'Where the porter was seeing to the soap dispensers?'

She hesitated. 'As a matter of fact, he wasn't. At least, I didn't see him . . . He'd have had plenty of time to do it and go, of course.'

'Of course.'

'Why?' In spite of her hurry she was intrigued. 'Is he saying something different?'

He stood to one side. 'I won't keep you, Nurse Landon.'

She smiled and so did he. There were things he couldn't tell her. She passed him and went downstairs, and he watched her, feeling quite unreasonably cheerful: her answers had been exactly right.

She wasn't a fool, of course. She knew that he'd been down in Punishments and that, talking to Captain Wilson, he'd have been bound to come up with the ten-minute discrepancy. But she'd got the porter's absence right too, and he believed her. Admittedly she hadn't mentioned her visit to the toilet earlier, but why should she? It wasn't the sort of thing you —

'Chief Inspector? Chief Inspector Duncan?' Daphne was hissing at him, one hand over the telephone mouthpiece. 'Chief Inspector, Dr Mellish has the governor with him just at present. He says could you please — '

'That's fine, Miss Tilder. Absolutely fine. I'll have a chance to see them both, then. No bother at all.'

He beamed at her and strode away before she could protest, gave the director's closed door a token couple of taps, and went straight in. Dr Mellish was at his desk, Mr Ransome stood by the window, sheets of computer print-out in his hand.

The director surprised Alec – he'd expected someone niggardly (Why? From his name? From his job? From something Peggy Landon said?), not this bulky expansive person. But his attention was quickly drawn to the news-papers scattered beneath the brilliant lamp on Dr Mellish's desk. He tried briefly to read the upside-down headlines, then dragged his gaze away. There was also on the desk a shiny new edition of Burton's *Pharmacological Yearbook*.

'Dr Mellish? My name is Duncan. Chief Inspector Duncan of Merseyside CID. I'm investigating yesterday's murder in your department. I believe you wanted to see me.' He turned to the governor. 'Good morning, Mr Ransome.'

The courtesies over, he went further into the room and closed the door behind himself. 'So far, Dr Mellish, I'm afraid I have little to report. I've talked to all the main suspects, and – '

'Sit down, Chief Inspector. Seat yourself . . .' Dr Mellish indicated the chair in front of his desk. His tone was warm but his gesture was a command. 'The governor and I have been discussing the newspaper coverage so far.'

Alec evaded the chair, joined Mr Ransome by the window. 'The tabloids are up to their tricks, I suppose.' From this angle he could see jokey headlines. 'They've nothing to go on but gossip, so – '

'It's their general attitude that concerns us, Chief Inspector. Anything that gives a clue as to how they'll react once the truth gets out.'

'I'd expect them to be friendly, sir. After all, it was the popular press that led the original campaign for – '

'They feed on outrage, man. Now they've got Justice City they could just as well turn on it.'

Alec thought that if he went on not being allowed to finish a remark he could easily get to dislike Dr Mellish. 'Aye, sir. I'm sure you're right. Luckily that's not my problem. I've got a murder to investigate, and – '

'Of course you have. Of course you have. And how's it going?'

Governor Ransome, always observant, a whizz at personnel relations, intervened. 'The Chief Inspector's had less than twenty-four hours, Iain. I don't think we can expect – '

'I'd look at the porter, if I were you, Chief Inspector. He's the one with the criminal record.'

Alec reminded himself that he was a public servant. And at least the director interrupted without fear or favour. 'Thank you very much, sir. I'll bear that in mind . . .' He paused. 'I believe the governor's more inclined towards the black nurse. Carole Serote.'

Dr Mellish frowned. 'Serote? What *are* you thinking of, Digby? Nurses don't kill people.'

'I was thinking of the dead man's crimes, Iain. The possibility of a racial motive.'

The lamp on the director's desk flickered, dimmed, then picked up strength. Dr Mellish glanced at his watch.

'Aha. Eleven o'clock . . . EAT, Chief Inspector. When it switches in it causes what I believe is called a power surge.'

Now he thought about it, Alec wasn't surprised. The iron mouths had looked hungry. He closed his eyes.

After that he changed the subject. 'What *is* the newspapers' general attitude?'

Dr Mellish poked his desk top. 'Facetious. Not helpful. Only to be expected, given the cover story.' He glanced sideways, not quite at Mr Ransome. 'Makes my people look like fools.'

A studied silence descended. Alec retreated to the door, his eyes discreetly observing the pattern of the carpet. He'd done his duty by the director and there were feuds here he didn't need. 'I'll be on my way then, Director. Was there anything in particular you wanted to – '

'Only this, Chief Inspector. I have a small team here and I trust them completely. I have every faith in them. I wanted you to know that. It was unfortunate, my being out of the country, but it really made no difference. No difference at all.'

'No, sir.' It was an adroit speech. The governor would be impressed. It exonerated everybody, but particularly the speaker. 'I'll be on my way, then.'

Alec nodded to Mr Ransome, went out, closed the door . . . and stood for a moment in the passage, stock still. He'd recognized the print-out in Mr Ransome's hand. He'd thought before that it was familiar, and now he realized it was that morning's post-mortem report on Beech from Manchester. As governor here, Mr Ransome would naturally have received a copy – the point for Alec was that it made sense of Mr Ransome's visit to Inductions. With an illegal drug, probably self-administered, present in the dead man's bloodstream, Mr Ransome would want to know when it had got there – while Beech was still in Manchester's care or after he'd been signed over to Justice City. The tiny quantity, no more than a residue, seemed to rule out the latter possibility, but Mr Ransome would want to make certain.

The only difficulty with this explanation was that if – as seemed likely from the PM print-out in the governor's hand and the pharmacology yearbook on Dr Mellish's desk – the two men had been discussing the drug found in Beech's bloodstream, why had Dr Mellish told Alec they'd been talking about the newspapers?

As Alec dithered in the passage Nurse Serote came up the stairs from the foyer at the far end. He didn't move. He was thinking that he ought to have a word with Dr Peck. The Manchester inspector had already talked to him but . . . And then again, he was remembering the power surge and now there were the iron mouths screaming.

'Chief Inspector?'

He snapped out of his trance. 'Nurse Serote. I'm sorry. I was miles away.'

'You were counting your blessings . . .' She touched his arm. 'You never heard that, Chief Inspector?'

'Counting my . . .?' He retreated from her. 'Of course I have. The phrase, that is.'

'I've embarrassed you. Well, when I was dreaming, my mother'd say to me, "You counting your blessings, Carole?" I never was.'

'Nor was I.' He shrugged ruefully. His mother had been altogether a tighter soul. 'I was counting my problems, I reckon.' He looked down at her. 'So? You wanted a word with me?'

She picked up on his formality, smoothed out the bib of her apron. 'Thing is, Chief Inspector, I've been thinking. You remember you said like I should tell you if I thought of anything . . . Well, Jake and I have been thinking, and – '

A sudden shout came from inside Alec's incident room. The door opened and Frank hurried out. He slithered to a halt.

'Chief – I was just coming for you.'

'Aye. Well, I'm just having a wee talk with Nurse Serote here, and – '

'It's in the computer, Chief – what we're looking for. Young Padmore's found it.'

Alec took a step towards him, hesitated. Nurse Serote spotted it. 'Let's talk later, Chief Inspector. Mine can keep. It really isn't all that much.'

Alec hesitated again, saw Frank's excitement, gave in to his own. 'Later, Nurse. I'll not forget. And thank you.'

He left her. In the office Padmore was at his keyboard, reaching for a paper from the printer. He handed it to Alec.

'It's eight years back, sir.' His glasses were crooked, his hands shaking. 'Comes from a robbery investigation. London area, up in Hendon. Beech was involved, but they never

217

pinned it on him. Never pinned anything on him . . . Anyway, there's this interview with one of his heavies – '

Alec read the fragment of transcript:

Insp.M. It's the Friday night I'm talking about, Chas. The Friday.

C.L. I heard you. Lucky was nowhere near. Over Clapham way that night. Strictly business. Some things Lucky sees to himself. Wishbone's one of them.

Insp.M. Wishbone?

C.L. Nom de bloody plume, Mr Miller. You know how it is.

Insp.M. Talking drugs, are we?

C.L. Talking business, Mr Miller. Just business.

Insp.M. Don't suppose this Mr Wishbone would come forward, would he?

C.L. Wishbone? Who's Wishbone? I never said a word.

Insp.M. But you did, Chas. I've got it here in my book. You said –

C.L. Look, Mr Miller – forget it. If Lucky ever got to hear I'd been shooting off my mouth, he'd . . . But I'll tell you this for nothing – if it's Friday night you're asking about, you're wasting your bloody time. Take it from me, Mr Miller – Lucky was miles away. Like I said, Clapham. South of the river.

Alec looked for a second sheet. 'Is this all there is?'

'Inspector Miller was the investigating officer,' Padmore told him. 'And C.L. stands for Charles Long. That's Chas for short.'

'I thought it might be. Is this all there is?'

Padmore wilted. 'It's all I've found so far, sir . . .'

'This Miller was investigating a Hendon robbery, Chief,' Frank put in. 'The Clapham yarn won't have seemed much of a goer. It's a start for us, though, At least we know this Wishbone's a person.'

'We do indeed.' Alec pulled himself together. 'I'm sorry.

218

Well done, Peter. Eight years ago, you say? You've done a fine job.'

Padmore was cheered. 'They were only handwritten notes, sir. We're lucky someone bothered to key them in.' He looked from Alec to Frank, saw an opportunity to elaborate. 'You see, sir, he could perfectly well have photo-scanned them as they were, stored them just as a picture. It's a great time saver. But then individual characters never enter the memory, only a general file description . . . That way my search would have missed Wishbone altogether. You see what I mean? It would have been in the file but not individually in the memory. That's the snag with photo-scanning, of course. It's very limited in its usefulness. There isn't always time, though, for – '

'Great.' Alec had been off again, thinking about drugs, and Wishbone, and their connection with Justice City. Now: 'That's really great. So what's Inspector Miller doing these days? Did he follow up, maybe unofficially, on the Clapham alibi? And where's this Chas Long? I need a word.' He took Padmore's eager upturned face in his hands and turned it back to the computer screen. 'And I need it yesterday.'

Inspector Miller proved easy. If Padmore minded Alec's bold black grasp he didn't show it. Taking Miller's first name and service number from the interview record, he was immediately able to call up the inspector's retirement date, due to ill health, three years later, and his death in Hammersmith Hospital, presumably due to the same ill health, eighteen months after that. He left a widow and two sons, now – Padmore did the sum – now fourteen and twelve.

Chas Long was less obliging. He made the one brief appearance in the records of the Hendon robbery investigation, he wasn't charged, and he disappeared. The name wasn't unusual, eight years had intervened, and Padmore settled in for a lengthy search.

Around noon Alec rang May's office. She was in court and they didn't know when she'd be back.

fifteen

It's one fifteen and Peggy Landon's coming up in the lift after delivering the morning's second batch of thresholding profiles to Mr Wilson. She isn't sorry to be leaving Punishments. Alec had been wrong about the silence there: despite state of the art sound-proofing, EAT creates acoustical unease in the corridors, a pressure on the ears that Peggy finds troublesome. On her visits when it's in operation she never stays longer than she has to.

Peggy's in a good mood. Her stance in the lift shows it: shoulders back, head high, welcoming her life. It's a fine day outside, sunshine after yesterday's depressing rain, the Herr Direktor's just phoned through to say he's lunching with the Governor when she'd feared he would expect to lunch with her, before that she'd dealt with the chief inspector's questions easily, and now she's looking forward to tonight's *Hedda* rehearsal. She's promised the director she'll be there and he isn't holding last night's defection against her. He can't afford to. He's always telling her, and she believes him, that there's no one else in Justice City who could possibly play the part.

He's working round to getting her to agree to a little horizontal exercise, of course. She believes this too, and it's less flattering, but she doesn't let it spoil the glow his words give her. They confirm the feeling she has in rehearsal, the feeling that she's getting Hedda right.

Looking at her, she probably is. She could with advantage be taller, but in a wig, and with high heels under a period long skirt, this will matter less. Her only difficulty (which she hasn't thought of) is that by the time of the performance she may not be available.

The lift doors open – the ride is only up one floor, far shorter than it's taken to tell – and she strides out into the corridor, along past the control room and through into the foyer. There she checks. Chief Inspector Duncan is at the foot of the stairs, talking to Carole. It's easy to see what's happened. Their attitudes tell it exactly: the chief inspector, still leaning towards the outside doors, has been stopped by Carole, who leans also, her hand almost, not quite, on his arm. The chief inspector, Peggy thinks, is a man who would rather not be touched.

She listens. '. . . could be important. Thank you very much.' His voice. 'What made you change your mind?'

'I haven't. Not really.' Carole smoothes her apron. 'Thing is though, a little mark like that's easy to miss and it doesn't do to be too certain.'

'I see.' He notices Peggy and raises a hand, which she acknowledges. 'And the later bruising?'

'Sometimes it doesn't show for hours, Chief Inspector. There's no rule.'

'Aye . . . Well. I'm very grateful.' He doesn't look grateful. Peggy understands his problem. If Carole's saying she might have missed a needle puncture mark when Beech arrived from Inductions, then that's thrown his case wide open. It was hopeless before: now it's global. She approaches them.

Carole and the chief inspector are parting but he suddenly calls her back. 'Nurse Serote – one more question. Do you remember seeing an acorn in any of the thresholding rooms?'

Peggy checks again – she remembers that acorn, the man in the room next to Beech had it, and she wonders how on earth the chief inspector's got to hear of it.

Carole remembers it too. 'An acorn, Chief Inspector? I

surely do.' Her smile, in this case at the recollection, is what Peggy likes best about her. It's a flower opening. It's the sun between clouds. 'One of the inductees had it. Peters... Petersfield, some name like that. He had it in his hand. Dr Landon took it from him. I think she put it on the table.'

'That's right.' Peggy decides she's obviously listening, so she might as well contribute. She walks forward, joins them at the foot of the stairs. 'I put it on the table. I felt sorry for him. He'd brought it so far, I thought he should have it when he went downstairs.'

'And did he?'

'I've no idea. I'm never around when Mr Wilson's men come for them.'

The chief inspector turns to Carole. 'And did he?'

She shrugs. 'By then we had a dead man on our hands. I guess I wasn't paying too much attention.'

There's an awkward pause. Peggy sees she can take the heat off a junior colleague and at the same time satisfy her curiosity. 'Is this acorn important, Chief Inspector?'

'I don't know.' He smiles. 'Probably not.' He turns back to Carole. 'Thank you for your help, Nurse. Even the smallest thing – we never know what it may add up to.'

She sees she's being dismissed, and goes.

His smile is very charming. Very sexy. There's been sexy black men around in Peggy's life, but until yesterday never to talk to. Never close up. In addition to which, this one's from Outside yet he's almost City. He fascinates her. He makes her wonder if perhaps a life in both might not be possible. She's happy in the City, of course she is, and of course this is her world and it's where she belongs, but sometimes, just sometimes, its walls close round her, cracking her heart and bones.

She's been half-planning to look in on Karl over in Research, to tell him thank-you for the good time he gave her last night at the City Bistro. Now, however, she doesn't think she will.

'If you're going to lunch, Chief Inspector, perhaps we could go together? The food's not bad in the staff canteen, but you need to know the pitfalls. If you like, I could advise you.'

He's surprised, but not displeased. She helps him to say yes. 'Unless it's unethical,' she suggests. 'Having lunch with a suspect.'

It isn't. 'Well, I *was* going to lunch, actually. . . That's very kind.'

She leads him through the grid of gates and covered walkways to the staff canteen. The wintry sun, already descending, casts long shadows, pillars, grilles, the low buildings of the library and education complex, creating a sombre, almost cloistered air. On a day like this, she thinks, Justice City is a good place to be.

They talk, their voices clear in the cold brightness. He says, 'Terrible thing, that IRA bomb.'

She hasn't heard about it and doesn't want to. She isn't political. Rapist or thief or IRA, in Justice City they're all the same, but she lets him explain, and then she's genuinely shocked. Attacking the healers is evil. Vile. And in the guise of a gift . . . vile. Living in Belfast, though, shouldn't people be more careful?

More careful? he says angrily. What sort of life would it be, trusting nobody?

She doesn't answer. It isn't her he's angry at.

In the canteen she reserves two chairs at a table by the windows, taking her white coat off and spreading it over them. Her coat does nothing for her. At the counter she steers him away from the lasagne and the moussaka, minced pussy-cat, she says, and they both have chips and glazed ham and pineapple. And coffee. He isn't a Jew, she notices, having read somewhere that there *are* black Jews. Not that she's bothered – Karl's probably a Jew, judging by his complexion and his prick, but she's never asked him. She avoids dessert and he takes the spotted dog and custard. They make a perfect pair.

There's no fuss at the check-out. He goes first, pays for his tray only, then she pays for hers. Their roles are clear, together but separate.

The window by their table looks out on asphalt tennis courts. On one of them a couple of brave staff members are whacking balls about. Beyond them, behind a row of trees, two sides of the square are filled in with low, two-storey LTI blocks behind their inner compound of electrified wire. The fourth side is occupied by the high blank wall of the covered swimming-pool, heated now only at weekends as a cost-cutting measure. Thus Justice City plays its part in government budget reductions.

Peggy looks around the canteen, waves at acquaintances, picks up her knife and fork. 'So . . .' She peers across at him and laughs. 'I'm not supposed to ask about your inquiry. What else is there to talk about?'

'The inquiry's boring. Tell me about yourself.'

Ask your bird to talk about herself. Christ, the oldest ploy. 'That's boring too.'

'Mebbe. I'll stop you if it is.'

That's a new twist, so she tells him the easy things, about her father's death, and her wanting to become a psychiatric nurse.

'You blamed yourself, of course.'

'I did then.' She remembers Karl. 'I don't any more.' She picks up her coffee mug. 'Your turn now.'

'Not yet. You said about becoming a psychiatric nurse. You didn't say about entering the prison service.'

'Of course not. That isn't so admirable.'

'Not admirable? I'd have thought it was very admirable.'

She tells herself this is a game. It started out, in the foyer, as a game. She doesn't go on at herself all the time about being a murderer, she's more useful things to think about, but that's what she is. And he's a policeman. But the point is, need that be so terrible?

She really likes him. 'I did it for the prospects.' Likes him enough to tell him the truth. 'Promotion requirements are easier. It's never admitted, but ... Well, look at me now. Outside, at my age, with my qualifications, I'd be wiping bottoms and handing round tranks. Here I virtually run the department.'

'You can't have known that when you joined.'

'I knew the odds were good ...' He wants to make her virtuous. She isn't virtuous. 'The leaflets talk about "unrivalled opportunities" and you get the message. It's a self-contained service — auxiliaries, nurses, doctors, the lot. I'm not saying standards are necessarily lower. I'm saying there's less fuss made about pieces of paper.'

He nods. 'All the same, not everybody gets to work in Justice City.'

'You're right. Some of the places I've seen ... You know, people outside talk about dealing with the violence in society. Mostly we don't deal with it — we simply move it into the prisons.' She pauses, frowning. What happened to the game? But if he asks a serious question then he gets a serious answer. 'What I do's violent. I admit that. But it's kept within bounds ... And it stops with incarceration. You've seen the long termers here.' She points through the window. 'You've been in the LTI blocks, haven't you? No punch-ups. No slashings. No buggery.'

He nods and she sits back, rests her case. He spears chips and eats them, watching her thoughtfully. She's not sure he's convinced and she wants him to be. This isn't like her harangue yesterday about not being a torturer. This is personal. She wants him to be convinced because he's a bit like Karl, though that sounds ridiculous, looking at the two men, but she wants him to be convinced because he's a ... because he's a weighty person. That's it. He's got a sexy smile and he's a weighty person.

'As for my job,' she says, 'I don't do it to keep tabloid readers happy.' Nor politicians, she thinks, remembering the Prime Minister whose speech writers let him say, *We understand too much and punish too little.* 'If you leave out retribution, Chief Inspector, sending men to jail's just social engineering. Judges need a moral context. They need retribution.' She's paraphrasing the governor's manual, but he won't have read it. 'The acceptance that wrong's been done. Call it penance if you like.'

He clears his throat. 'Isn't being sent to prison enough? Being sent away?' He breaks off, flings down his knife and fork. 'I'm sorry. . I'm badgering you . . . but I think about it, in my job, you know . . . and . . .'

'It would be enough for you,' she tells him. 'For me too.'

It's a tough answer, forcing him to recall, in contrast, the villains he's arrested. She's worked with them, read their crime sheets, listened to their troubles. Their troubles are status, and finding victims to brutalize, and prisons offer them both. He knows this as well as she.

He knows it. 'Aye,' he says, 'you're right . . .'

She reaches across the table and touches his hand. What happened to the game? She wants to comfort him, but she's not sure why he needs it. In due course she takes her hand away and he heaves the conversation into a different gear.

'It's pathetic,' he says, 'two law people talking nothing but shop.'

They find something else. She asks him about himself and he tells her about his childhood in Edinburgh. They talk about the Festival, and get round to plays, and *Hedda Gabler*, and he says he didn't know there was a theatre here. She tells him there isn't: the drama society records its shows on video, for transmission over the City's closed-circuit channel. In the summer they did a farce, now it's Ibsen. There'd be no use for a theatre — staffing ratios are so tight that enough officers are never off duty all at one time to make up a decent audience. But the TV channel's popular

226

and there's talent shows and all sorts, as well as films officers can write in for.

He eats his spotted dog. Eventually he says he was married once but he isn't any more. She asks him if he's got children. He tells her about his nephew, Jamie.

It's long after two now and they must both get back to work. She gathers up her coat. The canteen has a piano, a tea-stained upright, and as they leave they pass close by it. He pauses, plays a couple of bars with his left hand, a walking bass, enough to show her he can.

Two hours later, around four thirty, Jake de Carteret is in the communal kitchen on his floor of the unmarried men's staff quarters. As usual, he has it to himself, and this afternoon he's baking a birthday cake for Davey, whose shift in the motor pool runs till six. Davey shouldn't eat cake, he's trying to watch his figure, but what are birthdays for, for heaven's sake?

Jake is planning a towering chocolate edifice, with layers of coffee filling and coffee butter icing, and he works with one eye on the clock because he wants it to be a surprise. He's made an arrangement with one of the other kitchens on the block to store it in their fridge: Davey doesn't do much in the kitchen, but he's a terrible one for helping himself to cold beer at all hours.

Jake has been beating egg-whites for the last ten minutes. There's an electric beater in the drawer but he believes in the human touch. He says he can make egg-whites dance. Machine-beaten whites have no life in them.

Also, the ten minutes are an act of love.

Along the corridors prison officers bang in and out of their rooms. Four thirty is a shift change for some, and they're off to play squash or work out in the gym. Jake met Davey in the gym. He used to hang around the locker-room, for the tight briefs and the manly sweat, but now he never goes near the place. Hasn't done in nearly two years. He's promised

Davey. In any case, he doesn't want to. It's hard for Davey, the two of them having to live on a block where hunky men parade around at all hours *en déshabillé*, but Jake's never tempted. The old days were a constant hassle, God forbid he should ever return to them.

He tips his bowl, brings the whites into peaks. They dance for him. The blue enamel double boiler's on the stove, a present from his mother, already simmering, and he breaks a block of the darkest chocolate into it. French. The Swiss are the kings of milk chocolate, and possibly the Dutch, but only the French understand about plain. Sharp and smooth, bitter without being acidic. Never *sweet* . . . it's a national characteristic. *Toujours raffiné*. He prods the broken squares, helping them melt. Beside him the oven's preheating nicely.

In his and Davey's room across from the kitchen the telephone rings. Jake frowns, lowers the heat under the double boiler, gives the egg-whites a tweak, checks in his recipe book, wipes his hands on his apron, and goes to answer it.

'The de Carteret residence.'

'Jakey? It's me, love. Carole.'

La Serote? He's astonished. They've never spoken before, as far as he can remember, outside the House.

'And hail to thee too, blithe spirit.'

'Thing is, Jakey, I've been thinking, and I wanted to ask you . . .'

He waits, but she's died on him. Jakey . . . nobody, only she, ever calls him that, and only she when she wants something.

'So ask me.'

'It's about that acorn. Well, not really about that acorn. It's – '

'Acorn? Did you say *acorn*?'

'The Inspector asked me about it. The acorn Mr Petersfield had in his hand. You remember.'

'Petersen.' He does remember. 'The man's name was

228

Petersen. Unpaid child support. Six-six-three, I think his number was. And he did have an acorn.'

'That's what I said. And Dr Landon took it, and put it on the table, and I clean forgot it. Maybe Mr Petersfield got it back from the guards or maybe Granny scooped it up, but I've been thinking and I can't remember. All I know is, it wasn't there this morning.'

'I'm sure you're right.' Jake peers out at his double boiler. Did he leave enough water in it? 'So we won't be having an oak tree.'

'But the acorn got me thinking about the petals, and them I do remember. They wasn't there.' She's working up to something. 'When I found Beech dead the petals wasn't there.' She perorates triumphantly. Whatever it was, she seems to think she's proved it.

'Petals? You're going to have to help me.'

'Petals. Off the plastic flowers. You bashed into him, man, and – '

'He was just inside the door.' He's excited. He's caught up with her. 'And if the petals weren't there when we found Beech, and they weren't, then Granny must have swept them up. And he didn't sweep them up there and then because Herself sent him off on another job, so he must have done it later. In which case . . . in which case he was in Beech's room again between when we left him and when we found him dead. In which case – '

'In which case, maybe he saw something.'

'In which case, lovey mine, maybe he dotted our Albert.'

There's a silence between them. At her end, in the background, he hears children arguing.

Finally she says, 'I asked him that straight out. This morning. He said he didn't.'

'What else? You wouldn't expect him to – '

'I believed him. When he said he didn't he said it . . . you know . . . he said it *well*. I believed him.'

Jake has to admit he too had gone off Granny as the killer.

It would be tidy, though. Dr Peck was never more than a last resort.

'Have you told our gorgeous chief inspector?'

'About the petals? I wanted to talk to you first. Had they really gone . . . Besides, he's talked to Granny. What if he already knows?'

'They really had gone. I remember the room exactly. You standing by the bed. Beech's shoes on the floor under it. No petals. Not a single bloody petal . . . It's not up to us, lovey, whether he knows already. Tell him again. It can't do any harm.'

'Tell him now?'

'It can't do any harm.'

'I got kids to see to. Rachel's asked in friends.'

'Call him up. He's in Terrible Tilder's room.'

'Would *you*? I bothered him once already.'

'If you really want me to.' Jake's delighted. He's been feeling left out. 'I'll let you know what happens. What he says.'

'Granny was in Beech's room again, Jakey. No one else could have swept them up. He must have seen something.'

'I'll tell him. Leave it to me. Good luck with the tea party.'

He rings off and hurries back into the kitchen. Chief Inspector Gorgeous may take time, and he doesn't want the cake hanging over him. It's got to be cooked before Davey gets back. He's already creamed the butter and sugar and stirred in the flour and his secret ingredient, a generous pinch of ginger. Now he adds the chocolate, and a little milk, then folds in the beaten whites. Into the lined tin and it's ready for the oven. The heat gusts out when he opens the door.

He pulls on bunny rabbit oven gloves, places the tin reverently in the centre of the centre shelf, and closes the door with hardly a click. He stands for a moment, taking off the gloves and looking in through the oven's window, then he goes back into the bedroom, bed-sitting-room really, looks up Daphne Tilder's number in the City directory, and dials.

The telephone rings and rings. It's four forty-five and everyone's gone home. That's the police for you — can't even make it nine to five. Nobody answers and he gives up, disappointed. He'll see the chief inspector in the morning.

sixteen

Alec Duncan got back from his lunch with Nurse Landon feeling heartened. They had a line on Wishbone now and all they had to do was reel it in. Wishbone meant drugs, and drugs were a motive for murder any day. Add drugs to the murder profile and you were looking for a different sort of person. Sly. Cynical. Streetwise. Never Nurse Serote and probably not Granny Porter. A de Carteret sort of person.

Frank had lunched on his good lady's sandwiches, over a wad of papers just in from Manchester. Padmore had been in the canteen somewhere, but now he was back at his computer. Neither man shared Alec's good spirits. Chas Long had fallen off the edge of the earth, the police earth at any rate, and the wad of Manchester papers was less than helpful. Requisition forms for staff, equipment, and office space, so that Justice City could bill the county police authority; an application from Beech's next of kin for visiting privileges; a copy of Home Office regulations relating to deaths from unnatural causes while in custody; and a forensic report on the plastic gloves and disposable syringes sent for examination.

Alec read the report, warned by Frank's expression. He expected little and received nothing. The syringes were clean of all fingerprints and had been used solely for the thresholding cocktail. In the gloves a few microscopic flakes of dead skin had been found: these might possibly be attributed after complex DNA analysis but the process was very expensive – was it strictly necessary? The gloves also contained a great deal of residual liquid soap ingredients, from the brand used throughout HM prisons.

He let the report fall gently on to his desk. What it proved was that all the suspects washed their hands with prison soap. He wanted very much to demand the DNA analysis (cheese-paring like that insulted him), but he didn't feel justified. There weren't enough samples. All his suspects, except Granny Porter, had worn at least two pairs legitimately, and if Granny turned up in the analysis he'd be amazed. He simply couldn't believe in the silly old man as this particular killer.

He could imagine, in any case, what a half-way decent defence counsel would do with microscopic flakes of dead skin attributed to his client by means of a new and controversial process. To her client. He corrected his sexist thought and was reminded of May. He rang her office again. She was back from court but she wasn't available. She was with a client. She might be avoiding him but it wasn't like her. He left a message saying he'd called.

Getting nowhere with Chas Long, Padmore had gone back to Wishbone. Nine years, ten, then eleven . . . it seemed incredible that in all these millions, literally millions of entries there would be just the one mention. He'd been trying it in upper case so he tried it in lower. Lower case produced a couple of Christmas reminiscences from rambling witnesses, both innocent. He returned to Chas Long and looked for ways to widen the trawl.

Alec had got round to Nurse Serote's minor bombshell and was discussing it with Frank. If she *had* missed the puncture mark, and Beech had somehow received a thresholding dose *before* Nurse Landon got to him, then her injection would have been the one, unwittingly, that killed him. It shifted the time frame. It also widened the geography. Alec wondered suddenly if the governor could have known about this — if so, then it explained his questions over at Inductions.

But Mr Ransome couldn't have known. And if he *had* known he'd have told Alec. He wouldn't have gone off on his own. Would he?

'We're buggered if she *did* miss something,' Frank said. 'That'd mean the whole thing started up long before bloody Wishbone. We're back at square one, looking for a motive.'

'And we're left with an unexplained extra disposable syringe.'

Frank scratched his head. 'I suppose syringes *do* get dumped for innocent reasons. That'll be why they carry spares.'

'Nobody's mentioned it.'

'Perhaps we haven't asked the right question.'

'In any case . . .' Alec closed his eyes, concentrating. 'In any case, who could have got to him? I gather the people over at Inductions don't have much medical training . . . I'll have to go and see them.'

'There's always the doctor.'

'Peck? Aye. Well, he's on my list.' He remembered Peggy Landon saying something about Dr Peck. He looked through the transcripts piling up in his tray as Frank got to them. Nurse Landon's was at the bottom, one of the first. He leafed through it: *He's lazy. He compensates by giving everyone a hard time . . . He's got that idiotic grin . . . He's not an early riser*. Alec smiled. She didn't like Dr Peck, and now that he knew her better he could see why. She suffered fools, and the lazy, less than gladly . . . it had been an interesting lunch. She was an interesting person. Not just a pretty face, maybe not pretty at all, but alive. Dramatic, with the dark eyebrows and hair. Black, really. You didn't often see English people with true black hair. She walked well. Even so, he thought she'd make a rotten Hedda Gabler.

He looked up. 'Ring Dr Peck for me, will you, Peter? As soon as he's free I'd like a — '

Padmore wasn't listening. He was pointing at his screen.

'Bloody hell,' he said. 'Look at that. Bloody hell.'

From where he sat Alec could see a list scrolling by.

'Never underestimate the bloody programmers,' Padmore told him. 'I did. I should've asked it for help. Right at the bloody beginning. For suggestions.' He pointed again. 'Look at that.'

Alec got up and went to stand behind him. The list was of crime sheets and subsequent action. Each entry was considerable and the list ran off the screen. The name in the box was Chas Lang. One letter different. Not Long – Lang. An easy mistake for whoever keyed in the original handwritten interview notes. One letter, *o* instead of *a*, maybe written in pencil . . .

'Do we know where he is right now?'

Padmore scrolled some more. 'You're not going to believe this, Chief.'

'I am, lad.' The young man's voice had given it away. 'Mr Lang's here in Justice City. He may be down in Punishments, but my guess is he's serving LTI.'

'LTI, sir. Fifteen years.'

'Great. He'll welcome a break in his routine.'

Alec was already back at his desk, running a finger down the internal directory. He rang the LTI captain, identified himself, requested an immediate interview with Charles Lang, City number – Padmore scribbled it down on a pad and passed it to him – City number 7588396.

The LTI captain said it was after three o'clock and –

Alec said he didn't care if it was the middle of the night.

The LTI captain said he'd have to talk to the governor. There were regulations concerning visitation rights, and –

Alec told him he could talk to the Queen herself for all he cared. He was coming over immediately and he'd expect immediate admission.

He missed what the LTI captain said next because he'd put down the receiver.

He and Frank gathered notebooks and recorder. They

paused by the door. 'You've done a fine job, Peter,' Alec told him, 'but you're not through yet. We may need Lang's criminal associates and their whereabouts. I'll expect a list.'

He'd been to LTI Admissions before. He didn't need Frank's map. They walked fast. The sun was already below the roofs to the west, gathering in what little was left of the day. The air was icy cold and the night would be long. When they reached LTI Admissions the captain was on the phone, the receiver clamped between jaw and shoulder, and he was filling in a visitation slip on the desk in front of him. Alec and his sergeant entered his office unannounced.

'. . . Yes, Governor. Yes, they're here now. Yes, sir. Of course. I'll do that thing.' He rang off, tore the slip off the pad, and held it out to Alec. 'We've met before, haven't we, Chief Inspector?'

Alec didn't remember him, but there were bridges to be mended after his phone call — there could well be other, future cases when he might need a favour. 'Aye, we have that,' he said, taking the slip. 'And less inconveniently. I really do appreciate this, Captain. I wouldn't be bothering you if it wasn't that — '

'I don't need to know, Chief Inspector. I don't want to know. You do your job, I do mine. I could make a guess at what you're on, but . . .' He tailed off, nodded towards the door. 'You know the procedure. Lang doesn't have to see you if he doesn't want to.'

He wasn't pleased. Clearly Mr Ransome had been his usual robust self, but damage limitation would have to wait. Alec left the office. Alec's need to rush was foolish — five or ten minutes here or there wouldn't signify — but he didn't feel up to fighting it. If Lang could be persuaded to identify Wishbone his case was over.

He and Frank showed their City ID and visitation slip at the gate through into LTI. The accommodation was fenced, a fortress within a fortress, and they were spared much of a walk because Lang was in the nearest block. Three officers

236

accompanied them: no cell door was opened without three officers present.

'Cell' was the official designation, for political reasons (just as Supervision in the Community had had to be retitled Punishment in the Community in order to get it past the judges), but in reality each prisoner's accommodation was more a suite, a sitting room with sleeping annexe, with toilet and shower attached. Money spent here was saved many times over in staffing ratios and rationalized security, for the excellent conditions kept the do-gooders quiet. With free association abandoned (a liberal fetish – all it did was invite trouble) prisoners very rarely left their rooms, and then only in small numbers, and never more than two from any one block. Drug use was down, intimidation, violence, sex. So was danger to prison officers. The need for high staffing levels.

The corridor Alec and Frank were led down by their three minders was as quiet as Punishments had been. It was hard to believe that fifteen hundred asocial men, on two floors, were living here.

They stopped by a door. One of the officers checked the monitor, then tapped in the day's lock code. Nobody carried keys. Eager for a sight of Lang, Alec looked over the officer's shoulder. The monitor screen showed a balding, thick-shouldered man in a chair surrounded by a litter of magazines, reaching forward to turn off a television set. His face, as he turned towards the clicking of the electronic door bolts, was scarred and boxerish. It didn't seem that much of Lucky Beech's luck had rubbed off on his lads.

The door opened and one of the prison officers went in. The other two stayed outside, thumbs hooked theatrically over their belts.

'Couple of visitors for you, Mr Lang.'

Lang leaned sideways to peer out through the door. 'Bloody filth?'

'Police officers. Chief Inspector Duncan and Sergeant Grove.'

'I know it. White or bloody nig-nog, tell the filth a bloody mile off.'

'You don't have to see them.'

'Already have, haven't I? Spoiled my bloody day.'

'You don't have to talk to them.'

Lang considered. Outside in the corridor Alec looked away, at the ceiling, the floor, anywhere . . . He could get to Lang whatever the man said, but it would take form-filling. Time.

'Why not?' Lang decided. 'Make a change from the bloody TV.'

From the furtive way Lang had turned the set off, Alec doubted he'd been watching a film or a networked programme. The City offered a huge video libary, something for all tastes, and games from chess to hi-tech Nintendo, but prisoners also had staff-secure hook-ups available with each other, plus conference facilities. These warmed the cockles of their hearts but the subject of their conversations wasn't always warder friendly.

The officer came out. 'All yours,' he told Alec. 'We have to close the door but we'll keep an eye out.' He nodded at the monitor. 'Lang's not a bad old matey. Not as mateys go.'

Alec didn't smile. 'There's two of us,' he said, 'and we're bigger than he is.'

Aggro was unlikely. The threat of the Punishments Building loomed constantly over LTI inmates. It had a depressing effect on their aggressive inclinations.

Alec and Frank Grove went into the cell and the door was closed behind them. Frank set the ball rolling. 'Afternoon, Lang. Nice place you got here.'

'It *was* nice. Till you bloody liked it.'

Inmates got what was called a paint-and-paper allowance, and could do up their own cells. Some didn't bother, or slung paint around and lived with it. Lang's was neat, in beige and crushed strawberry.

He eyed Frank sourly. 'So which of you's the chief inspector? You or Jungle Drums here?'

Alec clenched his jaw, spoke through it quietly. 'We're not here to quarrel with you, Mr Lang. We're not here to be insulted either.'

'Ah. Sounds like you're the boss man. A nice change, that – I'm a bit of a Jungle Drums meself. You wouldn't bloody think it but my grandpa was a nig-nog. Boxed, he did. Black as the ace of bloody spades.'

Frankly, Alec wouldn't have thought it. A curious admission. Maybe for once his colour would be an asset.

'May we sit down?'

'Please yourselves. Pull up a pew.'

Lang was sprawled in an easy chair in front of the TV. Alec and Frank took upright chairs at the table and Alec produced his recorder.

'Mind if we tape this?'

'Do me a favour. All you filth are wired anyway.'

It was a popular myth. In fact personal bugging devices were illegal and, more importantly, expensive. Alec came to the point. 'You used to work for Lucky Beech,' he said.

'A while back. What if I bloody did?'

Alec chose his next words carefully. 'The courts have put Beech away. For a long time . . . I reckon you know that.'

'In here, ain't he? Bastard. We always knew he was loco, but not that way – not into cutting bloody tarts.'

'Only one.' Beside the point, but truth demanded it.

'Same bloody difference. A black too, poor kid.'

'Aye.' The magazines on the floor were about motor bicycles. He'd expected them to be porno. 'He's in for thirty-five years, Mr Lang. That's minimum.'

'Cheap at the price. You don't see me bleedin'.'

'The point is, Mr Lang, we're trying to clear up old

239

business. Lucky spread a wide net, you know that, and we'd like to sort it out.'

'I bet you bloody would. '

Frank cleared his throat. 'It could be there's people we're hassling that we shouldn't. Jobs that were really Lucky's.' Coming in with nothing to offer Lang, they had to make him believe that if he told them what they wanted to know, no one would suffer. 'You know his operation. You could help us.'

Put like that, Chas Lang became Lucky's right-hand man. He didn't contradict them. 'Try me.'

Alec took out his notebook, flipped some pages. 'Start at the beginning, shall we? A few years back. Tidy up some details. How's your memory?'

'It's what I bloody live on, stuck in here.'

'We have information that Lucky ran drugs, Mr Lang. In south London.'

'He ran drugs all over. That's going back a bit, mind. Eight, nine years. Then life got hot and he quit. It wasn't as if he needed them, he had the clubs lined up, and the girls, and – '

'I'm talking about south London. Clapham.'

'That was his base. That's why he quit, come the bloody inquiry. Too close to bloody home.'

'What inquiry was that, Mr Lang?'

'The Home Office bloody inquiry. Wandsworth. Wandsworth jail. Don't tell me you sods never made the connection?'

Alec kept his voice casual. 'What connection was that?'

'Bloody hell – Lucky always thought the filth knew all about it, just couldn't prove nothink.'

'Lucky was Wandsworth's supplier?' He remembered there *had* been a Home Office inquiry into drug abuse at Wandsworth but, given Clapham, he hadn't put the two together. He didn't know his London boroughs. They were probably side by side.

'If you're still trying to hang bloody Wandsworth on someone else, don't bother. Lucky had the whole place tied up tight as a nun's twat.'

'He had a contact? Someone on the inside?'

'How else? He dealt with them personal. No bloody names, no bloody pack drill.'

'But you knew what he was doing?'

'You talking about me? I bloody knew, all right. Them was nights he didn't need me and Spicer. Spicer was my oppo. Lucky'd take off in the Merc, south of the river. "Off to see Whatsit," he'd say. "Won't be bloody needin' yer."'

'Whatsit?' A gentle prompt.

'That's right. Some bloody stupid name or other . . . First it was Haystack. I ask yer. Then it was someone else. Haystack got transferred out . . . then it was bloody Fishbone. No. I tell a lie. Wishbone. Later it was Wishbone.'

Alec chewed his pen. He asked, lightly, 'You never got to see these people?'

'How could I? I mean – like I bloody said, Lucky kept that side of things to himself. He liked playing games, the names and all. Always give me and Spicer the bloody night off.'

'You were never curious?'

'Do me a favour. Did I check up on him, you mean? Check up on *Lucky*? I wanted to go on living, didn't I?'

'But you knew they worked in the prison. This Haystack and Wishbone, they worked in the prison.'

'They came from the prison. That's all I know. I mean, half of Wandsworth was shooting up. Don't trust me – that's from the Home Office bloody report. And it was Lucky kept the stuff coming, so they bloody must of . . . Look, what is this? The Spanish bloody Inquisition?'

Alec closed his notebook. Frank took over; he yawned and stretched. 'You know how it is, Chas. Bent screws are good for neither man nor beast. That drug lark was a killer.'

'Never worried me. Take it or leave it, that's my bloody motto.'

'So you never knew if this Fishbone was a man or a woman?'

It was a question, Alec realized, that he'd been avoiding.

Chas Lang turned away. 'Bloody Martian, for all I know. Or care.'

Alec said, 'Don't be like that, Mr Lang. It's all ancient history. Just for the records. Then we can move on.'

In fact he had a decision to make. He could continue this interview, inventing questions about Beech's later career to obscure the purpose of their visit. If he didn't it would be all over the LTI Blocks in half an hour that the nig-nog copper was on a drugs case going back to Wandsworth. Did that matter? The news would filter through to the staff and eventually reach the Punishments Building. Did that matter either? If warned, what could the murderer do? Make a run for it?

Lang hunched his shoulders. 'I told yer, didn't I? It might've been a screw, it might've been the sainted governor himself. Spicer and me didn't hang around. We – '

'Thank you, Mr Lang.' Alec stood up. 'You've been very helpful.'

'That's all, then? I thought you bloody said – '

'That's all for the moment.' The delay involved in a long line of invented questions was beyond enduring. Five minutes at Padmore's computer would tell him if one of their suspects had been at Wandsworth eight years ago. If so, that person would be the murderer. He couldn't wait. He didn't mind the rumour factory, he aimed to stay ahead of it. 'If there's more, we'll contact you later.'

'Later? You'll be lucky, mate. I said, you'll be bloody lucky.'

Once out in the corridor with Frank, Alec had to make an effort not to run. He thanked the LTI block officers for their help, then set off at a brisk walk. There wasn't any hurry. Nothing would go away.

As they climbed the stairs in the Punishments Building a

242

telephone was ringing. It sounded as if it had been ringing for a while. It was ringing in the incident room ahead of them and as they went in and Frank reached for the receiver, the ringing stopped. Without it the room was unpleasantly silent.

The time was four forty-five and Peter Padmore, whose duty ran till four thirty, had gone. He'd left, as requested, a list of Charles Lang's now irrelevant criminal associates and their whereabouts, propped against his screen.

List in hand, Alec flung himself into the chair behind his desk. What he needed was a run-down on Wandsworth staff and inmates, and he needed it now. He glared at the computer. 'I don't suppose you've picked up how to work that thing?'

'Access the Yard's mainframe, Boss? You need the codes.'

'It's all fucking codes these days,' Alec said savagely. 'You should have made it your business to know them.'

Frank wisely let this injustice go unchallenged. 'Maybe young Padmore's left a note of them somewhere.'

Padmore hadn't. Frank tried for a while to enlist the computer's help, without success. It had been told to keep its secrets.

Alec gave up. '*Ah, fuckit . . .*' It was still only Wednesday and he'd got till Saturday. There was plenty of time. 'We'll call it a day, Frank. It's knocking-off time anyway. Home by seven, with any luck.'

'I did promise.'

'So did I.'

Morag, like Frank's good lady, knew what a policeman's promises in such matters were worth. Even so . . .

Alec's Rover was still in the yard outside Reception, where he'd left it the previous day. They passed the drive back to Liverpool mostly in silence. Discovering the identity of Wishbone was only a beginning. It provided motive but no proof. It pointed to the murderer – the person Lucky Beech could finger as a prison drug dealer would clearly want him

243

dead — but offered nothing in the way of evidence. The plastic gloves were still unhelpful, and the disposable syringes. The suspects all still had opportunity, even the newcomer, Dr Peck.

The crime had grown uglier: it was now one of ruthless self-preservation, from a starting point of the evillest trade known to man. This new profile changed that of the murderer: they were now looking for someone capable both of murder and of drug-dealing ... Alec surveyed the suspects and came back, on account of the drugs, reluctantly to Jake de Carteret. He said as much to Frank, who didn't argue.

He drove hard: even after dropping Frank off at his home he almost kept his seven thirty promise to Morag. She and Iain were sitting down to dinner. They knew better than to wait; Jamie was in bed, but only after a promise from his mother that Uncle Alec would go up and say goodnight.

Alec slowly climbed the stairs. Jamie's door was open so that the landing light would shine in. The boy was asleep. Alec paused in the doorway, then went in, his head hitting the cardboard fish mobile that hung from the ceiling. Jamie slept very neatly, on his back, one hand holding the edge of the sheet, his eyelashes long and dark across his cheeks. Alec leaned against the wall by the head of his bed, trying hard to be still, and there, and nowhere else. He couldn't manage it.

He touched Jamie's hair, and went downstairs again. Morag was filling his plate.

'I'll be there in a minute,' he said. 'I just have a phone call to make.'

He dialled May's number on the telephone in the kitchen. It wasn't answered. He stared at the receiver, frowning, then hung up. May was having dinner out. She wasn't avoiding him, she was having dinner out. She'd gone to a restaurant.

He joined his sister and brother-in-law in the dining-room, took an empty chair in front of a full plate. 'I missed the news in the car,' he said. 'Anything more about the IRA bomb in the hospital?'

Iain pushed the wine in his direction. 'Nothing much. Apparently a woman delivered it. Claimed to be a grateful parent. They've issued a photofit. Might be anybody.'

Alec helped himself. 'You'd be surprised. Those pictures really work – I've known them produce dozens of sightings.'

'You've talked to these IRA people,' Morag said. 'You know them. Do you suppose that woman gloated?'

'Gloated?'

'What I can't bear is to think of that woman delivering the bomb, and going away, knowing it would go off in one or two hours' time, and kill or maim someone, and gloating. Getting pleasure from the thought . . . Do you think she did, Alec?'

He sampled the wine, which was villainous. Iain's wine always was. 'Those people consider themselves soldiers, Mor'. They're fighting the good fight.'

'Isn't glorying in someone's pain different? Iain – what do you think? Do soldiers do that?'

'I was never a soldier, thank God, but I expect so. Another bloody Commie bites the dust and all that . . . for Commie, read Jerry, Gook, Argie, bloody Proddy.' He raised his glass. 'Your health, Alec. And welcome.'

Alec drank up bravely.

'Which is why catching these people,' Iain went on, 'is such a waste of time. You're not allowed to shoot them, so you stick them in jail. By rights, because they claim to be soldiers, you ought to be able to keep them there until the war's over, which in this case probably means for ever. But you can't so you let them out again eventually, and back they go to the barricades . . .'

He paused as a thought occurred to him. Alec cringed, seeing where this was leading.

It led there. 'You could say the same thing about incarcerating common criminals. Prison turns them into victims and they come out more alienated than ever.'

It was an old argument. Alec had been told the statistics

endlessly. As a policeman he attracted them: people who cared about them accused him of them. Of all the European nations, Britain imprisoned the largest percentage of its population, a hundred thousand at the last count, and for the longest, and ever-lengthening sentences, and this despite unanimous research findings that neither measure had the slightest effect on the incidence of crime . . . What was more, keeping a man in a conventional high security jail cost as much as sending him to Eton.

And so it went. Alec didn't have an answer. If a course of action didn't work, why keep on with it? The prison population kept on rising and so did the crime rate. If a thing didn't work, why go on doing it? Alec didn't have an answer. He was part of the system, and it didn't work, and he didn't have an answer, and he wished people would leave him alone.

It was all people talked about, all the people he knew, outside the police force, talked about. And if he asked Iain now what he would do with the IRA woman if he caught her, Iain would say treat her as the soldier she wants to be, institute a policy of taking no prisoners, and shoot her. And if he asked Iain about criminals he'd say there were worse places to send them than Eton.

Popular acclaim for each new jail conversion within the Punishment and Protection Programme on the Justice City model made him deeply ashamed. As did his country's success as an international arms and EAT unit exporter.

Alec did his job. He had a murderer to catch. He kept his eyes on his plate and drank his wine.

Morag covered the silence. 'I must say though,' she murmured, 'living in Belfast, shouldn't those nurses have been more careful?'

Alec had been there before, also. It was Iain who turned on her. 'A box of chocolates, for God's sake! What sort of life would it be if you ended up trusting nobody?'

*

246

The following morning, Thursday, at shortly after six, as Alec was driving across town to collect Frank Grove for the trip out to Justice City, the telephone buzzed in his car. He picked it up, heard the Merseyside chief superintendent.

'Alec? Jack here.'

'You're up early.'

'Alec . . . I'm afraid I've got very bad news for you.'

He knew at once. 'It's May,' he said.

He'd rung her again last night and got no answer.

'She's dead?'

'A neighbour found her last night, Alec. He went to borrow some milk. It was after ten. We didn't call you till now. You couldn't have done anything.'

It wasn't his case and he needed the sleep.

'She's been murdered,' he said, drawing the car carefully into the side of the road. 'Stabbed? A knife?'

'Someone caught her as she came home from work. They –'

'I know who it was, Jack.'

'They'd been waiting in the shrubbery. You know how dark it is there. They waited till she'd opened her front door, and –'

'I'm coming in.' He looked in the mirror, slowly swung out to turn. The road was deserted, orange street lights against a black sky.

'It's not our case, Alec. Paul Hallet's on it. You're needed out in Justice City.'

'I know who it was, Jack. I'm coming in.'

'We have fingerprints, masses of them. We'll get him. The bastard was incredibly clumsy.'

'Clumsy?' Alec reversed, completed the turn. 'With the knife, you mean?'

'With the robbery.' But there'd been a tiny pause. 'Her wallet's gone. God knows what else. The front door's still open . . .'

Jack's pause had been hardly a beat, but enough. May

hadn't died easily. He'd seen it – they struggle and get stabbed again and crawl and get stabbed again and cry out in the dark and get stabbed again. May had cried out in the dark and he hadn't heard her.

'I'm coming in, Jack. I don't care what you say.'

'Her body's not here, Alec. You don't want to – '

'I know the killer. You can pick him up as soon as it's daylight. He's . . .' Alec closed his eyes, remembering. 'He's in his early twenties, five foot seven or eight, with stubbly hair and a wispy ginger beard. He has blue eyes and a broken front tooth, and he'll be wearing a black felt jacket with silver astrological symbols hand-painted on it. He told me his name was Humphrey, for what that's worth. You'll find him wherever your people dumped the guys from Needle Heaven. He's an addict and he'll be wearing the dead woman's jeans. He's probably pissed in them.'

He drove off, slowly and carefully.

'I'm coming in, Jack. I want to see him.'

thursday

seventeen

It's one o'clock, lunch-time, the darkness long gone from Justice City, and Peggy Landon's finished thresholding early. She's upstairs at her desk, sorting out office chores with Daphne. Now that the director's back there'll be fewer of these, but they built up while he was away – a whole week of drug invoices, daily returns, staff time-sheets, and an indent for a new ophthalmoscope – and she doesn't want him to know. Daphne works Wednesday, Thursday (today) and half of Friday. She's married to the Justice City chaplain, Graham, with a single parent daughter who works weekends in the Education office, and two grandchildren, so she needs her Saturdays and Sundays free. Friday afternoons go on housework and shopping, and Mondays she keeps for Graham after his Sunday labours. They win nationwide prizes for their imaginative needlepoint.

Peggy and she don't exactly get on, they're very different people, but they have a working arrangement. They both believe in the House and they both have a poor opinion of Dr Mellish.

Peggy's just passed over a stack of papers and she's waiting to get them back for signature. She goes to the window, squeezing past the desk that's been moved out from against the wall for Daphne. She always hopes she'll be able to see the moor from her window but she never can. There are Justice City's bars in the way, and the nearby generator building. And beneath it, the roof of Holding. The latter reminds her, beneficially, that Captain Wilson hasn't had to send a man into Holding for weeks, not since his eight new EAT rooms came into service. Nobody likes Holding.

The morning is grey and raw and it matches Peggy's mood. Last night's rehearsal has left her restless, dissatisfied with herself. Not with her performance as Hedda. With herself.

'Our black policeman was in late this morning,' Daphne tells her. 'I passed him on the stairs when I went down to the loo at around eleven . . .' She pats the front of her blouse. 'That man's too big for his boots. I hope I'm not a racist but that does happen sometimes when you give these people authority. They've no experience of it. No historical context.'

Peggy turns back from the window. She thinks, what an incredibly boring old fart you are! Christ knows how many centuries of historical fucking context you've come from and look what it's done for you . . .

She says, 'I think he's rather attractive.' This is the same remark but gives less excuse for Daphne to resign or complain to the vicar.

Mrs Tilder responds with a significant silence, chin tucked in to suppress her outrage, eyebrows raised to display it. She's not surprised at the sentiment, she's always known Peggy is a sex-crazed nymphomaniac, but at its bare-faced expression, there at the desk, in her office. She processes at arm's-length the papers Peggy's handed her.

Peggy returns to her chair. She's done her anti-racist bit and she doesn't feel much better. She feels worse. Its tameness makes her feel worse. Beside Hedda's, the emotional fires of her life seem so pathetic. The games she plays. The game she's been playing. In the big things she's not often burdened with a need for truthfulness, but she's an ex-drug dealer and a murderer, for God's sake – what hope, truthfully, has she of a relationship with a divorced black policeman? Yesterday's canteen lunch was games. And the moments in the lunch that weren't games, were games.

Hedda is incapable of games. She's willing to die, to kill herself rather than —

'For your signature, Charge Nurse.'

Daphne holds out the papers and Peggy takes them and lays them carefully down in the partially cleared space on the desk in front of her. She's come to a decision. She stands up. If she can't have emotional fire, at least she can have Karl. She walks to the door. She might, one day, tell him the truth. In an odd way, in her book, truth and sex go together.

'I'm going for lunch,' she says. 'If anyone needs me, I'll be over in Research.'

Daphne Tilder, who nibbles Ryvita and never takes a lunch break, makes no comment. She doesn't have to. All Justice City knows about Charge Nurse Landon and Dr Stanna.

Ten minutes later Carole Serote surfaces in the upstairs passage, braces herself, and knocks on Dr Landon's door. Last night, on the telephone, when Rachel was in bed, thank the Lord, she had a run-in with Freddy, and she's got to get things sorted out.

She'd decided it was time to brush Freddy off, but he didn't brush off easy. The current story about an injured inmate was for the birds, he said. He knew it and so did she. He'd invested in her down a good few years, he said, and now he was calling in on his investment. The tit-bits she'd fed him in the past had been shit. She was sitting on a big story, he felt it in his water. She was going to cough and if she didn't like it she could do the other thing. He could ruin her. Any time, he could ruin her.

And he could, so she's asked for till this evening to think about it, and she can never let him get away with that, so her best chance is a clean breast of things.

She knocks and marches in, but Dr Landon isn't there, only the old string-bag who usually works next door.

'Charge Nurse Landon has gone to Research,' the string-bag tells her. 'She'll be with Dr Stanna.'

This comes loaded with significance. Carole's surprised that the string-bag will share anything with her, even her dirty mind, but sometimes these things build up and have to be let out somewhere. Carole thanks her and goes out.

As she stands outside the door, uncertain what to do next, Dr Mellish emerges from his office just down the passage. He's not a man she would approach in the normal course of events, but he always smiles proprietorially when they pass. She may not know the word, but she knows what it means. Proprietors look kindly upon their possessions. In any case, she's there, her mind made up, Dr Landon isn't, and Dr Mellish is.

She calls, 'Excuse me,' and advances, blocking the passage. 'Excuse me, sir. Could you spare me a moment?'

Left little choice, he glances at his watch then manages a smile and steps back, holding the door open for her to go in.

'Nurse Serote. Of course. Sit down. What can I do for you?'

She sits. On the director's desk, beneath his lamp, is a large book, Burton's *Pharmacological Yearbook*, lying open. As Dr Mellish returns to his chair he quietly places a strip of paper in the book as a marker and closes it.

'So how are you, Nurse? And your daughter? Rachel, isn't it?'

'I'm fine, sir. Rachel's fine.'

'Good. Good . . . not working you too hard, are we?'

'No complaints, Dr Mellish.'

'Good. Good . . . so what can I do for you?'

It has to be said. It has to be gone through. The shameful story has to be told, and she tells it. No excuses. She doesn't mention her father, his crappy bedsitter. And across the desk Dr Mellish remains carefully neutral.

At the end, a reaction needed, he frowns. 'You realize you've broken the terms of your contract?'

'Yes.'

'And almost certainly infringed patient–nurse confidentiality?'

'Yes.'

'So what do you want me to do?'

'I'm a good nurse, sir.'

'You're also a dishonest nurse.'

This is terrible. Dr Landon would have spared her that. But she deserves it.

'Yes.' She stares at her fat black-stockinged feet in her small black shoes. She's been on them since six and her varicose veins are giving her hell.

Dr Mellish is still considering. 'So what do you want me to do?'

'Talk to Freddy, sir. A word from you and he's got no ground to stand on.'

'Forget what you've done, you mean? Overlook it?'

'I did come to you.' She's hardly audible. Such a big, proud woman. She rubs one calf. 'Of my own accord. Sir.'

Dr Mellish, who has been very still, like her, suddenly explodes into action. He moves papers, opens a drawer and closes it, takes a ballpoint pen out of his pocket, clicks the ball into position, leans back in his chair, then forward again.

'If we were to, as it were, come to some arrangement about the past, Nurse Serote, what could we, as it were, what could we expect in return?'

She lifts her gaze. 'I don't understand.' What does he want, her *gratitude*, for heaven's sake? What else has she?

'I'm sure you realize, Nurse Serote, that the next few days are going to be difficult. For this department and for the entire P & P programme. We have a death on our hands, an announcement will have to be made, and we're by no means certain what that announcement will be.' He pauses, draws speculative figures of eight in the air with his pen. 'And whatever the nature of that announcement, we're by no means certain what public response we should expect . . .'

He looks across at her, past his pen, and sees her baffled.

'A leak. Nurse Serote, at the right time, to the right source, might, as it were, put a toe in the water . . . Prepare people for the governor's eventual press release. Give us a guide as to its best . . . shall we say its best presentation?'

She's still baffled. 'Prepare them for Mr Beech's murder, you mean? And whoever done it?'

Dr Mellish frowns, turns away, clicks his pen, pockets it. 'If you were willing to communicate on just one more occasion with this Freddy, Nurse Serote — for the good of this department, for the good of Justice City — I think we could see our way to overlooking past . . . transgressions.' He turns back, flashes his proprietorial smile. 'And remove him from your life thereafter.'

There's stuff going on here she can't fathom. But she's so relieved to have past transgressions overlooked that she feels faint. She needs this job. She has Rachel to think of, as well as herself and Pa.

She asks, 'What'll I have to say?'

Dr Mellish is suddenly sharp. 'How can I possibly tell you that?' he reproves her. 'Chief Inspector Duncan hasn't finished his investigation.'

She nods but she doesn't believe him. There's stuff going on here she can't fathom.

eighteen

That morning Frank Grove drove out to Justice City in his own car, alone. The chief inspector rang him while he was polishing his shoes after breakfast, and told him about May Calcott. The chief inspector sounded fine. He had a good idea who the killer was, a starting point, and he'd be in the station for a while, and Frank should go on without him. Padmore should be put on to researching the Wandsworth connection, and after that Frank should use his own judgement. Maybe Dr Peck would need looking into, or maybe the Wandsworth answers would make that unnecessary. Frank should use his own judgement. He, Alec, would get out there as soon as he could.

He, Alec, was sounding fine. So fine that Frank was gut worried. There'd be photographs at the station, the preliminary PM, and Alec had admitted that the Chief superintendent had tried to keep him away, but he was going in all the same. Frank had sat in the car with him, in cafés with him, in the Liverpool nick with him, had stood on street corners with him, in doorways, for the two years Alec had known May. He knew how Alec felt. Now she was dead, bloodily, and Alec was sounding fine.

Frank drove fast, hating a world that gave and took back so lightly. He knew Alec had been eyeing Charge Nurse Landon and he knew it was a great nonsense. The row with May had been bloody silly. She was the woman for Alec.

Policemen like him deserved so much and usually got so little. Policemen were beleaguered, an ethnic minority. Frank drove fast, till he nearly killed himself and many other people on an icy curve to the east of Manchester. After that he drove at fifty all the way. He still worried and hated.

Up in the Justice City incident room Padmore was at his keyboard. They'd left no instructions so he'd filled in by adding to Lang's criminal associates and looking up Dr Peck's background. Neither was helpful. According to the Medical Association's databank, Peck had been a partner in a wealthy Southampton surburban general practice. Ten years ago he had suddenly resigned and joined the prison service. No reason was given, but it could as easily have been ill-health as misbehaviour. His medical records might be available, but breaching their confidentiality required another level of access coding.

Frank put Padmore on to finding a connection between Wandsworth and one of their suspects, and sat down at the chief inspector's in-tray. It contained little, principally the invoice for a limo and driver, from Justice City to Liverpool and back, twice, a flyer for a fund-raising bingo on behalf of the Justice City Conservative Association, and a new forensic report from Manchester. They'd been able to identify the designer drug in Albert Beech's bloodstream: its chemical ingredients meant nothing to Frank, and the only new information with it suggested that it was a widely available euphoric if you knew where to look, and it had probably been administered orally rather than intravenously. Popped, not shot.

If you knew where to look included Beech, and *euphoric* meant that he'd died happy – always assuming there was enough still in him for it to notice. Frank was just off downstairs to make Padmore and himself their first dose of the nurses' instant coffee when Padmore's Wandsworth screen came up with WILKS, Timothy, Richmond Crown Court, eighteen months for petty larceny. No record of the exact nature of the crime, but apparently Granny was such an old friend of the Wandsworth governor that he was made a trustie just about from day one. They gave him the prisoners' laundry to collect and deliver, and let him out into town on an easy-going basis. He was well into his sixties even then, no family worth mentioning, and the only trouble he got himself into – setting fire to the newspapers in the reading room, for God's sake – coincided with the day when he'd have been coming up for maximum remission. Frank could see them having literally to throw him out at the end of his sentence.

For drugs distribution the laundry set-up had been perfect. The only problem as far as Frank was concerned was what Granny'd done with all the money. Even a few months as Lucky Beech's go-between would've earned him a tidy packet. That, and why he hadn't been sussed out during the Home Office inquiry – a few more of Padmore's well-chosen search codes produced the dates of the inquiry and they coincided with the final months of Granny's sentence. He must have given the Home Office boys one hell of a good story.

Frank slapped Peter Padmore's shoulder. They had their murderer.

Padmore dared to have his doubts. Even if the Beech/drugs/Wishbone/Granny connection were established, it didn't provide the old sod with a motive. He liked jail, didn't he? He was virtually in it now – what more could they throw at him for an eight-year-old crime? Solitary on special diet? EAT? On a seventy-six-year-old man? Besides, wasn't there a statute of limitations?

'The trouble with you, Pete,' Frank told him, 'is that you're thinking normal. Granny Porter isn't normal. You said it yourself – he's seventy-six . . . seventy-six coming up a hundred and two. He's missing his marbles. You've seen him – isn't he missing his marbles?'

Padmore took off his glasses, breathed on them. 'You won't mind, Sarge, if I keep on with the search.'

Frank sighed, took a print-out of the Wilks entry, put it reverently on top of the papers in the chief inspector's in-tray, and went downstairs for the coffee. By the time he returned Padmore had located a Nurse Probationer Margaret Landon working in the Wandsworth prison infirmary.

Frank slapped the mugs down so hard they slopped over. 'And a de Carteret scrubbing bedpans, I suppose. And a bloody Serote mopping the floors.'

'Not yet, Sergeant,' Padmore told him. 'Give me time.'

Time proved unfruitful. No other Wandsworth staff member, from the highest to the lowest, matched any Justice City name, and no other inmate either.

Frank didn't like it. Nor, he knew, would the chief inspector, and that – on this morning of all mornings – mattered. Even so, accepting Padmore's reasoning as to motive (which he reluctantly did), if the field was only Wilks and Landon, then Landon, with so much to lose, came out undeniably the leader ... He read their two interview transcripts, plus the chief inspector's notes. Both stories looked good, but were unsupported. They had only Wilks's word that he'd been in the nurses' room, and only Landon's that she'd gone to the loo. What he needed – and what he coincidentally was about to receive – was evidence for or against one or other suspect.

In his break at ten thirty Nurse Jake de Carteret came up to the incident room. The chief inspector's absence clearly disappointed him – Sergeant Grove was less *sympatique*, frankly not *sympatique* at all – but he made the best of things. He explained about the plastic flower petals.

Frank frowned and made muddled notes. 'You're saying the petals were on the floor when Nurse Landon injected Beech . . .'

'I'm saying they were on the floor when Nurse Landon injected Beech.'

260

'And they were gone an hour later, when you found Beech dead.'

'And they were gone an hour later. You've got it exactly.'

'So what are you suggesting?'

De Carteret cast his eyes up to the ceiling. 'I'm not suggesting anything, lovey. Someone swept them up. It wasn't me. La Serote could have, she was there before me, surfacing, but she says she didn't.'

'And you say no outsider could have got in without your seeing because you say you were in the dispensary, out in the foyer, the whole time.'

'I do say.'

'And nobody did.'

'And nobody did.'

Frank stared at his notes. Sweeping up petals was harmless enough, yet no one was admitting to it. Granny Porter was the obvious candidate. Frank could easily construct a scenario in which Granny was in Beech's room, busy with his dustpan, when opportunity and impulse came together and he grabbed a syringe from the wagon and used it . . . Nurse Landon on her hands and knees with a brush was harder to imagine. Both had unsupported alibis.

'I'll need to confirm this with Nurse Serote. No offence, mind, but – '

'Be my guest. She's downstairs, resting her poor legs.'

Frank took the hint. Instead of summoning her he went downstairs. She confirmed de Carteret's story: the petals had definitely been there, they'd definitely gone, and she definitely hadn't touched them.

'Why should I tell a lie?' she demanded. 'I'm a tidy soul – I could've swept them up easy, but I didn't.'

Frank went back upstairs. Padmore had switched off the computer, loosened his collar, and put his feet up.

'That's it, then,' he said. 'You reel in the Landon bird.'

Frank scowled at him. 'The chief inspector sees you like that, boy, and you won't know what hit you.'

261

He sat down at his desk and started typing up the new de Carteret and Serote evidence, getting it into shape for his boss. The time stood at nearly eleven, time to begin expecting him.

Frank's typing slowed, stopped ... A mental picture, unwanted, had come to him: the Merseyside nick, smokey interview rooms, chipped green corridors, a desk with photographic blow-ups, preliminary interviews and reports scattered across it, on a chair somewhere the neighbour who'd found the body, scuffed floors, full ashtrays, all the grubby odds and sods of the investigative process. And Alec, in his grey, go-to-Justice-City suit, an uncomfortable presence, deferred to in whispers, the victim's lover, an intruder, pushing to be a part of what wasn't his. May's death was Chief Inspector Hallet's. It didn't matter that Alec could name her killer; her death was Hallet's.

Frank went back, saddened, to his notes. Landon had the better motive, Wilks the more plausible opportunity. The chief inspector wouldn't like her fingered as Wishbone.

Where's the proof? Can we make it stand up?

They couldn't. Nurse Probationer Margaret Landon had been exonerated by the Home Office inquiry. They'd have looked into opportunity, contacts, financial situation ... They hadn't known about Wishbone at the time, of course, but now, with Beech dead, the only person who knew for certain about Wishbone was Wishbone. Reopening an eight-year-old case posed problems, particularly of time – of which they had very little.

The chief inspector would like her as Beech's murderer even less. It was a question of capacity.

Wilks and Landon must be re-examined. If they both denied all knowledge of the bloody petals, then ... Frank looked up at the clock again. He'd gone as far as he cared to on his own – the second go round at those two was too important. He drank his coffee, which was cold now, and willed the chief inspector to arrive.

He could disguise his own inactivity behind bits of paper, but not Padmore's, so he set the young man to tracing Margaret Landon's monthly staff assessments at Wandsworth and Timothy Wilks's discharge sheet. For a man who knew what to look for there might be something in them.

Alec arrived at two minutes past the hour. He was tense but very steady. Much older. 'I've been thinking on the drive out,' he said as he sat down carefully at his desk, wincing. 'We've neglected the Peck man disgracefully. This Wishbone thing could be a total red herring . . .'

There was to be no discussion of his morning. Frank said nothing, pointed to his in-tray, let him read. The Wishbone thing wasn't a red herring. He moved from page to page, his eyes scanning faster.

'Padmore . . . Padmore, this is great stuff. Great – you're a genius, lad. I mean that . . .'

He read the de Carteret evidence twice. 'Someone's lying to us, Frank. Shouldn't be too hard, finding out who.'

Frank stood up. 'You'll need to talk to them. Which one first?'

'Try the old gent.' Alec looked at his watch. 'At this sort of time Nurse Landon has her hands full.'

Asked for his boss's choice in advance, Frank would have bet on Granny Porter a hundred to one. The other's charms had become a liability – before he went after her the chief inspector would assemble all the background he could get. He was good at detail, good at the close-up: it was the overall that sometimes eluded him.

Downstairs Nurse Landon and her team were going round the thresholding rooms. Granny Porter wasn't with them. Frank tried the washroom and the nurses' room. He remembered the second floor washroom and, heart beating faster than was comfortable, got lucky. A familiar haze of roll-up met him as he opened the door.

Granny's protests lasted down the stairs, died in front of the unsmiling chief inspector.

'You lied to us, Wilks.'

'Lied? You can't say that.' Granny buttoned his white coat. 'I want my solicitor.'

Alec tapped his desk. 'I have it here in writing.'

'Bugger off. You haven't fucking charged me. I don't have to fucking answer.'

'You dealt in shit, Wilks. In Wandsworth. You got it from Lucky Beech and you sold it on.'

'Me? Shit? Pull the other fucking one.'

The denial, although automatic, came after a moment's surprise, a moment's incomprehension, and a moment's relief – he'd been expecting something else, some other accusation, and the fleeting parade of emotions across his scraggly features, none of them cancelled soon enough to be missed, told Frank that the old man was hiding something. Granny was an actor, but of the old, broad school. If he'd *wanted* to register surprise he'd have registered it till his jaw fell off. Nuances, the half-seen, were beyond him.

Frank caught his boss's eye. Alec had seen it too.

'And the petals you swept up in Lucky Beech's room?'

'Petals? Never touched no fucking petals. Like I fucking said, I was in the nurses' room all the fucking time.'

Alec leaned forward. 'All what time, Wilks? All what time?'

'Don't be fucking stupid.' Granny's few teeth hissed. 'All the time the petals were on the . . .' He reconsidered. 'Besides, I swep' them up later.'

Alec gave him a couple of minutes to worry in. 'Bring a chair for Mr Wilks, will you, Sergeant? He's not looking too good.'

Frank fetched a chair. Having Padmore in the room might have inhibited the interrogation, but Granny wasn't much of a challenge. He sat on the chair, his knees together, pulling his coat tightly across them. For all the world like a tart afraid of showing her knickers.

Alec cleared his throat. 'I gather you *do* know what petals we're talking about.'

'I swep' them up. Afterwards. Later. I swep' the fuckers up.'

'You swept them up twice?'

'Piss off. What the hell d'you think you're – '

'You certainly swept them up once, Mr Wilks, before Nurse Serote found Beech dead. We've got witnesses. Now you're saying you swept them up again.'

It was pathetic. Frank didn't like it. Nobody should be tied up in such obvious knots, so obviously. The Chief talked about capacity – what capacities did this old man have, for God's sake?

'Your witnesses are wrong. I swep' them up after.'

'After what, Mr Wilks?'

'Just *after*. I don't know. Later. It was all go. After lunch. Tea or something. Later. Your witnesses are wrong.'

It was a promising stance. Frank could imagine what a sharp defence counsel would make of the presence or otherwise of a few plastic flower petals. Flower petals that had presumably disappeared long ago in the House garbage.

The Chief could imagine it too. 'So you were in the nurses' room, Mr Wilks. And if Nurse Landon says you were in the washroom?'

'She fucking can't. She never came near the fucking place.'

He looked round defiantly. It took a long silence, and their faces, and the way they watched him and didn't move, to tell him what he'd said.

He wound his feet round the chair legs and pulled his coat hem closer. 'I didn't kill him,' he said. 'He was dead when I fucking got there.'

Frank believed him. He believed Granny's whole story, brought out piece by piece. The door to the washroom opened from the right, towards the foyer. Granny'd been in the washroom half an hour, doing a job that should have taken ten minutes. He'd opened the door a crack – a way of life, his life – and seen her coming out of the door nearly opposite. *Her. Missy Landon.* She'd stood by the lift, close to the wagon, looking along towards the foyer. Nobody'd come, she'd put something in the bin on the wagon and gone down in the lift, he'd left the washroom with his brushes and bits . . . He dusted round the first room, then went on to the next, Lucky Beech's, where he swept up the petals. He didn't want to look at Lucky, the man was crazy, he scared him stiff, even strapped down on the bed, but finally, his shoulder ready against the door, he did look.

Lucky was staring up. He looked dead and his screens said the same thing. Granny Porter wasn't daft. Straight lines like that meant only one thing.

Then he heard someone going by, the fat blackie going past his window on her way to the room at the end, and he didn't want to be caught there, there with Lucky dead, and he nipped next door. The bloke in there was snoring. Granny reckoned Nurse Serote wouldn't get past Lucky when she found him dead, and he was right. And when she fetched de Carteret and they were in with Lucky, he pushed off, dumped his cleaning stuff under the stairs, and that was fucking that. Bob's your fucking uncle. He was over in Inductions when Dr Polly Peck arrived, telling him not to start bringing over the next batch.

The chief inspector asked him about Nurse Landon, was she definitely coming from Beech and not just along the passage from the control room, and he said she was definitely coming from Beech, no skin off his nose. And he added in a detail: it was plastic gloves she dumped in the bin on the wagon. The chief inspector asked him about a syringe and he said she might have had one, but he never saw it.

The chief inspector told him he didn't believe him about Nurse Landon and he said he wasn't fussed, they could do the other thing. Next the chief inspector told him he'd murdered Beech and was making up the whole story.

'Me?' he said. 'Me do for Lucky? You must be joking. Cunts like that don't go quiet. I'd never sleep easy in my bed again.'

Frank and the chief inspector questioned him for over an hour. At the end he was chirpier than they were. He had his story and he stuck to it. He wasn't saying Missy Landon had done for Lucky. He'd nothing against her – she was a nice lady. She'd been coming out of Lucky's room, was all.

Frank told him they'd be typing up a statement for him to sign, and sent him away. The time was after one. Elbows on his desk, the chief inspector pressed his pale fingertips wearily into his eye sockets.

'We're going to have to talk to her.'

Frank felt sorry for him. 'It's the obvious story for Wilks to tell, Chief. Caught out, proved a liar, he shifts the blame. He's not stupid.'

'Wrong. Frank. Wrong . . . Stupid is what Granny Porter *is*.' He picked up the telephone, fumbled for the City directory which fell on to the floor. '*Ah, fuckit* . . . nip next door, will you, Frank? Tell Nurse Landon we could do with a word.'

Nurse Landon wasn't in her office. The formidable Daphne Tilder was, and she said Nurse Landon had gone over to Research. She was visiting Dr Stanna.

Hearing this, Alec hesitated. 'Take a walk, shall we, Frank? I seem to have been sitting down all my life.'

nineteen

Going down the stairs of the Punishments Building and out into the highways and byways of Justice City, Alec walks carefully. He chats carefully with Frank. He smiles carefully and turns up his jacket collar against the cold. He's careful. It's how he keeps his act together. He's been careful ever since he arrived in Justice City. Before that, ever since he left the Merseyside nick. Before that, he's been careful ever since the chief superintendent called him and told him about May.

He dreads leaving the Punishments Building now and going out again into Justice City, but it has to be done. He's faced the City once already this morning, its anger, its violence, and its terrible calm, and they nearly floored him. They showed him his own. But he faces them again because there's a chance, a strong chance, that Peggy Landon may be Lucky Beech's murderer, and he needs to know, so it has to be done.

Now there's been another murder. *Ah, fuckit.* If a bell rang every time there was another murder it'd play 'The Bonnie Earl of Murray' day and night, non-stop.

By the time he'd left the Merseyside nick they hadn't found Humphrey. They soon would, though. His face wasn't in any of their books, but a couple of young officers said they knew him from Alec's description. The beard, the broken tooth, the black felt jacket . . . they'd take a ride down to the ferry terminal. They'd pulled him in once or twice in recent months and let him go again. He hadn't been vicious, they thought: just an addict.

Had the man who'd killed May been vicious? Alec couldn't say. One thing leads to another. Maybe all he'd wanted was the price of a fix or two. Maybe she'd brought her death on herself, refusing to give it to him. It was impossible to tell from the blow-ups Inspector Hallett had tried to hide from him. All the blow-ups showed was that she'd struggled and got stabbed, and crawled and got stabbed again, and then maybe she'd cried out in the dark and got stabbed again. The blow-ups showed the abrasions her knees had suffered from the crawling, and the abrasions her hands had suffered from the struggling and the crawling. There was no evidence that she'd cried out in the dark, no neighbour had heard her, no passer-by in Sefton Park, but it had certainly been dark and there was a good chance that she'd have made some sort of noise, some sort of protest. He'd been much too far away himself to hear, of course. He'd been driving to Morag's, or arriving there, or having his dinner.

He remembers all this very carefully. He works it out. He doesn't think about what he'll do with his life, now that May's dead. He doesn't think about Humphrey's future either. His carefulness doesn't allow that sort of thing. His carefulness keeps him safe: inside it he still has a measure, a considerable measure of control.

He and Frank reach a gate at a junction in the walkways and pause to consult Frank's map, looking for the Prison Procedures Research Unit. The day hasn't improved from its grey, raw beginning. Alec shivers in his expensive double-breasted chief inspector's suit. They stand beneath the granite wall of the City chapel and he helps Frank hold the map flat against a wind gusting straight down off the high fells. The Research Unit proves to be nearer than they thought, just up the slope beyond the Hospital Wing.

Alec is surprised to see, marked on the map, a small graveyard alongside the chapel. He's noticed that the staff of

269

Justice City don't go out much, but are they really, ultimately, so unwilling to leave? It hardly seems possible, but the graveyard can hardly be for the inmates so he supposes they must be. After all, if they left, where would they go? Who are they? The graveyard's on the other side of the chapel and he and Frank don't make a detour now to visit it.

The Prison Procedures Research Unit is a small building, but lavish. Uniquely within Justice City, a Japanese architect based in Dallas, Texas, was given a free hand and worked in stainless steel under massive red cedar timbers, enclosing a central glassed-in ice garden. Alec sees the point. The Research Unit has to look special. It does a special job. Besides, the international flavour the architect created has turned out to be very suitable, for the work done here by Dr Karl Stanna and his team attracts a steady stream of expert visitors from abroad. The ice-garden, creating blue pinnacles and canyons, has become famous all round the world.

Security at the reception desk is tight, but eventually they are directed to Dr Stanna's workspace, which adjoins the animal laboratory. The receptionist confirms that Charge Nurse Landon arrived fifteen minutes earlier, and wants to telephone ahead, but Alec dissuades him. He doesn't really believe in Peggy fleeing through a back window at the mention of his name, but he's not taking any chances. He doesn't really believe she ran drugs or murdered Albert Beech either, but he mustn't let this influence him. He's got a job to do. He's being careful.

He and Frank have been warned that Dr Stanna conducts delicate experiments and may not be ready to let them in, but when they reach the door to his workspace they find it on the latch. Alec knocks, gets no response, pushes it slightly and calls, 'Hullo?'

There's still no answer so he looks round it, then enters. Dr Stanna has books, computers, a microfiche reader, chairs and tables, a sturdy day-bed, a large fishtank apparently containing a single octopus, an exercise bike, and a glass wall looking out on to a central panorama of ice caves and sparkling snow. The room has a faint smell in it that Alec can't identify. He calls again, more loudly, 'Hullo?'

A pause, then, through a half-open door into an adjoining room, sounds of movement. 'Coming ...' This is Peggy Landon's voice. 'Dr Stanna's been called away. He won't be — '

She appears in the doorway, breaks off when she sees the two policemen. She's carrying a large-ish brown chimpanzee that has its arms round her neck. Now Alec recognizes the smell in the room — it's the faint fecal tang that's found in even the best kept animal houses.

Peggy seems pleased to see him. 'Chief Inspector. What a surprise. Are you looking for Karl? He's — '

'No ... no, not Dr Stanna ...' Alec is amazed at the motherly picture she presents. This is an aspect of her life she's never mentioned. 'No, it's just that something's come up. We have a few more questions.'

'For me? Here I am, then. Oh, and this is Joshua.' She unwinds the chimpanzee's arms from her neck but he hangs on tightly and refuses to be introduced. 'We're old friends,' she says. 'I give him a break from his cage whenever I'm over here.'

Frank sorts out chairs, one for Alec at a table, Peggy Landon and Joshua a tactful couple of yards away across the floor, in case Joshua needs space. Alec sets up the recorder, takes out his notebook slowly and carefully, collecting his thoughts.

'It's about your visit to Captain Wilson with the thresholding profiles. I believe you went to the toilet on the way.'

'That's right.'

He waits, staring at his notebook, letting her wonder.

Then, 'And the porter wasn't there?'

'What's that?'

'The soap dispensers — the porter wasn't refilling them?'

She's having trouble with Joshua. He's restive and she

unwinds his arms again and this time she half rises and places him on the floor, well away from her chair; 'Who knows what Granny Porter's ever up to?' she says lightly. 'You tell him what to do, but heaven knows when he actually does it.'

'But he wasn't in the washroom.'

'In the washroom, Chief Inspector? I'm afraid I can't help you.'

For the very first time, Alec thinks she's prevaricating. Joshua, meanwhile, crouches meekly on his little bare bony arse, his arms folded across the top of his head. They're so long that his hands curl into his armpits on either side.

'Of course you can help me. You were there, weren't you?'

'In the washroom?' She stares at him, seemingly bewildered, then understands. 'Ah, I see what you mean, Chief Inspector. You think I used one of the toilets in the ground floor washroom. I didn't. There's a loo by the lift gates down in Punishments. I used that.'

'That's not what you told us.' Alec holds out a hand and Frank passes him the transcript. 'I asked you if Granny Porter was seeing to the dispensers in the washroom. The ground floor washroom. You answered, *As a matter of fact he wasn't. At least, I didn't see him.*'

She shakes her head. 'That's ridiculous. I couldn't possibly have seen him. I wasn't there. I must have got muddled somehow.'

'You didn't seem muddled. At the end of the interview, after you'd – ' Joshua begins a thin, pathetic wailing ' – as you were leaving, after you'd claimed that you hadn't seen him, you asked me if he was saying something different.'

'I'm sorry, Chief Inspector. There has to be a mistake here. Perhaps you misheard me.' She raises her voice above Joshua's. 'All this fuss about which toilet I went to. Why should I lie? It's ridiculous.'

Alec looks at her over the spiral metal binding of his notebook: there's a pain in his chest as he sees that she *is*

272

lying and he believes he knows why. But he makes no mystical claim to be able to spot liars at a hundred paces, and if he's right about this then he's been wrong about a lot of other things. Wrong about her.

In any event, if he's right, then she's thought her lie through so quickly – in the moment she gained for herself putting Joshua down on the floor – that it does indeed seem ridiculous, a ridiculous quibble that all the same may have to be the cornerstone of any case he eventually will present.

Maybe he's wrong. For heaven's sake – she's an able young woman, an intelligent young woman, a pretty young woman, a young woman who has taken him at something other than his (black and police) face value. She's treated him as a human being. So why is he doing this? Has he lost all sense of proportion? Have his duty and his professional pride really brought him to this, to picking over when and where and if some pretty young woman went for a pee?

He wants to be wrong. One lie. It doesn't amount to much. It's not automatically a dagger in someone's heart. In the famous words of the CID basic training manual, one lie certainly isn't automatically an extra injection in Albert Beech's arm.

She will not, of course, know this. She can therefore be badgered.

'I did not mishear you,' he tells her quietly. 'It's on the tape and in the transcript. And since you're lying, it has to be because the missing five minutes before you reached Captain Wilson were spent neither in the upstairs nor in the downstairs toilets – they were spent in Albert Beech's thresholding room. They were spent giving him a second injection. They were spent murdering him because he'd recognized you as his drug contact back in your Wandsworth days and you couldn't afford to risk your whole life here in Justice City by letting him live.'

She frowns and tilts her head as if she hasn't heard him. This may be fair: she may well not have. Alec has spoken softly, carefully, and Joshua's wailing has increased. It's a frail, desolate sound, a level of personal sorrow that Alec has never heard from an animal, and Joshua's body language reinforces it. He tries to fold himself ever smaller on the floor, within elbows and knees and small sharp shoulder blades that seem to Alec needlessly emaciated. Alec frowns. The weeping, too, is needless. The animal's perfectly safe where he is, and no one's hurting him. Both the sight and the sound of him are intrusive, and Alec wonders why Peggy Landon is allowing them.

He begins again, nearly shouting. 'I didn't mishear you.' He doesn't shout, it wouldn't be careful enough. 'It's on the tape and in the transcript,' he nearly shouts, 'and you lied because — '

She shakes her head. 'It's no use.' She leans forward, picks up Joshua, and the weeping stops. He tugs himself close against her. 'I'm sorry, Chief Inspector. I thought he might settle if we left him . . . You were saying?'

Alec sees that Joshua has left a puddle on the floor. Aren't these animals house-trained?

'He's very thin,' he says suspiciously. 'Is he ill?'

'Not ill. It's difficult, getting him to eat.' She strokes Joshua's forehead. 'He isn't like this just with me, I'm hardly ever here — he's like this with everybody. He likes a cuddle . . . Now, what were you saying?'

But Alec knows what happens to animals in laboratories — no, not true, he doesn't know, has never chosen to know, and there isn't a mark on Joshua.

Even so, 'He looks ill to me, Nurse Landon. Why doesn't he eat?'

'Well, he's blind and apparently chimps are very sight-oriented. They — '

'Blind?'

'Of course. I thought you realized. If he wasn't blind I could never let him off on his own in Karl's office. Chimps are very curious. They — '

'Blind? How did that happen?'

'It's a part of Karl's, of Doctor Stanna's research programme. He blocks impulses along the optic nerve. It's a tiny electronic implant. The purpose is to establish how long these blocks can remain in place before they become irreversible. Karl reckons we need around six months if the procedure's to be of any use.' She smiles at him. 'Karl has to use animals – he doesn't like to but he can hardly try it out on humans. We haven't yet hit a point of no return, but there has to be one.'

Alec glances at Frank. It's none of their business. They're wasting time. This is a murder inquiry. Even so, he has to ask her, 'This blindness is part of the research here?'

'Of course it is. It's a totally new sentencing concept. And it's brilliant . . .'

She leans forward, still clutching Joshua, and Alec sees that she's going to tell him all about it. Yet she's no fool. She can't be hoping he'll forget what he's there for. Maybe she still isn't taking his questions seriously. Maybe she simply finds Dr Stanna's work important and exciting. So important and exciting that she can't bear not to share it.

'Once Karl can induce blindness in humans for set, predictable periods,' she says, 'with one hundred per cent reversibility and no after-effects, then the authorities can start winning the public round to its use by the courts as an incapacitor.'

'I don't understand what you're saying.' But he does.

She sits back, her chin on the top of Joshua's head. 'Just imagine, Chief Inspector,' she says, 'a court with the ability to impose a sentence of so many weeks or months of clinically induced blindness. During his sentence the criminal will need only the lightest of supervision. He won't have to be taken out of society. Not only will this save money – it also brings back the old-fashioned social stigma of measures like the stocks and branding, but more humanely. And with any luck the criminal's total dependence on others during his blindness will reshape his character, his antisocial assumptions. The deterrent effect on others, and against re-offending, will be enormous and at ridiculously little cost . . . Don't turn away, Chief Inspector – think about it. Really *think*. Do-gooders moan about the number of criminals we imprison. This has to be the answer – a single, simple, virtually painless surgical implant. Punishment, incapacita-tion, denunciation, deterrence, rehabilitation, all rolled into one. EAT's crude – we won't need it. And no jails either, except for remand prisoners and the lightest offenders . . . Public education will be needed, but this has to be the right answer. Don't you see, Chief Inspector? Don't you see?'

Again, please.

'I don't understand what you're saying.' But he does.

She sits back with her chin on the top of Joshua's head.

Again, please. What she has to say is remarkable enough to be worth repeating.

'Just imagine, Chief Inspector,' she says, 'a court with the ability to impose a sentence of so many weeks or months of clinically induced blindness. The criminal will need only the lightest of supervision. He won't have to be taken out of society. Not only will this save money – it will also bring back the old-fashioned social stigma of measures like the stocks and branding, but more humanely. And with any luck the criminal's total dependence on others while he's blind will reshape his character, his antisocial assumptions. In any case the deterrent effect on others, and against re-offending, will be enormous, and at ridiculously little cost . . . Don't turn away, Chief Inspector – think about it. Really *think*. Do-gooders moan about the number of criminals we imprison. This has to be the answer – a single, simple, virtually painless surgical implant. Punishment, incapacita-tion, denunciation, deterrence, rehabilitation, all rolled into one. EAT's crude – we won't need it. And hardly any jails, except for remand prisoners and the lightest offenders. Public education will be needed but this has to be the right answer. Don't you see, Chief Inspector? Don't you see?'

He sees.

He sees her. He sees her capacity for far worse than murder.

The pain in his chest is like breaking ice. It grinds and echoes.

In a precise revelation he sees her and, within her, looking brightly out at him, an unnumbered eager multitude: the punishers, the beaters and lashers, the short sharp shockers, the no holiday campers, the lock 'em up and throw away the keyers, the let's think a bit more about the victimers, the hangers and gassers and electrocuters, the punishers, the punishers, the punishers . . . She distils their righteous outrage. It doesn't matter a damn that punishment has never helped one single solitary soul. It doesn't matter a damn that they, the punishers, have no right, are not God, hold no dominion, have earned no dominion, have no right, no right at all, certainly not in the name of justice, to increase the world's already incalculable suffering. Their outrage burns with a hot, unquenchable flame, and she's their vengefulness, the servant of their destructive folly.

He sees them in her, and Humphrey in her, and May and Morag and Iain in her, and himself in her, himself in her, himself in her, and he can be no longer careful.

He flings himself at her, blaring. He hoists her to her feet with one fist, hits her face with the other. She falls, scrabbles away from him amazed, Joshua fleeing. He lifts her again, drives her backwards against the wall. He cannot endure her plausibility, the devious violence of her ways. He cannot endure her wiles. Keep crime off the streets – put it instead in jails, the crime of clanging iron doors and buggery and slopping out and despair and men hanging from window frames by their knotted pissed-in underpants, the crime of Justice City's gates and granite walls and silent antiseptic corridors, of LTI, of smugness and snugness and videos running H and C in every room, the unspeakable crime of EAT . . . all the crimes that non-criminals require in the name of righteousness. Keep them off the streets: there are better places, places where all people can secretly, not so secretly, rejoice in them. No nation is ever short of torturers, only of outlets for their talents. He hits her face again, breaking teeth on his knuckles, and hits her again, mixing his blood with hers across splits in her cheek and nostril.

All his working life he's been delivering people to Nurse Landon.

He beats her against the wall, her head against the wall, and hits her again, breaking her jaw. He puts everything he has into these blows. He's a large man and she's everything he fears. May has died, and Humphrey whom he helped has killed her, and the infliction of so much suffering on her, on him, on them, on the world, revolts him, and jails feed the dark souls of the righteous, and Peggy Landon, able and intelligent and pretty, has taken him at other than his face value, has treated him like a human being, and has seemed to lack the capacity for murder – but not for justice, for Justice City, for Joshua.

As a result of which he can no longer be careful, can no longer wish to be careful, can no longer care if he is careful or not. May is dead and nowhere is safe. He's no right to expect it, so he hits Nurse Landon again, crushing more flesh in a face that's already red and meaningless.

She's been silent since her first sharp, astonished cry, just gasping a little each time he hits her, and the only sounds he can hear are his own grunts, and Joshua's maimed, stupid bleating. But now Frank stands close behind him, first swearing then running out of breath as he embraces, wears down and finally smothers Alec's huge arms, anger, despair.

Another man arrives, the man Alec saw Nurse Landon go to the City Bistro with. It's clever Dr Stanna: he bends over her where she's collapsed down against the skirting board.

278

He turns her head on one side and cleans her mouth out with one finger so that she can breathe. Frank releases Alec and he walks away, sits at the table. A couple of Peggy's small toothmarks are still drawing blood from his knuckles: otherwise he's physically undamaged. He's as good as new.

epilogue

twenty

Alec leaned on one elbow, attentively watching and listening as his broad black left hand, on its pale, flexible fingertips, walked in elusive major/minor steps, with chromatic regressions, up the bass octaves of the piano standing in the big bay window of the house in Sefton Park. He put in three notes against the beat, dropped down a tenth, began to climb again, and lifted his elbow to release his right hand for a stab at the tune he was hearing.

He had a gig booked that night at a club in the city centre, ten o'clock till three, and he was laying out chords. The gigs he played weren't anywhere near a livelihood but they were all he had for the moment and they might become one. He had savings, but no police salary, and no pension.

January was past. February had come and gone, and March, and now, in the twilight outside the window, April daffodils crowded the flower beds and mossy grass in the narrow front garden behind the hedge. He sat there playing often, looking out as his fingers moved harmonies round in his head. May had left him the flat in her will. He was surprised and touched, and felt bad, remembering how they'd parted, but he'd left her his dockside place in his will, similarly, and would have wanted her to have it had he been the one to die that Wednesday night and not she, so he could only hope she felt the same. Wherever she was, which he rather thought was nowhere.

He'd lived here ever since he left Morag's. They'd wanted him to stay but he couldn't do that, and he chose May's place because he'd been happier there than anywhere else, ever. He changed a few things, and hung wallpaper that they'd talked about and nearly bought a week before she died, he had plenty of leisure now, but mostly he'd let the rooms be. On his first visit to the flat, two days after her death, he'd dragged out the hall rug she'd died on and burnt it on the green gravel outside the garage, but he regretted that now. It hadn't wanted to burn, and he'd splashed paraffin about and got himself hot and sooty. The rug had had only one very small bloodstain. He needn't have behaved so theatrically.

His own place he'd sold quickly, for what he could get. He offered it to his mother, but all her friends were in Edinburgh and she didn't want to leave. He spent a few days up there with her, after moving into Sefton Park. She didn't understand about bereavement. This wasn't surprising – he didn't either. And his was twofold, May and his job, his life, what he *was*, the only life he'd ever had. Now he knew only that he was waiting for something to happen and it hadn't happened yet.

He stopped playing, switched on a standard lamp, and sorted through piles of sheet music that had somehow spread across the top of the piano. He was looking for 'A Slow Boat to China': he thought he could wind it up into a good end to his first set. Nat King Cole had done the fastest, niftiest 'Slow Boat' in the business.

He'd resigned from the police force, over the telephone with a letter following, that Thursday afternoon in the Prison Procedures Research Unit. Nobody tried to dissuade him: not Frank and certainly not – after he'd been put in the picture – the chief superintendent. Resignation accepted, as from that moment.

It didn't spare him a court of inquiry but Nurse Landon never pressed charges. She spent six painful weeks in hospital while doctors made a wonderful job of straightening out her face and her teeth, but she resisted a lot of official and family pressure for her to see him brought to justice. She said, what with the difficult Albert Beech case and a personal bereavement, she thought he'd suffered enough. It had been an unwarranted attack, and it had lost her *Hedda Gabler*, but she accepted that she'd been tactless and she didn't feel resentful. He'd been under a great deal of stress, one way and another.

Alec often thought about her. He tried to be grateful. She was monstrous, obscene, abhorrent, and what she stood for even more so, he'd changed his mind about nothing, but she had, somewhere, a generous spirit. He didn't understand this, and it worried him. His position required people to be consistent, and they weren't. Mr Ransome was consistent. The governor of Justice City had wanted a quick and painless outcome to the Albert Beech affair. He'd worked consistently towards that end, and he'd got it. He and Dr Mellish, together, had got it.

A scapegoat was needed and found, the unappealing Dr Peck, and Albert Beech's death became technically accidental. It was the *Pharmacological Yearbook* that provided them with the breakthrough. Once Mr Ransome had read Manchester's detailed analysis of Beech's designer euphoric, he'd been able to find in the *Yearbook*, among its possible side effects, a dangerous reaction to a paralytic ingredient in the thresholding cocktail. All that then remained was for an error to be discovered in Manchester's initial calculation of the exact amount of this euphoric present in Albert Beech, and that was soon accomplished. A nought had been omitted by a lab assistant and the amount was in fact considerable, more than enough to bring about respiratory paralysis and death.

The governor's visit to Inductions cleared them, and therefore him, of neglect as far as intravenous injection within the purlieus of Justice City was concerned, and Dr

Mellish's conversation with Nurse Serote resulted in one final Friday leak to Freddy that took the worst of the edge off Mr Ransome's Saturday press conference. It was clearly unfortunate that a Justice City inmate had died, but the fault was entirely his own: medical regulations in Justice City required all new arrivals to inform the examining doctor of the drugs they were taking or had recently taken, and Albert Beech had failed to do this. Copies of his medical report sheet, signed by the examining doctor, were available at the door.

The examining doctor was meanwhile left in the regrettable position of having failed to discover either the euphoric in pill or capsule form on Beech's person, or its presence in Beech's bloodstream. It didn't matter that blood tests were no part of Dr Peck's routine examination: they should have been.

Dr Peck, his head bent, was front page news for a couple of days, and took early retirement. He was replaced by a Royal Navy medic squeezed out in the most recent round of defence cuts.

Nurse Landon took up her job again as soon as she was fit, welcomed by Dr Mellish who'd had to fill in in her absence. Alec didn't know this, but coolness had developed between her and Karl Stanna, who was a man more capable than most of putting two and two together, of deciding his attitude to the result, and of adjusting his private life accordingly.

The other three people at one time seriously suspected of Beech's death – Jake de Carteret, Carole Serote and Timothy Wilks, *aka* Granny Porter – returned to their routines with, for the first two, a small new understanding of their moral priorities. Jake's Davey's birthday was a triumph and Carole's Rachel never again had to pretend she didn't know what was going on when her mother muttered down the telephone at someone called Freddy. For the third suspect, there was no change whatsoever. Granny Porter scurried to and fro, complaining, a happy man, with trolley and buckets and brushes, for another couple of months. Then, in the natural course of events, one night in late March, he died in his sleep of being Granny Porter and seventy-six. He was discovered in his bed next morning, warm on account of his electric blanket and, for the first time in years, on account of a muscular spasm, smiling.

Alec found 'Slow Boat' and propped it on the music stand. A simple arrangement, but user friendly: F major, D major, G minor, E seven . . . He tried it a tone lower, for the velvet of E flat. He played for maybe twenty minutes, as the evening drew in and the room darkened round the single bright cone of the lamp. He didn't mind shadows. May was never in them.

It was unreasonable to feel her death so deeply. Humphrey – his real name was Trevor, Trevor Winterburn Bladen – had been brought into the Merseyside nick forty minutes after Alec had left it. Interviewed, fingerprinted and charged, he was now awaiting trial. This gave Alec no comfort. Sentencing guidelines for addicts who murdered to pay for their habits were harsh and exemplary, and society had to be protected and he'd no better suggestion, but May stayed dead. There'd been a time before her death, maybe ten minutes, which particular ten minutes he couldn't remember, when he'd thought that if she'd really dumped him Peggy Landon might replace her. He'd been mistaken, but had the idea really been so crass? How different were they?

He'd been unfair to Nurse Landon: she was responsible finally, like May, only for her own failings, not for the nation's. In her case this was bad enough, but she was less of a leader than May had been, and they'd served the same system.

As he had.

He stopped playing. In the darkness outside, distantly, a siren wailed. One day soon, if Nurse Landon was right, the nation would be asked to approve judicial blinding. Why was that worse than the punishments they traditionally sanctioned? Was it worse?

In any case, penal systems in democracies required that justice should be seen to be done and therefore that criminals should be seen to be punished in ways the people thought suitable . . . He stared at the backs of his hands. This was the point he constantly came to. In the motorway café on his and Frank's way up to Justice City, Mr and Mrs Lawford had thanked him for putting away the murderer of their son: Mrs Lawford slept more easily in her bed, she said, knowing that, thanks to him, a blow had been struck for justice . . .

It had seemed fair enough.

But then, the following night, when he was talking to Iain and Morag about the IRA bomb in the chocolate box, Morag had wondered if the woman delivering it had gloated afterwards, knowing that, thanks to her, a blow had been struck for the Republican cause . . . Put like that, it seemed to him that Mrs Lawford's satisfactions and the IRA woman's were perilously similar.

It was a point he constantly came to.

He turned off the light and played on in the dark. He was waiting for something to happen and it hadn't happened yet. Meanwhile, he had a gig to get ready for.